Kaiju Task Force: Rise Of The Hybrids

Kaiju Task Force, Volume 2

Benjamin Stetser

Published by Benjamin Stetser, 2024.

This is a work of fiction. Similarities to real people, places, or events are entirely coincidental.

KAIJU TASK FORCE: RISE OF THE HYBRIDS

First edition. November 28, 2024.

Copyright © 2024 Benjamin Stetser.

ISBN: 979-8224092666

Written by Benjamin Stetser.

To my awesome nephew Reese, May your passion for gaming and streaming take you on incredible adventures. Always remember, every game is a new world waiting to be explored, and every stream is an opportunity to connect with others who share your dreams. Keep playing, keep creating, and never stop believing in the magic of your journey. The sky's the limit!

Chapter 1: The Calm Before the Storm

The world had never been the same after Omega. Sure, the cities were left in ruins, and once-thriving coastlines were now ocean debris, but the real change? The awkward silence. The kind that felt like someone forgot the punchline to a joke—except the joke was the world's destruction. And everyone was holding their breath, wondering if another disaster was lurking just around the corner.

The Kaiju Task Force had slimmed down after the chaos, which was surprising to exactly no one. Bubba, the mountain of muscle and sarcasm, had been shipped off on a super-secret mission so classified, not even the janitors knew where he went. And every time someone asked General Strayer for more details, she'd shut them down with her patented "look." You know, the one that could freeze a volcano mid-eruption? Yeah, that one. Bubba's absence left a void, like when you take the last bite of pizza but are still hungry—just emptier, quieter.

But life marched on. Blake had stepped into his role as second-in-command, growing into a capable leader under Alpha—who, let's be real, looked like he moonlighted as a metal-clad action figure. No one had ever seen Alpha out of his armor, which added to his mysterious "I'm definitely hiding something" vibe. What Blake didn't know was that Alpha wasn't just his mentor. He was David Bennett, their father. Yep, dear old dad was pulling the ultimate "I'm your father" reveal, but like, way after anyone would expect it. For now, the suit was as much a shield as the secret.

Blake found himself in the control room of their shiny, newly rebuilt headquarters. He stood behind a wall of reinforced glass, staring at the horizon. The world believed the Kaiju threat was over—after all, they had taken down Omega, the queen of the deep blue sea. But Blake? He had a bad feeling. And not just your typical "forgot where I left my keys" kind of bad—more like "something huge is about to drop" kind of bad.

"Yo, are you seriously... thinking?" Riese's voice cut through the silence like a knife through stale bread. His brother—resident science nerd and sarcasm machine—strolled into the room, casually tossing his lab coat over one shoulder like he was auditioning for a detergent commercial.

"Yeah, man, it's wild. First time for everything, huh?" Blake smirked, his usual grin creeping back. "Might be all the radiation in the air. Messing with my head."

"Well, if your brain's starting to work, we're all in trouble." Riese leaned against the console, arms crossed. "What's up, really? You look like someone told you there's no coffee left."

Blake sighed, rubbing the back of his neck. "It's just too quiet. Everyone's acting like we've wrapped up the whole Kaiju thing because Omega's gone. But that's the thing, Riese—how many times has the world thought it was done with something, only for it to come back worse?"

Riese raised an eyebrow. "You got any evidence, or are you just going full conspiracy theorist on me?"

Blake shrugged. "Dad used to say paranoia's just being ready for when things go south."

Riese couldn't help but chuckle. "Dad also said not to panic until we actually have to. So, until another giant lizard shows up, I'm sticking to upgrading our tech. You can keep being the doomsayer."

Blake grinned, even though the knot in his stomach wasn't going anywhere. "Fine, go play with your toys. I'll just be here, keeping an eye on the end of the world."

"Good. We need someone to keep the family paranoia alive." Riese winked, turning back to his work, but both brothers knew the tension in the room wasn't going anywhere. Something was coming—they could feel it.

Alpha—David Bennett—stood nearby, watching them. They had no clue who he really was, and he preferred it that way. If they knew, everything would change. They'd be distracted, and distractions were the last thing they could afford with the world still hanging by a thread.

As the days passed, though, the government felt... confident. Omega was gone, the cities were getting rebuilt, and the Kaiju threat? Well, it seemed to be on hiatus. The Kaiju Task Force was being repurposed for—wait for it—ceremonial appearances. Yep, they weren't battling giant monsters anymore; they were showing up in fancy suits to wave at parades and press conferences. Not exactly what the team had signed up for.

Blake sat outside the Task Force building on a metal bench, staring at his gleaming mech suit standing nearby. The sunlight reflected off the armor, making it look more impressive than it felt. Reese sauntered up, looking like the cat who swallowed the canary.

"You look like you just ate a lemon," Reese quipped, smirking. "Another round of ceremonies?"

Blake sighed, running a hand through his hair. "Yep. Because, you know, I totally signed up to fight Kaiju and make public appearances like I'm on the cover of a magazine."

"Come on, bro. Admit it—you love it," Reese teased, leaning against the bench. "We look like walking tanks. Who wouldn't want that kind of attention?"

"Yeah, except we're not doing anything," Blake shot back, annoyed. "I didn't sign up to play dress-up for politicians. I wanted to fight monsters, not smile for the cameras."

"Well, welcome to government work," Reese replied, deadpan. "Optics are everything. They're trying to make the public feel safe, even if it's just a dog-and-pony show."

"Optics don't kill Kaiju," Blake muttered, frustration thick in his voice. "We should be out there, preparing for whatever's next—not playing mannequin for photo ops."

"Maybe. But hey, at least we look good while doing it," Reese said with a shrug. "And remember that kid at the parade last month? Thought we were superheroes."

Blake couldn't help but laugh at the memory. "Yeah, that was pretty cool. But seriously, if I start giving speeches about how great the government is, you have to promise to put me out of my misery."

Reese grinned. "Deal. But until then, relax. We'll be the first ones called when the next Kaiju decides to crash the party. Just enjoy the downtime. We both know it won't last."

Blake sighed, nodding, though he couldn't shake the feeling that something was coming. "Here's hoping it's sooner rather than later. I can't stand being a glorified action figure."

Reese laughed. "Don't worry, bro. I've got your back. And if the world does end? At least we'll go out looking fabulous."

New York City was in chaos, the aftermath of Omega's attack still palpable in the air. Streets once bustling with life were eerily silent, punctuated only by the distant hum of generators and the shuffle of cleanup crews. The remnants of destruction lay scattered across the landscape—abandoned vehicles, shattered glass, and remnants of the panic that had ensued.

Federal agencies had descended upon the city like vultures, their black SUVs lining the streets, blocking off entire blocks as they cordoned off areas deemed hazardous. Scientists in white lab coats moved about with grim determination, collecting samples of Omega's biological material from the site of the devastation. The enormity of the task weighed heavily on them, but there was a sense of purpose in their movements.

"The body needs to be moved quickly," a sharp voice cut through the haze of activity. Agent Collins, a seasoned operative with the Department of Defense, was barking orders into a radio. "Ensure it's contained. We can't afford any further contamination."

A large containment vehicle, reinforced and heavily shielded, stood ready at the edge of the recovery site. The massive, blue-scaled form of Omega had already been meticulously covered with thick tarps, its immense bulk drawing the attention of onlookers from behind barricades, their expressions a mix of horror and awe.

As teams worked, a palpable tension hung in the air. Discussions of radiation levels were hushed but fervent. Omega's blood, rich with bioluminescent properties, was suspected to be highly radioactive. There was hope among the officials that it hadn't infiltrated the city's water supply, but the fear was a ghost that lingered in every corner.

"Have you checked the levels at the filtration plant?" another scientist in a lab coat asked, her brow furrowed in concern as she scanned her handheld device. "We need those results ASAP. If any of this got into the system, we could have a public health crisis on our hands."

"Still waiting on confirmation," a tech responded, his eyes darting between the readings and the grim face of his colleague. "But the preliminary scans show no signs of contamination. Just high radiation levels around the body itself."

Amid the bustling activity, a shadow loomed—General Strayer, her Pomeranian, Kevin, trotting beside her. She surveyed the scene, her expression steely. Despite her cool demeanor, the weight of the moment pressed down on her. She had witnessed the destruction firsthand and felt the dread of what Omega's presence meant for humanity.

"General," Collins approached, adjusting his cap as he saluted. "We've contained Omega's remains, but we need to discuss our next steps. The media is already spinning wild stories, and we can't let panic spread."

"Agreed," she replied, her voice steady. "We need to control the narrative. Brief the press on what we know, but don't give them any details that could fuel conspiracy theories. We have enough to deal with without adding public hysteria to the list."

As the day wore on, the city continued to grapple with the reality of the situation. Residents watched from a distance, a mixture of relief and lingering fear washing over them. News crews gathered, broadcasting the surreal sight of a once-mighty Kaiju's body being carted away like some twisted trophy, a testament to humanity's survival against a force of nature.

Yet, in the hearts of those who had witnessed Omega's wrath, questions remained unanswered. What had caused Omega to come here from her realm? What other creatures might follow? And how could they prepare for an uncertain future where giant monsters roamed the earth?

In the shadows, eyes watched the chaos unfold. Vance Hadrian, tucked away in a hidden laboratory, monitored the situation through a series of screens. A sinister smile crept across his face. The world was ripe for exploitation, and he intended to capitalize on every ounce of fear and confusion that had erupted in the wake of Omega's attack. The Kaiju had opened the door to possibilities he had only dreamed of.

"Let them clean up the mess," he muttered to himself, fingers dancing over the keyboard as he plotted his next move.

As the sun dipped below the horizon, casting long shadows over the city, a new chapter began to unfold, one that would push humanity to its limits and challenge their very understanding of life on Earth.

It was late at night in their cramped New York City apartment, and the glow of the television flickered in the dim light. Reese lounged on the couch, a bowl of popcorn perched on his stomach like a prized possession, while Blake sat cross-legged on the floor, looking like a kid at a comic book convention. Norah, their younger sister, sprawled on a bean bag chair, her expression a mix of curiosity and really, guys?

Dave Hogan's late-night talk show was in full swing, the audience clapping and laughing at his usual parade of terrible jokes. "And speaking of monsters," Dave chuckled, "I told my cat I was watching a movie about Kaiju, and he said, 'You mean another sequel?'" The audience howled, but Blake grimaced.

"Ugh, that joke should be outlawed," Blake muttered, shaking his head like someone just ruined his favorite superhero movie.

"Right? It's like he's trying to compete for 'Worst Joke of the Year,'" Reese replied, popping more popcorn into his mouth. "But wait—hold your breath! The movie trailer is coming up. I can't wait to see how badly they mess this one up."

As if on cue, the screen shifted to a flashy trailer for Guardians of the Universe, the upcoming film based on the Kaiju Task Force. The images were explosive: massive Kaiju rampaging through the streets, the Task Force suited up in their mechanized Valkyrie armor, with epic music blasting in the background like they were auditioning for a Fast & Furious sequel.

Norah wrinkled her nose. "That looks... awful."

"What do you mean?" Reese asked, his excitement temporarily unshaken. "It's got all the big action scenes! It's going to be epic!"

"No, it looks cheesy," Norah retorted, crossing her arms. "Like they took all the real drama and turned it into a dumb spectacle. And those special effects? They look like something out of a bad video game."

Blake nodded in agreement, eyes glued to the screen. "Yeah, they're trying to make it look cool, but it feels more like a Saturday morning cartoon. They're missing the real stakes. This isn't a joke—this is our lives! I mean, where's the part where I almost got squished?"

"Exactly!" Norah exclaimed, sitting up. "They're turning it into a joke! It's all explosions and flashy lights, but what about the chaos, the fear, the real danger? They glossed over it like we were in a parade instead of fighting for survival."

Dave Hogan's voice cut through their banter again as he introduced the star of the film. "And here's the thing, folks—next up is THE Kaiju Queen herself, Alyssa Knight!"

The audience erupted in applause as the camera panned to a glamorous actress decked out in red, looking more like a model on the runway than someone who'd just faced down a monster.

Blake shook his head. "That's their version of me? I look nothing like that. And who fights monsters in heels?"

Reese smirked. "Look on the bright side, bro—they got your height right."

Blake rolled his eyes. "I swear, if they turn us into action figures..."

Norah grinned. "Oh, they already have, Blake. I saw your figurine at the toy store. It's got a Kung Fu grip!"

They all burst out laughing, the absurdity of the situation momentarily lifting the weight of reality from their shoulders. But as the laughter faded, a quiet determination settled over Blake.

"Right? Like, what's next? Kaiju dating shows? I'm sure Omega would've swiped left," Blake joked, standing up. "I can't take this anymore. I'd rather watch paint dry."

Reese stretched his arms, grinning. "Agreed. Let's find something more grounded. Maybe an actual documentary about Kaiju sightings. You know, real monsters—no love stories required."

Norah perked up. "Finally! Let's watch something real instead of this garbage. They'll never capture what we went through on that screen."

Blake smirked as they started flipping through channels. "Yeah, but if they ever do make a realistic movie about us, I better be played by someone cool. Like a superhero or something."

The apartment grew quiet as the night deepened. After a few more half-hearted jokes and grumbling about the sad state of Kaiju-based movies, the siblings finally decided to call it a night.

"Alright, time for bed. Big day tomorrow," Blake said, stretching with an exaggerated yawn.

Reese rolled his eyes, tossing the empty popcorn bowl onto the coffee table. "Big day, sure, if by 'big' you mean another boring briefing about nothing happening."

Norah, already halfway to her room, paused at the doorway. "Yeah, well, just because nothing's been blowing up recently doesn't mean we should let our guard down."

"Tell that to the movie studios," Blake quipped, grinning. "Night, guys."

They exchanged half-hearted goodnights, each disappearing into their rooms, but there was an unspoken agreement hanging in the air.

The next morning, the siblings made their way to the Kaiju Task Force building. The imposing structure stood as a reminder of the battles they'd fought, the victories they'd claimed, and the losses that still weighed on their hearts. The world may have been at peace, but the scars left by Omega's rampage were still fresh.

"Why do I feel like this is going to be a waste of time?" Reese muttered as they walked through the main corridor.

"Because it's probably going to be a waste of time," Blake replied, grinning as he flicked Reese's ear. "Maybe General Strayer's just calling us in to tell us how amazing we are. I mean, that would make sense."

Norah shot them both a look. "You two have no idea what's coming, do you?"

"Enlighten us, wise one," Reese said with a smirk, but Norah just rolled her eyes and pushed open the door to the conference room.

Inside, General Sarah Strayer sat at a large round table, her expression as unreadable as ever. Behind her, Alpha stood like a silent sentinel, his armor gleaming under the fluorescent lights. Blake always wondered how Alpha managed to pull off the whole "mysterious warrior" vibe 24/7. It was like he never took the suit off. In fact, they had never seen him outside it.

But it wasn't the General or Alpha that caught their attention. Sitting beside Strayer was a man they didn't recognize—a tall, stern figure with gray hair and an expensive-looking suit. He had the unmistakable air of someone who thought they were important.

"Kids, have a seat," General Strayer said, her voice clipped.

"Well, this doesn't look ominous at all," Blake whispered as he plopped down in a chair. Reese slid in beside him, hands behind his head in a mock-relaxed pose. Norah, arms crossed, sat stiffly next to them, already on edge.

Once they were settled, Strayer cleared her throat. "This isn't my meeting. I was asked to convene it, but the Senator here has something he wants to say." She gestured toward the gray-haired man, her tone making it clear she wasn't exactly thrilled about the situation.

The Senator gave a thin, polite smile, though it didn't reach his eyes. "Thank you, General. I'll get right to the point. My name is Senator Caldwell, and I've been tasked with evaluating the continued need for the Kaiju Task Force in light of recent developments."

"Recent developments?" Reese scoffed quietly. "What, peace?"

Caldwell shot him a quick glance but continued without acknowledging the comment. "The Kaiju threat, as we understand it, is over. Omega is dead. The world is safe. The destruction has ceased. As such, the government can no longer justify the enormous expense of maintaining this force. Effective immediately, the Kaiju Task Force will be disbanded."

There was a long silence.

Blake blinked, then raised his hand like he was in school. "Uh, sorry, Senator... Calzone—"

"Caldwell," the Senator corrected, clearly unamused.

"Right, right. So, just to clarify—you're saying we're done here? Pack it up, go home, move on with our lives, that's the plan?"

Caldwell's lips tightened. "Yes. Exactly."

Reese leaned forward, smirking. "Cool, cool. Just one problem with that: What happens when the next Kaiju decides to take a stroll through Central Park? We just send it a politely worded letter asking it to leave?"

"Or maybe you want us to make a rom-com about it?" Blake added with a grin.

Norah, however, was not in a joking mood. She slammed her hands on the table, leaning forward aggressively. "This is a mistake. You can't just disband us because things have been quiet for a while. We've been on the front lines! We know better than anyone that these things don't just disappear."

Senator Caldwell's expression hardened. "Young lady, I understand your passion, but the Kaiju threat has been neutralized. There's no need for panic or conspiracy theories. The world is moving on, and so must we."

Norah's eyes flared, but before she could launch into another argument, Alpha spoke for the first time, his deep, commanding voice filling the room. "Stand down, team."

The three siblings turned to face him, surprised. Alpha rarely intervened, especially like this.

"We follow orders," Alpha continued, his helmet hiding any hint of emotion. "There's nothing we can do. This is the government's decision. We don't have a choice."

Blake, Reese, and Norah exchanged uncertain glances. They could all feel the frustration boiling beneath the surface, but Alpha's words left no room for argument.

"Fine," Blake muttered, throwing up his hands. "Guess we're going into early retirement. Anyone up for golf?"

Reese shook his head, but the humor had drained from his face. "This is a mistake, and you know it."

Norah, teeth gritted, said nothing more but glared at Senator Caldwell like she could burn a hole through him.

General Strayer stood, signaling the end of the meeting. "You're dismissed."

As the siblings walked out of the room, Reese couldn't help but toss a parting shot at the senator, who had just finished delivering yet another long-winded speech about the government's commitment to national security.

"Thanks for the riveting update, Senator! I can't wait for your next gripping episode of 'The Bureaucratic Chronicles.' I hear Season Two is coming out just in time for the elections," he quipped, smirking as he glanced back.

Blake snorted, shaking his head as the senator's face turned a delightful shade of crimson.

Alpha cleared his throat, a sound that cut through the tension like a knife.

Reese raised an eyebrow at Blake. "You think he always sounds this serious? I'm half expecting him to pull off his helmet and reveal himself to be a stand-up comic from a parallel universe."

Blake chuckled, but they both knew there was no time for humor now. They needed to head to the battle room and start packing their belongings. As they walked down the sterile corridors of the Task Force headquarters, the sense of finality hung in the air.

Once inside the battle room, they began shoving various gear into their duffel bags.

"I can't believe we're being disbanded. This is like the ultimate team breakup," Blake lamented, tossing a helmet into his bag with more force than necessary.

Reese nodded, his expression exaggeratedly serious. "Yeah, but instead of a heartfelt farewell dinner, we get packed lunches and a memo from HR. 'Thank you for your service, here's a gift card to Applebee's.'"

"Great, nothing says 'thank you for fighting giant monsters' quite like microwaved nachos," Blake shot back.

Norah, who had been quietly organizing her equipment, chimed in, "Well, I'm taking Elon up on that job at Tesla. I hear they're making electric cars that can dodge Kaiju."

"Oh, that'll be fun," Reese replied, feigning enthusiasm. "Picture it: 'Tesla Model X, now with 50% more 'not getting crushed by a giant sea monster' features.'"

"Hey, don't knock it till you try it!" Norah retorted, grinning. "At least I won't be running around in mech suits anymore. I could actually wear something other than body armor for once."

Reese shrugged, "I'm headed back to the agency. They're studying Omega's biology, and I've been given the green light to take a blood sample with me. It's about time they start understanding what we're dealing with."

"Nice! What do you think they'll learn from it?" Blake asked, his curiosity piqued.

Reese started listing off potential findings as he shoved a couple of vials into his bag. "Well, they might discover some radical cellular regeneration properties, which could explain why Omega healed so quickly. There could be unique genetic markers indicating her adaptability to different environments, which might lead to breakthroughs in evolutionary biology. And who knows? Maybe we'll find some hints at her immunities, which could help us create defenses against future Kaiju threats."

"Wow, you've really thought this through," Blake said, rolling his eyes. "What am I supposed to do while you guys are off doing important science stuff?"

"Probably something equally riveting, like getting back to the zoo full-time," Reese teased. "What are you going to do there? Train the penguins to be your backup dancers?"

Blake grinned. "Actually, I'm thinking of going on some expeditions looking for Bigfoot. You know, doing my part for cryptozoology. Maybe he's been hanging out in a corner of the zoo this whole time."

"Yeah, because that's what the world needs right now—Blake the Bigfoot Hunter. Imagine the headlines: 'Local Zookeeper Becomes Best Friends with Legendary Cryptid!'"

Blake laughed. "Hey, if I find him, it's a scoop of epic proportions. Maybe I'll convince him to help with Kaiju defense. Who needs fancy tech when you have a hairy giant on your side?"

Norah shook her head, chuckling. "Just make sure he doesn't eat you first. I can see the headlines now: 'Cryptid Cuisine: How Blake Became Dinner.'"

The banter continued as the siblings packed their bags, feeling a mix of apprehension and excitement about the next chapter in their lives. Despite the uncertainty, they found solace in the fact that they would still be there for each other, even if they weren't fighting monsters together anymore.

As they finished packing, Blake took a moment to look around the battle room, filled with memories of their time as a team. "You know, I'll miss this place," he said, a twinge of nostalgia creeping into his voice.

"Me too," Norah replied, her expression softening. "But we're not gone yet. There's still time for one last adventure."

"Agreed," Reese said, slinging his bag over his shoulder. "But for now, let's see if we can avoid being crushed by the weight of our own glory."

With a shared laugh, they headed out of the battle room, ready to face whatever awaited them next.

Chapter 2: Vance Hadrian

Vance Hadrian sat in his expansive, glass-walled office atop the Hadrian Industries skyscraper, surveying the city below with cold detachment. The world buzzed beneath him, people going about their daily lives, unaware of how much of it was influenced—directly or indirectly—by him. Real estate, tech startups, government contracts, even cutting-edge scientific research; his fingers were in everything. But despite all his success, the vast empire he had inherited from his late father felt as hollow as the praise he had long craved but never received.

Victor Hadrian, the towering figure who had built the Hadrian empire from nothing, had been as distant as he was ruthless. To the world, he was a titan, a billionaire real estate mogul who commanded respect with every deal. But to Vance, he was an unapproachable ghost, a man who never seemed to notice the son desperate for his approval.

Vance's early years had been defined by two things: the loss of his mother and his exile to cold, isolating boarding schools. His mother, Sarah Hadrian, had died of cancer when Vance was just eight years old, leaving him without the one source of warmth in his life. His father, never one for sentiment, buried himself in his work and shipped Vance off to elite boarding schools, where his name and wealth painted a target on his back.

The bullying started early and never let up. Vance was different—he wasn't just the son of a billionaire, he was introverted, bookish, and awkward. The other boys saw him as weak, a boy whose father couldn't even be bothered to show up to parents' weekends or sports games.

They tormented him relentlessly—pushing him down stairwells, stealing his clothes, humiliating him at every opportunity. But no matter how much they hurt him, the emotional pain of his father's absence cut deeper.

Vance excelled in academics, pouring himself into his studies as if trying to earn some invisible approval. Every accolade, every perfect report card, was met with silence from Victor Hadrian. The few times his father did acknowledge him, it was with a nod, maybe a cold word of encouragement, but never the affection Vance so desperately sought.

It wasn't until Vance attended university—the best in New York, naturally—that he started to gain the respect he deserved. He majored in both business and science, earning degrees that positioned him not only as a sharp executive but also as one of the most promising scientific minds of his generation. But even as he rose in the ranks, even as he stepped into the CEO role at Hadrian Industries after his father's death, the hunger for validation never left him.

Now, Vance ruled over the very empire his father had once held. Real estate, tech ventures, and, most importantly, GeneSys Labs—the company's flagship scientific division—were all under his control. GeneSys was where the most important work happened, where Vance's true passion lay. The company had secured several high-profile government contracts, particularly in biotechnology and weapons research, making it an invaluable asset to national security.

"Mr. Hadrian, your ten o'clock is here," came the voice of Michelle, his efficient and ever-calm assistant, through the intercom.

Vance pressed a button. "Send them in," he replied, his voice crisp and controlled, betraying none of the turmoil underneath.

The man who entered was a government liaison, clearly nervous despite his attempts to hide it. Vance barely acknowledged his presence with a glance. He didn't care for bureaucrats. What interested him was power—real power. Not the fleeting recognition his father had amassed, but control over life, death, and the forces that governed them.

"Thank you for meeting with me, Mr. Hadrian," the liaison began, his voice shaky. "We're very pleased with the progress GeneSys Labs has made, particularly in your research on Kaiju biology."

Vance's eyes flicked up at the mention of Kaiju. His top scientist, Reese Bennet, had been working tirelessly on Kaiju samples, trying to unravel the biological mysteries of the creatures. Their regenerative properties were of particular interest to the government, especially for potential military applications.

"You're impressed," Vance said flatly, gesturing for the man to sit, though his tone suggested he didn't care if he did. "Good. But that's not enough. What do you need from me?"

"Well," the liaison fumbled with some papers, "we're hoping to accelerate the research on cellular regeneration. Dr. Bennet's reports suggest it could be groundbreaking, and we believe it could lead to... advancements in human health, even military defense."

Vance's interest piqued, though he masked it well. Reese Bennet was brilliant, but he lacked the ambition Vance possessed. Reese saw his work as science; Vance saw it as a key to godhood.

"You let me worry about the science," Vance said, leaning forward slightly. "You'll get your results when they're ready."

The liaison nodded quickly, clearly intimidated by Vance's cold, unrelenting gaze. The meeting ended shortly after, the man scurrying out as quickly as he could. Vance hardly noticed his exit.

Standing, Vance moved to the massive window that dominated his office. The city stretched out before him, endless, sprawling—full of people he could control, systems he could manipulate. But as always, the power he wielded still felt insufficient. He wanted more. He needed more.

His gaze fell to the one personal item on his desk—a framed photograph of him as a child, standing with his mother. It was taken before the cancer had claimed her, before his world had become a cold, lonely place. His mother had loved him; he could still feel the warmth of her embrace in the photo. But his father? Victor Hadrian had been an absence more than a presence, even when he was alive.

It was this void, this unquenchable thirst for approval, that still drove Vance to this day. But the approval of a dead man meant nothing now. What mattered was power. And GeneSys Labs held the key.

Vance didn't just want to be a great CEO. He wanted to be something more—someone who could conquer even death itself. Kaiju biology could give him that, if he could unlock its secrets. Immortality wasn't just a fantasy; it was a future he intended to claim for himself.

Victor Hadrian had built an empire. But Vance Hadrian? He would build a new world. A world where the limitations of life no longer applied.

And unlike his father, he would not fail.

Reese Bennett stood in his lab, hunched over a table cluttered with holographic projections and digital readouts, engrossed in the latest results from his research on Omega's blood. The sample throbbed with life under the microscope, shifting and pulsating in ways no ordinary cell should. Omega's cells could heal almost instantly, adapt to harsh conditions, and seemingly regenerate indefinitely. Reese couldn't help but grin at the possibilities, thinking beyond the obvious military applications.

Imagine a fighter jet that could repair itself mid-air, or a car that regenerated after a crash. Heck, why stop there? Buildings, bridges—anything could be infused with this kind of biological resilience. It was science fiction becoming reality, and Reese was right at the heart of it.

"Hey, Bennett! Are you playing mad scientist again, or did you just spill your lunch on the equipment?" Vance's voice broke through Reese's thoughts, followed by the sound of heavy footsteps.

Reese smirked, not even looking up from his work. "Well, well, if it isn't the man who wears suits so tight, I can hear them scream for mercy. What brings you down to the dungeon, Vance? Miss me already?"

Vance Hadrian, the CEO of GeneSys Labs, walked in, flashing a grin as sharp as his tailored suit. "Just checking on my favorite science geek," he quipped. "You look like you're one weird thought away from growing a second head."

"Second head? That's cute, coming from someone who has the personality of a brick wall," Reese shot back, still focused on the glowing sample. "But yeah, I'm good. Just figuring out how to make the world a better place, one Kaiju blood sample at a time. No biggie."

"Right," Vance chuckled, walking up to the holographic display. "So, how's it going? Still thinking of merging biology and technology so we can have fighter jets that heal themselves? Or is this about building cars that can regenerate their paint job after you scratch them?" Vance chuckled.

Reese finally glanced up, his eyes gleaming with excitement. "Oh, it's way bigger than that, my friend. Think about it: machines that don't need repairs, factories that never break down, even ships that fix themselves after taking damage. I'm talking a full-scale revolution here. Omega's biology could make all that possible. You've got your flying death machines, sure, but I'm looking at a future where everything—literally everything—can heal itself."

Vance's eyes gleamed with interest, though his smirk didn't fade. "You always were the dreamer, Bennett. Now, about Project Iris—"

Reese raised an eyebrow. "Oh, you mean the little side project where we're creating Frankenstein's menagerie? How could I forget?"

Vance snorted. "Yeah, that one. How's it going?"

Reese sighed dramatically, turning his chair to face Vance fully. "Well, let's see. In theory, splicing animal DNA to create hybrid supersoldiers sounded brilliant. In practice? Let's just say the animals don't exactly play nice together. The DNA starts rejecting itself after two months. It's like trying to get you and a personality into the same room. Just not compatible."

Vance laughed, shaking his head. "You wound me, Bennett. But seriously, how bad is it?"

"Not a total failure, but not great either," Reese said, pulling up images of three embryos on the holographic display. "These three here—Titanax, Aquila, and Lynxara—are the survivors so far. Titanax is a gorilla-elephant hybrid, built like a truck with a bad attitude. Aquila's a shark-eagle combo, so, y'know, wings and fins. And then we've got Lynxara, part lion, part hyena, all trouble."

Vance stared at the embryos, his expression turning serious. "Impressive. So what's the issue?"

Reese leaned back in his chair, crossing his arms. "The DNA works for a while, but then it just... falls apart. The cells start rejecting each other. It's like the animals realize they don't belong together and just break down. We've kept these three stable, but it's only a matter of time unless we find a solution."

Vance rubbed his chin thoughtfully. "And Omega's blood? Could it help with the DNA rejection?"

Reese gave him a sideways glance. "You want me to mix Kaiju blood into these hybrids? Are you trying to create unstoppable monsters, or are you just bored with regular world domination?"

"Bored," Vance deadpanned. Then he broke into a grin. "Look, I'm just thinking out loud here. If Omega's cells can regenerate endlessly, maybe that could stabilize the hybrids. Keep them from falling apart. Worth a shot, don't you think?"

"Sure, let's give our science experiment the healing powers of a giant, world-destroying lizard. What could go wrong?" Reese said, his voice dripping with sarcasm. But then he sighed, more seriously.

Reese rubbed his temple, glancing between the holographic displays and the bubbling tanks that housed the embryonic hybrids.

The weight of Vance's expectations pressed down on him, and though the possibilities were staggering, the risks were equally terrifying. He turned back to the CEO, who was still studying the screen with laser focus.

"Look, Vance," Reese began, trying to sound measured, "I get that you're excited about this—heck, I'm excited too—but mixing Omega's blood with the hybrids... it's not something we can just jump into. We barely understand Omega's biology ourselves. There's no telling what kind of side effects could happen if we tried to introduce it into these embryos. If Omega's regeneration went out of control or mutated the hybrids beyond recognition, we might not even be able to stop them."

Vance raised an eyebrow, his posture still composed but his expression slightly more thoughtful. "You're saying you don't trust your own work, Reese?"

Reese snorted, crossing his arms. "It's not about trusting my work—it's about trusting that Omega isn't some walking biological nightmare waiting to happen. This Kaiju's blood doesn't just heal; it adapts. It changes. Who's to say those hybrids wouldn't start changing too? What if we give them Omega's cells and they start mutating in ways we can't predict?"

Vance let out a sigh, rolling his eyes just slightly. "Come on, man. You're always the cautious one. You act like I'm asking you to combine Frankenstein's monster with Godzilla."

Reese raised a finger, smirking. "You are asking me to combine Frankenstein's monster with Godzilla. And as much as I'd love to see you get squished by one of your own creations, I'm going to have to say we should slow down. Omega's biology is dangerous. We don't even know how it'll react inside a human-sized hybrid."

Vance paced for a moment, letting the tension simmer between them. Finally, he stopped and faced Reese, his cool facade cracking just enough to reveal some genuine concern. "You're right, alright? I hate to admit it, but you're right. Last thing I need is one of these things growing an extra head or turning into some unstoppable monstrosity before we even have a leash on them."

Reese chuckled, shaking his head. "Appreciate the vote of confidence, boss. We'll figure it out—we just need more time. Maybe once we understand Omega's healing process better, we can give it another shot. But for now, we stick to the plan, no shortcuts."

Vance sighed again, this time with a little more resignation. "Alright, alright, no shortcuts. You're the expert. I'll hold off on the Frankenstein-Godzilla combo for now."

Reese smirked, feeling the tension in the room lift just a little. "Glad you're seeing sense, for once. It's rare, but I'll take it."

Vance shot him a dry look, then glanced down at his watch. "Speaking of rare moments, I assume you and Jessica will be joining us for dinner tonight, right? Alice's been planning this thing for a week, and she's threatening to kill me if you bail again."

Reese raised an eyebrow, grinning. "Oh, so that's why you're so tense. Scared of the missus, huh?"

Vance smirked back, rolling his shoulders. "Hey, I'd rather face down a Kaiju than disappoint Alice. She's scarier than any of those monsters."

Reese laughed, leaning against the counter. "You sure? Because I'm pretty sure she could take you out even without Kaiju blood."

Vance crossed his arms, shaking his head with mock irritation. "Keep it up, Bennett. Just remember, if you don't show, I'll be telling her it was your idea to cancel. See how that works out for you."

Reese gave him a sarcastic salute. "Yes, sir, Mr. CEO. I'll be there—wouldn't miss a chance to watch you squirm under Alice's thumb."

"Good. Bring wine. Lots of wine," Vance added with a smirk, already turning to head out the door. "You're gonna need it."

Reese called after him, "Don't worry—I'll bring enough to drown your misery after Alice grills you about work."

Vance waved a hand dismissively but couldn't hide the grin. "Yeah, yeah. Just don't be late, or I'll lock you in here with the hybrids. And don't think I won't."

Reese chuckled, shaking his head as Vance left. "Looking forward to it, boss. See you tonight."

As the door closed behind Vance, Reese turned back to the tanks, watching the hybrids float peacefully in their containment. The science was moving fast, almost too fast. But at least, for now, they were staying cautious. He could only hope they wouldn't unleash something far worse than what they could control down the road.

Vance stepped out of Reese's lab, the door hissing shut behind him as the cool, sterile air of the facility greeted him. The hum of machines and the distant whir of equipment filled the hallway, but all Vance could think about was Reese—and the fact that, once again, the guy had managed to turn a perfectly thrilling idea into a long-winded debate about ethics. He couldn't help but smirk. That was Reese for you, always the buzzkill, armed with just enough logic to make you rethink your entire life.

As he reached his office, Vance pulled out his phone and dialed his wife, Alice. The phone barely rang before her cheerful voice answered.

"Hey, sweetheart," Alice greeted. "Finally escaping the mad science for the night?"

"Not quite yet," Vance leaned back in his chair, feeling the weight of the day settle into his shoulders. "Just finished with Reese. You might want to set two extra plates tonight. Looks like he and Jessica are coming over for dinner."

"Oh, so you managed to drag him out of his lab?" Alice chuckled. "I was half expecting him to cancel with some excuse like 'saving humanity.'"

Vance snorted. "I wouldn't put it past him. But no, he's actually showing up tonight. Probably just for the roast, though. You know how he is about food."

Alice's laughter was music to his ears. "Well, I'll make sure it's perfect. Should I also be prepared for Reese's signature blend of sarcasm and overthinking?"

"Guaranteed," Vance said, grinning. "And more wine than necessary to drown our collective misery."

Alice laughed again. "Sounds like a plan. You guys deserve a good night."

Vance nodded, feeling a little lighter. "Thanks, love. I'll be home soon."

After hanging up, Vance leaned back, letting the quiet of his office wash over him for a moment. His office, filled with sleek tech and stacks of reports, suddenly felt empty. His thoughts drifted back to Reese—his best friend since their wild college days, back when neither of them had a clue where life would take them.

God, those college days. The memories alone made Vance chuckle. Reese was always the smartest guy in the room, and of course, he knew it. The two of them were constantly in competition—whether it was over grades, who could build the better robot, or who could hold their liquor after one too many keg stands. Reese had once drunkenly declared he could "cure hangovers" by sheer willpower and a ridiculous amount of caffeine. Spoiler: he couldn't. He ended up in the campus nurse's office, looking like a zombie with a PhD.

And the parties. Vance remembered that one time Reese built an actual miniature flamethrower for a dorm party, because apparently, it wasn't a "real event" without fire. That little stunt nearly got them both kicked out. But somehow, Reese sweet-talked the dean into believing it was a "physics demonstration." Classic Reese—charm a professor while casually risking everyone's lives.

But despite all the hijinks, there was no one Vance trusted more. Reese had always been the one who had his back, even when they were competing. And yeah, sure, Reese's ego was massive, but Vance wouldn't have it any other way.

When Reese had left to join the Kaiju Task Force, it felt like a chunk of Vance's life had gone with him. They'd kept in touch, but something was always missing. Reese was off saving the world, while Vance was stuck in meetings, wading through paperwork. It wasn't the same without his best friend around to make every situation just a little more ridiculous.

Now that Reese was back, though? The future looked bright—well, as bright as it could be. Still, Vance couldn't help but feel that old excitement bubbling up. Whatever came next, at least they'd face it together, like they always had. And knowing Reese, it would be just as chaotic and twice as entertaining.

He stood up, grabbing his coat and shutting down the holographic displays on his desk. Tonight wasn't about the lab or the experiments. It was about catching up with an old friend, maybe making fun of each other a bit, and enjoying the good food Alice had cooked up.

As he headed toward the elevator, Vance smiled to himself, thinking about the dinner ahead. Reese would probably insult his cooking knowledge, Jessica would roll her eyes, and Alice would have to referee the whole mess. Yep, it was shaping up to be a great night.

For the first time in a while, Vance felt like everything was falling back into place.

Stepping outside into the cool evening air, he looked forward to heading home.

Vance arrived home to the cozy sight of his daughters bustling around the living room, filled with laughter and the aroma of Alice's cooking wafting from the kitchen. As he walked in, he spotted his youngest daughter, Lily, who was frantically smoothing down her dress in front of the mirror. The sixteen-year-old had just enough time to perfect her look before heading out on her first official date with a boy named Ethan.

"Dad! You're home!" Lily squealed, her eyes sparkling when she caught sight of him. She dashed over, throwing her arms around him. "Did Uncle Reese come with you?"

"Not yet, but he should be here any minute," Vance said, ruffling her hair affectionately.

"Yay! I can't wait to see him!" Lily squealed again, her excitement palpable. She had always called Reese "Uncle Reese," even though he wasn't technically her uncle. But to Lily, he might as well have been part of the family.

Just then, the doorbell rang, and Vance opened it to find Reese and his girlfriend, Jessica, standing on the doorstep, both wearing wide smiles.

"Look who's here!" Vance called, stepping aside to let them in.

"Hey, Uncle Reese!" Lily shouted, running up to him and wrapping her arms around his waist.

"Hey there, Lil' Firecracker!" Reese laughed, playfully lifting her off the ground. "Ready to light up the town tonight?"

"Yeah! I'm going out with Ethan!" she announced proudly.

Reese raised an eyebrow, feigning concern. "Ethan? That kid who wears those dorky glasses? Are you sure you want to date a guy who looks like he just crawled out of a science fair?"

Lily grinned, shaking her head. "At least he's not a huge nerd like you, Uncle Reese! Besides, I think he's cute." With that, she scooted past them and out the door, shouting over her shoulder.

As the door clicked shut behind her, Reese turned to Vance, his face a mixture of amusement and mock indignation. "I'm not a nerd! I'm...technically skilled in various scientific disciplines!"

Jessica laughed, shaking her head as they stepped inside. "Only you, Reese. Only you."

Once inside, the atmosphere shifted to one of warmth and camaraderie. Vance guided them to the dining room, where Alice had set a lovely table adorned with candles and their favorite dishes. The four of them sat down, and laughter quickly filled the air as they passed around food and poured drinks.

After dinner, they cleared the table and moved into the living room for some board games. The competitive spirit ignited as they settled down with a classic strategy game, their laughter filling the room. As they played, Vance couldn't help but steal glances at Jessica and Alice. The two women chatted animatedly, their camaraderie forming another layer of warmth around the group.

At one point, Vance leaned closer to Jessica and Alice, lowering his voice. "So, speaking of adventures, did I tell you what Reese discovered while he was at work today?"

Reese shot him a warning glance, his eyes widening slightly. "Vance, maybe we should—"

But Vance continued, ignoring the look. "He's found evidence that mixing Kaiju blood or something like it with tech could lead to some serious enhancements. It's groundbreaking stuff!"

Jessica's eyes lit up with curiosity, while Alice leaned in, intrigued. "Really? What does that mean?"

"Uh, well—" Reese interjected, his voice tinged with discomfort. "It's not as simple as it sounds. We don't fully understand Omega's biology yet."

After a few more rounds of laughter and playful insults, Reese turned to Vance, a glint of mischief in his eyes. "How about we escape the gossip for a bit, huh? Let the ladies do their thing while we admire the skyline?"

"Sounds like a plan," Vance agreed, rising from his seat. They slipped out onto the deck, the cool evening air wrapping around them as they stepped outside. The city skyline sparkled against the darkening sky, a mixture of bright lights and shadows casting a tranquil glow.

They leaned against the railing, taking in the view. Vance breathed in deeply, savoring the moment. "You know, it feels good to have you back, Reese. It's like we're kids again, dreaming about the future."

Reese chuckled, glancing sideways at Vance. "Yeah, except now we actually have to deal with the consequences of our genius ideas."

"Speaking of which," Vance began, gathering his thoughts to bring up the delicate subject of hybrid experiments again. "I was thinking about the possibilities—"

Just then, a sharp knock echoed from the front door, cutting through the moment. Vance frowned, glancing back toward the house.

"Who could that be?" Reese asked, raising an eyebrow.

"Let me check," Vance said, moving back inside. As he opened the door, his heart sank at the sight before him: two officers from the Rockland County Sheriff's Department stood in his doorway, their faces serious.

"Mr. Hadrian?" one of them asked, stepping forward. The flashing lights of police cars illuminated the driveway, casting a stark glow across the living room.

"Yes, that's me. What's going on?" Vance's stomach twisted with unease.

"We need to speak with you and your wife. It's important," the second officer said, glancing over his shoulder.

Vance's pulse quickened as he called for Alice, his voice shaky. "Alice! Can you come here for a moment?"

She appeared almost immediately, concern etched across her face as she joined him at the door. "What's going on?"

The first officer took a deep breath before delivering the news. "I'm afraid there's been an accident. Your daughter, Lily, was involved. She's in the hospital in serious condition."

The room spun as the weight of the words hit Vance like a punch to the gut. "What? How? What happened?"

"There was a car crash," the officer explained, his tone steady yet somber. "Another vehicle ran a red light. She was taken to Rockland Medical Center, and we need you to come with us."

"Is she... is she going to be okay?" Alice's voice trembled, a mixture of fear and desperation.

"They're doing everything they can, but you should get there as soon as possible," the second officer urged, his eyes filled with compassion.

Without waiting for another word, Vance bolted toward the door, panic surging through him. "I'll drive! Let's go!" he shouted, urgency in every syllable.

As he raced past the officers, Reese followed closely behind, worry etched on his face. "Vance! Wait!"

"Stay with Jessica!" Vance yelled back, barely able to comprehend anything beyond the need to get to the hospital. "I'll call you when I get there!"

He dashed outside, the world around him fading into a blur. The comforting skyline had vanished, replaced by the overwhelming fear that had settled in his chest. All he could think about was Lily and the dread of what awaited him at the hospital.

As he jumped into his car, he fumbled with the keys, his hands shaking. The urgency of the moment was all-consuming, the sirens from the police cars echoing in his ears. He couldn't lose her. Not now. Not ever.

With a deep breath, he turned the ignition, the engine roaring to life. Vance hit the gas, racing down the driveway and onto the road, his heart pounding in rhythm with the speed. In that moment, nothing else mattered—only reaching his daughter and holding her close again.

Chapter 3: Shattered Dreams

Vance Hadrian entered the ER, his heart pounding as he pushed past the chaos of medical staff and worried families. The antiseptic smell burned his nostrils, but he barely registered it as he hurried toward the nurse's station.

"Where's my daughter, Lily Hadrian?" he asked, his voice strained.

"Room 12, down the hall to your left," the nurse replied, her gaze flickering with concern as she saw the urgency in his eyes.

"Thank you," he breathed, racing down the corridor, his mind filled with nothing but the image of his little girl.

As he reached the door marked with a small nameplate, he paused for a moment, collecting himself before stepping inside. The sight that greeted him stole the breath from his lungs. Lily lay in the hospital bed, her small body seemingly swallowed by the stark white sheets. Her face was bruised and pale, and various tubes snaked around her, beeping machines providing a haunting symphony of worry.

"Lily!" Vance whispered, rushing to her side. He took her tiny hand, feeling the coldness of it against his palm. "Oh, baby, I'm here."

Her eyes fluttered open, and a weak smile broke through the pain. "Dad," she croaked, her voice a mere whisper.

"I'm right here. You're going to be okay," he reassured her, though panic twisted in his chest like a vice.

Just then, a doctor entered the room, her expression grave and professional. "Mr. Hadrian?"

"Yeah, what's going on? How is she?" Vance asked, anxiety creeping into his voice.

The doctor hesitated, glancing between Vance and Lily. "Lily has sustained severe injuries from the accident. She has multiple fractures in her legs and a serious spinal injury. We'll need to perform immediate surgery, but I must be honest—the prognosis is not good. Unless some miracle drug comes along, she may never regain the ability to walk again."

Vance's heart dropped, the world around him fading into a blur. "What? No, there has to be something you can do. Please, we can't just accept that!"

"I understand how difficult this is," the doctor said gently. "We'll do everything we can, but I want to prepare you for the possibility of a long recovery process."

Just as Vance struggled to find words, he heard a familiar voice. "Vance!"

He turned to see Reese, Jessica, and his wife, Alice, rushing into the room. Alice's face was filled with worry, and as she reached him, she enveloped him in a tight hug.

"I'm here," she whispered, her voice steady despite the tears brimming in her eyes.

Vance held her tightly, feeling the strength of her embrace. "It's bad, Alice. They're saying—"

"I heard," she interrupted softly, pulling back to look at him. "We'll get through this. Together."

Reese stepped closer, concern etched across his face. "What can we do?" he asked.

Jessica, holding onto Reese's arm, looked between Vance and Lily. "Is there anything we can help with? Just tell us."

Vance took a deep breath, steeling himself for what lay ahead. "Just be here. I need you all here."

As they gathered around, the reality of the situation sank in, but for the first time since entering the hospital, Vance felt a flicker of hope. They would fight for Lily, and with his family and friends by his side, he wasn't going to give up.

The waiting room felt like a time warp, each second stretching into an eternity as Vance sat hunched in a plastic chair beside Alice. The sterile smell of antiseptic hung in the air, mingling with the tension that crackled between them. Reese and Jessica occupied the seats across from them, their faces reflecting the gravity of the situation.

As they waited, Vance's mind raced with thoughts of Lily. The little girl who used to bounce through their front door, giggling and brightening their lives, now lay under the knife, battling for her future. He rubbed the back of his neck, the stress weighing heavy on his shoulders.

After what felt like hours, the doctor finally emerged, her scrubs still stained from the surgery. Vance's heart pounded as he stood up, Alice clutching his hand tightly.

"Mr. Hadrian, Mrs. Hadrian," the doctor said, her expression somber. "I have an update on Lily's condition."

Vance nodded, his breath hitching in his throat. "How did it go?"

"We managed to repair some of the damage," she explained. "She has several fractures in her legs that were set and stabilized, but unfortunately, the spinal injury is severe. I must be honest—Lily will most likely never walk again."

The words struck Vance like a physical blow. He staggered back against the wall, his heart shattering into a thousand pieces. Beside him, Alice's breath hitched, and tears streamed down her cheeks.

"No, no, no..." Vance whispered, shaking his head in disbelief. "There must be something more. We can't just accept this!"

"I understand this is incredibly difficult to hear," the doctor replied gently. "We'll support you through the rehabilitation process, but I want to be transparent about her prognosis."

Vance felt like the floor had fallen away beneath him. "She's just a child! She's supposed to have her whole life ahead of her!" His voice cracked, frustration and despair swirling together.

Alice buried her face in her hands, silent sobs racking her body. Vance turned to her, reaching out to pull her into a tight embrace, wishing he could take away her pain, wishing he could do something—anything—to change the outcome.

After a moment, Alice whispered, "I need to see her. I need to be there for her."

"Of course," Vance said, nodding as she composed herself, wiping away her tears. "I'll be right here."

Alice nodded and walked toward the double doors leading to the surgical rooms. Vance watched her go, his heart heavy.

"Hey," Reese said softly, pulling Vance's attention back to him. "Let's step outside for a minute. We can talk."

"Yeah, okay," Vance replied, grateful for the distraction as he followed Reese through the waiting room and out into the cool night air.

Once outside, Vance leaned against the brick wall, staring into the darkness. The weight of everything pressed down on him, and he felt like he couldn't breathe.

"I can't believe this is happening," Vance said, his voice shaky. "We were just having dinner, laughing, and now... it's like everything's flipped upside down."

Reese stood beside him, his expression serious. "I'm so sorry, man. I can't even imagine what you're going through. But you're not alone. We're all here for you."

"I just keep thinking about all the things Lily will miss out on—her first dance, learning to ride a bike. It's not fair." Vance clenched his fists, frustration bubbling up again.

"It's okay to be angry," Reese said, his voice steady but soft. "You can be angry at the world for this."

"I just want to fix it," Vance said, running a hand through his hair. "But I feel so helpless."

"We'll figure this out together," Reese assured him. "And maybe there's a way we can help Lily in ways we haven't even thought of yet. You're a brilliant scientist, and you've always been creative. There may be options we just need to find."

Vance pushed off the wall, running his fingers through his hair in frustration. "You're right, Reese. Omega's blood—"

Reese cut him off, narrowing his eyes. "What about Omega's blood?"

Vance turned to face him, determination lighting his eyes. "You said it may have the ability to change medical science. It could help us heal people! What if we try it with Lily?"

Reese shook his head vehemently, his expression darkening. "No, Vance. Absolutely not."

"But—"

"Listen to me," Reese interrupted, stepping closer. "We don't know what Omega's blood can do. It's experimental at best, and we have no idea how it would react in a human body. It could cause more damage than good. It could kill her!"

Vance felt the heat rise in his chest, his frustration boiling over. "But what if it works? We have to at least consider it!"

Reese took a deep breath, trying to remain calm. "We are years away from being able to do something like what you're proposing. There are protocols, ethical guidelines. We can't just rush into this without knowing the potential consequences."

"But it's Lily! She's just a kid!" Vance's voice cracked, emotion pouring out of him. "I can't just stand by and let her life slip away. What kind of father would I be?"

Reese's expression softened, but he stood his ground. "You'd be a father who makes decisions based on reason and not desperation.

I get it, Vance. I really do. But jumping into a potentially dangerous experiment isn't the solution."

Vance ran a hand down his face, pacing the small space between them. "I know you're right, but it just feels so hopeless. If we don't try something—"

"Trying something doesn't mean throwing caution to the wind," Reese said, his tone firm. "We need to gather more information, see what we can do safely. We can't risk her life on a hunch."

Vance stopped, the weight of his words sinking in. "So what do we do then? Sit around and wait for the next bad news?"

"We support her," Reese replied, his voice softer now. "We stay by her side, help her through this however we can. But we can't rush into something that could make everything worse."

Vance felt the anger drain from his body, leaving him feeling hollow. "I just wish I could do more."

Reese placed a hand on Vance's shoulder. "You're doing more than you realize by being here for her. We'll figure this out, I promise."

Vance took a deep breath, grateful for Reese's support, even if it felt like a fragile lifeline in the chaos surrounding them. The quiet reassurance from his friend grounded him, but in the back of his mind, a different thought churned, growing louder with each passing moment: I am going to do what I have to do, old friend.

He turned to Reese, masking his inner turmoil with a composed facade. "Hey, can you tell Alice I'll be back soon? I just need to go for a drive and think."

Reese looked concerned. "Vance, are you sure that's a good idea? You don't want to be alone right now."

"I'll be fine," Vance insisted, forcing a smile. "Just need some fresh air to clear my head."

As he walked away, the heaviness in his chest felt unbearable. He exited the hospital, the fluorescent lights flickering above him as he made his way to his car. The night air hit him like a cold splash of water, sharp and invigorating, but it did little to cool the fire brewing inside him.

What am I going to do? He climbed into the driver's seat, the familiar scent of leather and metal filling his senses. Vance started the engine, the rumble a comforting sound as he pulled out of the parking lot and into the empty streets. The headlights cut through the darkness, illuminating the path ahead but doing nothing to illuminate the darkness clouding his mind.

He couldn't shake the image of Lily lying on that hospital bed, her small body so fragile, a mere shell of the vibrant girl he knew. *I can't lose her*, he thought fiercely. *Not like this.*

His thoughts turned to his personal lab. He had a small vial of Omega's blood locked away, the one thing he had kept secret from everyone, even Reese. It was a risk he had taken, driven by curiosity and ambition—one he had never expected to contemplate using so soon.

What if it could save her? The idea swirled in his mind, intoxicating and dangerous all at once. He thought about the potential—the possibility of something extraordinary happening. *Maybe this is the miracle drug we've been waiting for.*

But with that thought came the sharp edge of reality. He knew how reckless it was. The dangers of experimenting with something so volatile were enormous, but what choice did he have? *What if it works? What if it could help her walk again?*

As he drove, his mind raced with the implications. He envisioned the sterile walls of his lab, the cool, clinical environment where he could conduct the experiments away from prying eyes. *No one needs to know*, he reassured himself. *Just a few tests. Just to see if it has any potential.*

Vance gripped the steering wheel tightly, feeling the pulse of determination racing through him. *I'm her father. I need to do everything I can to save her. This isn't just about science; it's about my daughter.*

He made the turn toward his home, each mile bringing him closer to the moment of truth. The stakes were higher than ever, but deep down, he felt a flicker of hope igniting within him—a flicker he couldn't afford to extinguish.

As he pulled into the driveway, the house loomed in front of him, dark and quiet, but he felt the weight of what lay ahead. He had to be cautious, calculated. There was no room for error.

Vance parked, his heart pounding as he got out and made his way to the door. *This is for Lily. This is for her future.*

With resolve hardening in his chest, he stepped inside, the familiar surroundings offering little comfort as he headed toward his personal lab. The decisions he was about to make could change everything. In just a few moments, he would take a step toward something uncharted, crossing a line he had never imagined he would even consider.

He opened the door to his lab; the familiar sight of equipment and vials greeted him like old friends, but tonight, they felt different. Tonight, they were tools for a desperate act.

Vance approached the secured storage, his heart racing as he entered the access code. The lock clicked, and he felt a rush of adrenaline as the door swung open. There it was—the small vial of Omega's blood, gleaming ominously on the shelf.

I have to know, he thought as he reached for it. *For Lily, I have to know.*

Chapter 4: "Wild Side of the Stage"

Blake shifted uncomfortably in the small, cramped green room backstage at The Dave Hogan Show. It was his first time on live television, and the pressure was starting to get to him. He wiped his sweaty palms on his pants and checked the mirror again. He wasn't just here to talk cryptids or Kaiju—the stuff he usually thrived on. No, today, he had a very different task: showcasing animals from the Philadelphia Zoo.

Five of them.

The list had been curated for maximum cuteness, intrigue, and a little bit of danger. But still, this wasn't his usual gig, and the thought of messing up on live TV while wrangling animals made his stomach churn.

He snapped out of his anxious thoughts when a producer tapped on the door. "You're up in five minutes. Get ready."

Blake sighed, straightened his jacket, and stood. The animals were ready—five crates lined up along the wall. They'd been calm so far, though he could hear the occasional shuffle or grunt. He only hoped they'd behave once they were under the bright lights.

Then, the familiar booming voice of Dave Hogan echoed through the studio speakers.

"Ladies and gentlemen, we've got a wild treat for you today! Our next guest is someone who knows all about the wild side of life, whether it's in the forests hunting cryptids or today, here, with some real-life creatures from the Philadelphia Zoo! Please welcome, the man who's probably had more interesting close encounters than anyone else on this planet, Blake Bennett!"

Blake took a deep breath and rolled his shoulders back. Showtime.

As he stepped out from behind the curtain, the applause hit him like a wave. The audience was cheering, the stage lights were blinding, and at the center of it all was Dave Hogan, grinning like a mischievous kid.

"Blake, my man!" Dave called, walking over with outstretched arms. "You look like you're about to lead a safari!"

Blake laughed, shaking Dave's hand. "Yeah, but you know, I left the pith helmet at home."

The audience chuckled, and Blake relaxed a little. He could do this.

"So, Blake," Dave began, taking his seat on one of the chairs while motioning Blake to the other, "you've brought a few friends with you today, right?"

Blake grinned. "Oh yeah, I've got five little—or not-so-little—buddies from the Philadelphia Zoo who were more than happy to tag along. And don't worry, they promised to behave."

The crowd laughed, and Dave leaned in. "Alright, let's meet 'em! What's first?"

Blake turned toward the first crate and opened it carefully, reaching inside. "Let's start with a crowd favorite—a little something to ease us into the wild world."

Out came a Red Panda, its fluffy red and white fur contrasting beautifully under the lights.

"This little guy is Waffles," Blake said, cradling the Red Panda in his arms. "Now, red pandas are not actually pandas. In fact, they're more closely related to raccoons! Waffles here spends most of his time hanging out in trees, snacking on bamboo, and being so cute it's basically illegal."

Dave, always quick with a quip, leaned forward. "So, if I put a stack of waffles in a tree, will Waffles go after them?"

Blake smirked. "He might, but he'd be more interested in bamboo. Though, you could try maple syrup. I hear that's universal."

The audience chuckled, and Blake gently placed Waffles back in the crate.

"Alright, that's one down," Dave said. "What else you got for us?"

Blake moved to the next crate. "Next up, we've got something a little more exotic. This is Oliver, a Fennec Fox."

He lifted out a small, sandy-colored fox with enormous ears, drawing a chorus of "awws" from the audience.

"These little guys are from the Sahara Desert, so those big ears help them stay cool," Blake explained. "Plus, they have insane hearing. They can actually hear prey moving underground!"

Dave raised an eyebrow. "Kind of like my ex-wife at the ATM, huh?"

The audience erupted in laughter, and Blake shook his head, grinning. "Yeah, exactly. They're basically the desert's most adorable detectives."

Oliver was returned to his crate, and Blake moved on.

"Alright, now it's time to turn things up a notch," he said, giving a dramatic pause before opening the third crate. Out slithered a Green Tree Python, its emerald body coiled neatly around Blake's arm.

"This here is Jade," Blake said. "She's a Green Tree Python, and while she looks like she'd be at home in the grass, she actually spends most of her time in trees, waiting to ambush prey. She can sense heat with those pits near her mouth—so, Dave, be careful. She knows exactly where you are."

Dave recoiled a little for comedic effect. "I feel very seen right now, Blake. Very seen."

Blake laughed, "Don't worry, Jade's a total sweetheart—unless you're a mouse."

He placed Jade back into her crate, the audience still buzzing from the spectacle.

"Okay, okay," Dave said, raising a hand. "I'm not sweating or anything, but can we get something a little less... sneaky?"

Blake chuckled, moving to the fourth crate. "Alright, something a little more... 'fluffy.' Meet Nala, the African Pygmy Goat."

A small goat with tiny horns and a black-and-white coat stepped out, trotting around confidently.

"Now, pygmy goats are basically the comedians of the animal world," Blake said. "Nala here is curious, playful, and will chew on just about anything—including maybe my shoes if I stand here too long."

The crowd laughed as Nala nibbled on Blake's pant leg. Dave shook his head. "Okay, that's officially adorable. Can I keep her?"

"You'll have to talk to the zoo about that one," Blake joked. "But trust me, you don't want to deal with the insurance once she starts head-butting your furniture."

Finally, Blake moved to the last crate. "And for our grand finale, something a little more... majestic."

Out from the crate emerged a stunning Bald Eagle named Liberty. The room went silent in awe.

"This is Liberty," Blake said with pride. "Bald eagles, as you know, are a symbol of freedom here in the U.S. They've made a remarkable comeback from near extinction thanks to conservation efforts. Liberty here is a bit of a celebrity at the zoo. She's got a wingspan of about six feet and—let's be honest—she's the real star of the show today."

The audience burst into applause, admiring the powerful bird as it perched confidently on Blake's gloved arm.

Dave was beaming. "Alright, I gotta admit, that's pretty impressive. I think we've officially gone from cute to epic."

Blake smiled. "Yeah, she's kind of the Beyoncé of the bird world."

As the applause died down, Dave asked, "So, Blake, for anyone planning to visit the Philadelphia Zoo, how long do you think it'll take to see all these amazing creatures?"

"Well," Blake said, "the zoo is about 42 acres big and home to 1,700 animals. You could spend a couple of hours there or easily make it an all-day adventure depending on how much you want to explore. There's always something new to see."

Dave nodded, leaning back in his chair. "Sounds like an awesome day trip. Thanks for bringing a little bit of the wild into the studio today, Blake. It's been a blast."

As Blake was about to leave the stage, Dave leaned forward, his grin turning mischievous again. "Now, Blake, before you go, I gotta ask the big question."

Blake paused, sensing the shift in tone. "Oh boy. Here it comes."

Dave chuckled. "Look, everyone knows you've got this animal expertise, but I've done my homework. You're also a member of the Kaiju Task Force. You know, the group that deals with actual, massive, world-threatening monsters? So... what's that like? And—come on—what can you tell us about these Kaiju? Spill the beans, man!"

The audience gasped, and Blake couldn't help but smile. "I knew you'd bring it up eventually."

Dave threw his hands up. "You can't be out here wrangling zoo animals and not expect me to ask about that side of your life. So, what's the deal with these giant creatures? And let's start with the big one—Omega. She's, what, eight stories tall?"

Blake's eyes lit up, and his geek-out mode kicked in full throttle. "Yeah, Omega. She's a total force of nature. We're talking about a Kaiju that's roughly 30,000 tons of pure devastation. The queen of the ocean. Her powers? Insane. Aqua Beam, Tidal Surge, Regenerative Healing—you name it, she's got it. The first time I saw her, man, it was terrifying. Like, 'Oh, great, that's how I'm going to die' terrifying."

Dave leaned forward like a kid hearing his favorite superhero story. "No kidding? What was that like? You're out there, and suddenly, there's a skyscraper-sized dinosaur thing staring you down. What goes through your head?"

Blake shook his head, laughing. "Honestly? At first, it's like, 'Please don't let me pee my pants on live television.' But after that? You just know you've gotta do something. The team—Reese and Norah—we all knew we couldn't just sit there and let Omega tear through New York like it was a sandbox."

Dave was hanging on every word. "And what about the danger? I mean, I'm guessing this isn't like dealing with a rogue squirrel. How close did you actually get to Omega?"

Blake leaned back, raising his eyebrows. "Oh, we got close. Too close, if you ask me. Picture this: a Kaiju the size of a building, and I'm there with the team, trying to figure out how to stop something that can shoot laser beams from its neck vents. Laser beams. Like, what? Who even has that in their power set?"

Dave was practically bouncing in his seat, fanboying harder than ever. "That's so cool! Dude, you're like an actual superhero! Forget the zoo—this is the stuff I wanna hear about. What was the scariest moment for you?"

Blake scratched the back of his head. "You mean other than the part where I thought we were all gonna be crushed into tiny pancakes? That'd probably be when Omega used her Tidal Surge. We were in Manhattan trying to figure out where she'd strike next, and bam—this massive wave comes crashing through, courtesy of her. I swear, I thought the entire city was going to be wiped off the map."

The audience was dead silent, hanging on every word.

"And that's when we realized," Blake continued, "we weren't just fighting a monster. We were dealing with something on a scale we'd never seen before. It wasn't about survival anymore—it was about stopping her. And believe me, there were a few times where I was like, 'Okay, Blake, this is it. You're done.' But somehow, we kept going."

Dave shook his head in amazement. "Dude, you and the team are out here saving the world from Kaiju, and I'm over here worrying about whether or not I can finish a pizza by myself."

Blake smirked. "Well, in fairness, that's a pretty worthy battle too."

The crowd erupted in laughter, and Dave leaned back in his chair, clearly impressed. "You're telling me."

As the applause began to die down, Dave leaned forward, still grinning ear to ear. "Blake, I gotta admit, you and your team are awesome. I mean, actual superheroes! I'd love to get a tour of the Task Force building sometime, see those Valkyrie suits up close—maybe even try one on, huh?"

Blake's smile faltered a little. He rubbed the back of his neck, his expression softening. "Yeah, about that... I don't know if that's going to be possible, Dave."

Dave's grin slipped as he noticed Blake's change in tone. "Wait, what do you mean? Is it one of those top-secret, hush-hush government things? Come on, man, you can hook me up!"

Blake sighed and shrugged. "It's not about the secrecy anymore. The government shut down the Kaiju Task Force. Project's disbanded. The Valkyrie suits? Locked up. No tours, no nothing. It's all... over."

The audience collectively gasped at the revelation, and Dave's jaw dropped. He leaned back dramatically, slapping his hands on the desk. "You're kidding me! They shut you guys down? Why? You were out there saving the world from giant monsters! This is like finding out they canceled Christmas."

Blake chuckled at Dave's over-the-top reaction, shaking his head. "Yeah, trust me, I wasn't thrilled about it either. Politics, budgets, priorities shifting—all that boring stuff. Apparently, giant monsters aren't a top priority anymore." He shrugged. "Guess when you don't have a Kaiju knocking at your door, it's easy to forget how important it was."

Dave, always one to find the humor in anything, groaned and waved his hand in exaggerated frustration. "Man, the worst mistake of the century! These are the same people who made kale chips a thing. This is an outrage!" He pointed at Blake, eyes wide in mock indignation. "You're telling me I'm never going to get to see those awesome suits in person?"

Blake smirked. "Sorry, Dave. The closest you're getting is the action figures they sell at the gift shop."

The crowd roared with laughter, and Dave threw his hands in the air. "Well, that's just great. Guess I'll have to settle for dressing up as a Kaiju for Halloween instead. Do you think the suit comes in XXL?"

Blake burst out laughing. "You're going to have to get it custom-made, my friend."

The audience joined in the laughter as Dave dramatically slumped over his desk. "Man, I was really hoping to look cool in one of those suits. Fine, Blake, I'll let it slide this time. But the next time you take down a Kaiju, you owe me a selfie."

Blake shook his head, still chuckling. "Deal."

The show wrapped up, and after the cameras stopped rolling, Blake made his way backstage. He was packing up his gear and getting ready to head out when he heard someone clearing their throat behind him. He turned around to see Dave standing there, his usual goofy grin replaced by a surprisingly sincere expression.

"Hey, Blake," Dave started, his hands stuffed awkwardly into his pockets. "I just wanted to say... thanks. You know, for everything you and your team did. I mean, I know I was joking around up there, but what you guys did was huge. You saved a lot of lives. And if it means anything, I for one think the Task Force should be back up and running. I'll be out there rooting for you, man. Saying it loud to whoever I can, trying to get you guys reinstated."

Blake was taken aback by the sincerity in Dave's voice. He wasn't used to seeing this side of the comedian. "Thanks, Dave. That means a lot."

"And hey," Dave continued, his grin returning, "if they ever bring the Task Force back, you just tell 'em I'm volunteering to be the janitor.

Just let me in the building, give me a broom, and let me peek at the Valkyrie suits. I'll mop the floors, scrub the toilets—whatever it takes!"

Blake couldn't help but laugh. "You, a janitor? I'm not sure I trust you with cleaning supplies."

Dave puffed out his chest, pretending to be offended. "Excuse me, I'll have you know I once mopped a whole stage after spilling an entire gallon of coffee. I'm practically a pro."

Blake raised an eyebrow. "You spilled the coffee?"

Dave waved him off. "Details, details. The point is, I'm dedicated. And if cleaning the Task Force HQ is what it takes to get me in, I'm your guy."

Blake shook his head, still laughing. "I'll keep that in mind."

Dave clapped Blake on the shoulder, his grin returning to full force. "You do that. But seriously, man, thanks again. You're a real-life hero, and don't let anyone forget it."

Blake gave a nod, feeling a warmth in his chest. For all of Dave's goofiness, the guy had a good heart. "Thanks, Dave. I appreciate it."

With that, Dave gave a dramatic salute, almost bumping into a prop backstage as he turned to leave. Blake watched him go, shaking his head with a smile.

"Janitor of the Task Force," Blake muttered to himself. "That guy's something else."

But as he stood there, he couldn't help but feel a flicker of hope. Maybe, just maybe, the Task Force wasn't done for good. And if it ever came back, at least he'd know he had one very enthusiastic janitor ready and waiting.

Chapter 5: Behind the Tech and the Dream

Norah sat at her desk, her fingers flying over the keyboard as she fine-tuned the coding for Tesla's newest project—a fully autonomous driving system upgrade that would revolutionize the way people interacted with their vehicles. The hum of the bustling research and development department buzzed around her, but Norah was fully immersed in her work, her mind a well-oiled machine of innovation and creativity. This was where she thrived.

A few feet away, her colleagues gathered around a sleek new prototype—a drone-android hybrid that she had been pivotal in designing. The android looked like something straight out of a superhero movie: a sleek, metallic frame with built-in repulsor jets on its hands and feet, giving it an Iron Man-like appearance. Elon Musk had been particularly excited about this one, intending to use it as his own personal security detail.

Norah smirked, watching as the team tested the android's flight capabilities. It shot into the air with a soft hum, the jets propelling it gracefully through the air before it landed smoothly back on the ground.

"Not bad, huh?" one of her teammates, Sophia, grinned as she nudged Norah's shoulder.

"Not bad at all," Norah replied, a spark of pride in her voice. "Just wait until we get the laser systems fully integrated. Elon's gonna feel like Tony Stark himself."

Sophia laughed. "And to think, just a few months ago we were working on self-parking cars. Now we're building flying robots for billionaires."

Norah chuckled along, but her mind wasn't fully in the moment. As much as she loved her job, as much as she loved the thrill of creating cutting-edge technology and pushing boundaries, there was always something lingering in the back of her mind. Something that had never really left her since the day the Kaiju Task Force had been disbanded.

The Kaiju. The Valkyrie suits. The threat that loomed over the world, even if no one seemed to acknowledge it anymore.

Her mind drifted back to those days—long hours in the Task Force R&D labs, developing technology to combat creatures that defied human comprehension. She'd been working on weapons that could level the playing field against these titanic monsters. But now, she spent her days improving luxury cars and designing security drones for a tech mogul.

It wasn't the same. It wasn't enough.

She glanced at the notebook tucked discreetly under a stack of blueprints on her desk. It was worn, the cover faded from being opened and closed so many times. Inside it was a treasure trove of sketches, diagrams, and ideas she had never shared with anyone—not her team, not even Elon Musk.

The notebook was filled with concepts for new weapons, advancements for the Valkyrie suits, ways to make them faster, more efficient, and more comfortable for the pilots. She had even developed a new kind of neural interface that would allow the pilots to react more quickly to the Kaiju's movements. Every time a new idea hit her, she jotted it down in the notebook, keeping the dream alive in secret.

Norah sighed and pulled herself back into the moment as Sophia called her over to help with a new calibration. She grabbed a tablet and made her way over to the prototype, slipping into her professional mode with ease. But the flicker of that other life—the life she hadn't quite let go of—never left her.

Later that evening, as the team wrapped up for the day and the lab quieted down, Norah sat alone at her desk. The lights dimmed, casting soft shadows across the room. She flipped open her notebook, running her fingers over the sketches of the Valkyrie suits, the weapon enhancements, and the control room layouts she had been tweaking.

She had never been able to shake the feeling that they would need the Kaiju Task Force again. It wasn't just about the thrill of the work or the challenge of building something that could stand up to creatures of mythic proportions—it was the knowledge that the world was still vulnerable. No matter how many autonomous cars or flying security bots they built, humanity was still just as fragile as it had been the day Omega tore through Alaska.

Norah stared at one particular page in her notebook, a sketch of a revamped Valkyrie suit. She had added more ergonomic controls, redesigned the cockpit to give pilots better visibility, and even integrated an emergency self-healing system for the suit itself. It wasn't just a fantasy; it was practical, it was possible—if only they were given the chance to use it. She knew she could make the nanotechnology needed for it if only given a chance.

She tapped her pen against the page, lost in thought.

A part of her wished she could be back with the Task Force, working on these designs full-time, pushing the limits of what was possible to protect the world from threats it didn't even realize were still lurking. But the reality was different now. She was at Tesla, working on projects that, while groundbreaking, didn't hold the same weight in her heart.

"Maybe one day," she muttered to herself, closing the notebook and tucking it back under the blueprints. "Maybe one day they'll need us again."

But for now, she would keep her ideas safe, waiting for the moment when the world would wake up and remember that they still needed the people who could face the impossible.

As Norah shut down her lab for the night, the hum of the machinery fading into silence, she felt a deep sense of satisfaction. Another day of progress. Another day closer to bringing something incredible into the world. She gathered her things, placing her notebook carefully in her bag before flicking off the lights and heading toward the lobby.

In the gleaming lobby of Tesla's headquarters, she spotted Elon Musk standing near the front desk, chatting with a few executives. His presence always filled the room, and despite his eccentricities, Norah had grown fond of their brief interactions over the years.

"Good night, Elon," she called out with a small wave as she passed by.

Elon turned, offering her one of his trademark smirks. "Good night, Norah. Don't stay up too late inventing the future."

Norah chuckled as she stepped outside into the cool night air. The sky was clear, and the stars twinkled brightly above. She made her way to her electric car, the smooth lines of the sleek vehicle reflecting the lights from the parking lot. Sliding into the driver's seat, she activated the self-driving mode and leaned back, letting the car navigate its way home while her mind drifted.

Though her work was fulfilling, there was something even more precious waiting for her at home—her family.

When she pulled into the driveway, the lights of her smart house automatically lit up, welcoming her. As she approached the front door, it unlocked with a soft click, and the gentle hum of the home's advanced AI system greeted her with a warm, "Welcome home, Norah."

Inside, the house was a marvel of modern technology—automated lights, climate control, and even a kitchen that could prepare meals on its own. But as impressive as all that was, what mattered most to her was the sound of tiny feet rushing toward her.

"Mama!" Her two small children, a five-year-old boy named Noah and a three-year-old girl named Hannah, ran up to her, giggling as they crashed into her legs for a hug.

Norah's husband, Caleb, stood in the doorway of the living room, a wide smile on his face. "Look who finally made it home," he teased, crossing the room to kiss her on the cheek.

"I know, I know," she said, laughing as she wrapped her arms around him. "Long day at the lab. But I'm here now."

"Just in time for bedtime," Caleb said, glancing at their two rambunctious kids.

"No bedtime yet!" Noah protested, while Hannah clung to Norah, yawning but trying to stay awake.

Norah smiled softly, ruffling Noah's hair. "Alright, alright, how about a bedtime story first?"

Both kids' faces lit up as they ran to the bookshelf, searching for their favorite books. Norah followed them into their bedroom, where the walls were adorned with bright, interactive screens that could display anything from soothing nature scenes to educational games. Tonight, they had chosen a soft sunset.

Noah and Hannah finally settled on one of their favorites—a children's Bible storybook. Norah smiled as she sat on the edge of Noah's bed and pulled her little ones close. She opened the book to the story of Jonah and the whale, her voice soft but animated as she began to read.

"Once upon a time, there was a man named Jonah," Norah began. "God asked Jonah to go to a city called Nineveh, but Jonah didn't want to go. Instead, he ran away, and he ended up on a ship in the middle of a storm."

Noah's eyes widened. "A storm?"

"That's right," Norah said, nodding. "A big, scary storm. The sailors were so scared, but Jonah knew the storm was happening because he had tried to run away from what God wanted him to do. So, he told the sailors to throw him into the sea."

Hannah gasped, hugging her stuffed animal closer.

"But guess what?" Norah continued with a smile. "God sent a big fish to swallow Jonah and keep him safe. Jonah stayed in the fish's belly for three days, praying and asking God to forgive him."

Hannah, with her big, innocent eyes, looked up at Norah. "Was Jonah scared?"

"I think he was," Norah said softly. "Just like anyone would be. But even though Jonah was scared, he knew that God was with him. And because he trusted in God, he found the courage to face his fears and do what he was supposed to do."

Noah, ever curious, asked, "Did Jonah fight any Kaiju, Mama?"

Norah chuckled, shaking her head. "Not quite, but it wasn't too different in a way."

Her voice softened as she thought of the Kaiju Task Force. "You know, there were times when I felt like Jonah," she said, looking between her two children. "When the Kaiju first appeared, I was scared. We all were. They were so big, so powerful, and it felt like no matter what we did, we couldn't stop them. But I kept my faith. I believed that we were doing the right thing, that we were protecting the world, and that God was watching over us."

"And did God help you, like Jonah?" Hannah asked, her sleepy eyes wide with wonder.

Norah smiled, stroking her daughter's hair. "Yes, I believe He did. He gave us the strength to keep going, even when things seemed impossible."

As she finished the story of Jonah, Norah felt a deep sense of peace. She kissed her children goodnight, watching as they drifted off to sleep.

The house, with all its technology and advancements, was nothing compared to the warmth and love she felt in that moment.

Before she left the room, she whispered, "Just like Jonah, we have to be brave. No matter how big the storm—or the Kaiju."

Chapter 6: The Breakthrough

The dim, sterile light of Vance Hadrian's secret laboratory flickered as he hovered over his desk, eyes strained from days without proper rest. Scattered across the metal surface were vials of Omega's blood, microscopes, and charts filled with chemical equations and scribbled notes—each a testament to his tireless efforts. His face, once clean-shaven, was now marked by stubble, and dark circles clung to his eyes.

It had been days—no, weeks—since Vance had locked himself in his private lab beneath the house, determined to find a way to heal his daughter Lily. Every time he saw her in that hospital bed, immobile, his heart shattered. Her life would never be the same if he couldn't do something. He knew that. And as much as Reese had tried to talk him out of it, reminding him of the countless dangers, Vance couldn't just stand by.

Reese was brilliant, perhaps one of the sharpest scientific minds in the world, but Vance... Vance was something else. He thrived on pushing the boundaries, on bending the rules of what science could do. He had always been willing to go where others wouldn't dare—now more than ever.

The faint hum of the lab's machines filled the silence as he studied the latest sample. Omega's blood shimmered under the harsh light, almost alive with potential. Its regenerative properties were extraordinary—more potent than anything he had ever seen. For hours, he'd analyzed it, isolated its components, and theorized how to harness its powers.

But theory wasn't enough. He needed proof.

With his head down, deep in thought, Vance hardly noticed the hours pass. His only breaks were to grab a quick bite, kiss Alice on the cheek, and occasionally take a shower. Each time he emerged, he looked more disheveled, more lost in the depths of his obsession. His wife worried, of course, but she knew better than to question him. Vance had always been relentless when it came to the people he loved.

Finally, after what felt like an eternity, he felt something click. His eyes widened, scanning over the glowing screen in front of him. The data—it was all there. He'd done it. He had isolated the key factor in Omega's blood that allowed it to regenerate so quickly.

His heart raced as he reached for a syringe, drawing out a small amount of the solution he had created. If this worked, it could not only restore Lily's ability to walk—it could change medical science forever. But he couldn't risk testing it on her. Not yet. First, he needed to know if it would even work on a human being.

Taking a deep breath, Vance stood up, steadying himself. His hand trembled as he grabbed a small hammer from his desk. He hesitated for only a moment, knowing there was no turning back. Then, without another thought, he slammed the hammer down onto his thumb with a sickening crack. Pain shot up his arm, sharp and immediate, as his thumb swelled and turned a deep purple.

Vance gritted his teeth, eyes watering from the sudden agony. But he remained focused, reaching for the syringe and plunging it into his arm. He injected the solution quickly, watching with a mix of hope and fear as the liquid flowed through his veins.

Seconds passed. Nothing happened.

He glanced at his thumb, now throbbing with pain, and a wave of doubt crashed over him. What if this was all for nothing? What if it couldn't work on humans? Or worse—what if it backfired, and he ended up worse off?

But then, as he stared down at his hand, something remarkable began to happen. The pain started to fade, slowly at first, but unmistakably. His swollen thumb pulsed once, twice—and then the skin started to knit itself back together before his eyes. The discoloration receded, and the bones realigned with a soft, almost imperceptible click.

Within a minute, his thumb was completely healed.

Vance stared in awe, flexing his hand and wiggling his thumb as if testing to see if it was real. It worked. It actually worked.

He let out a shaky laugh, half from relief and half from disbelief. He had done it. He had replicated Omega's healing ability in a human. His mind raced, already leaping ahead to the next step. This was just the beginning. If it could heal his broken thumb, it could heal Lily. It could give her life back.

Vance's laughter faded, replaced by a solemn determination. He knew the risks. He knew this was uncharted territory, and there were no guarantees. But Lily was worth the risk. She was his daughter, and he would do anything—anything—to save her.

He would have to be careful, of course. Reese couldn't know about this, not yet. Neither could Alice, not until he was sure it would work. But now, with this breakthrough, Vance felt more certain than ever that he could restore Lily's ability to walk.

Clenching his newly healed hand into a fist, Vance whispered to himself, "I'll make you whole again, Lily. I promise."

The sterile hum of the hospital's fluorescent lights filled the quiet corridors as Vance Hadrian stepped cautiously through the entrance. It was late—well past visiting hours—but that didn't matter tonight. He had only one goal in mind. He walked past the darkened reception desk, his shoes making the faintest of sounds against the tiled floor, each step heavy with the weight of what he was about to do.

His heart pounded in his chest as he entered the intensive care wing where his daughter, Lily, lay recovering. The room was dimly lit, the soft glow of the machines casting faint shadows across her peaceful face. She looked so fragile lying there, as if the world had stolen all the energy from her once vibrant spirit. Vance paused at the doorway, overcome with a mixture of guilt and hope.

He pulled a small vial from his coat pocket, the faint luminescent glow of its contents reminding him of the hours he had spent perfecting the serum. Omega's blood had given him a chance—a chance to undo the damage done to his daughter. The serum that now rested in his hands was the key to her future, to her walking again. But it was also a gamble, one that no one else could know about.

He approached Lily's bedside, his eyes locked on her face. She was sleeping peacefully, her chest rising and falling in slow, rhythmic breaths. She looked so serene, as if the pain of her injuries didn't exist in her dreams. Vance leaned down, brushing a gentle kiss across her forehead. He lingered there for a moment, his lips pressed softly against her skin, whispering a silent prayer that this would work.

"I'm going to fix this, baby girl," he murmured under his breath, his voice barely audible. "I promise."

His hands shook slightly as he attached the syringe to the IV line that was feeding her medication. With one deep breath, he injected the serum into the drip, watching the faint blue liquid mix with the clear medicine and flow into Lily's bloodstream. He stood there for a moment, waiting. Waiting for something—anything—to happen. But nothing did. At least not yet.

Vance knew it would take time. The serum needed to bond with her cells, to work its magic the same way it had on him. It would be slow, perhaps even painful, but if it worked, she would walk again. She would have her life back.

He gently touched her hand, his heart swelling with both hope and fear. There was no turning back now. This was the path he had chosen.

"Sleep tight, Lily," he whispered, before turning away and quietly leaving the room.

The walk back to his car felt surreal. The weight of what he had done hung heavy on his shoulders, but there was also a spark of something else—hope. He slid into the driver's seat, staring out into the night as the hospital disappeared in his rearview mirror. He had done what any father would have done—he had given his daughter a second chance.

When Vance finally arrived home, the house was silent. The weight of the past few weeks settled over him like a fog as he made his way upstairs to the bedroom. Alice was already asleep, her body curled under the blankets, her face calm and peaceful. He stood at the doorway for a moment, watching her, before quietly slipping into bed beside her.

As he lay there, staring at the ceiling, his mind raced. What would tomorrow bring? Would the serum work as it had on him? Would he wake to a phone call from the hospital telling him something miraculous had happened? Or, worse, would it be the opposite? He clenched his jaw, willing the dark thoughts to disappear.

I had to do it.

He repeated the thought over and over again, as if trying to convince himself it was true. He had no choice. Lily deserved to walk again, to live a full life. And if this serum worked, she would.

He turned to his side, his hand gently resting on Alice's shoulder as he let out a soft sigh. The world felt heavy, but for the first time in weeks, there was a flicker of hope.

Tomorrow, he would find out if his gamble had paid off.

With that thought, Vance closed his eyes.

Vance was deep in a restless sleep, his mind a whirlpool of dreams and nightmares. The weight of his secret actions clung to him like a shadow, even in his unconscious state. Then, something pulled him from the murky depths—a voice. A familiar, joyful voice, shaking him awake.

"Vance! Vance, wake up!"

His eyes blinked open to find Alice standing over him, her face alight with excitement, tears welling in her eyes. Her hands gripped his shoulders, gently shaking him again.

"What? What's going on?" Vance mumbled, still groggy, as he sat up in bed, rubbing his face.

"It's Lily!" Alice exclaimed, her voice almost breaking with emotion. "Vance, she's—she's walking!"

His heart skipped a beat. He stared at Alice in disbelief, wondering if he was still caught in some kind of dream.

"What did you say?" he asked, his voice low, almost afraid to believe it.

Alice smiled, tears now streaming down her cheeks. "Lily woke up this morning... and she stood up, Vance. The nurses had to catch her because she almost fell, but she's walking! She's walking with the therapists right now, down the halls. The doctors—they don't understand it. No one can explain how, but she's walking!"

The room spun as Vance took in her words. His pulse quickened, and a swell of emotion rose in his chest—hope, disbelief, fear, joy—all crashing into him at once. He had imagined this moment, prayed for it, but now that it was here, he could hardly comprehend it.

"We have to go," Vance said, his voice shaking as he threw back the covers. He was already on his feet, pulling on a shirt with trembling hands. "We need to see her."

Alice nodded, already grabbing her purse, practically bouncing with energy. "I called ahead; they said we can come right now. She's... she's waiting for us."

They rushed out of the house in a blur. The drive to the hospital felt like an eternity, Vance gripping the steering wheel as tightly as his emotions. His mind raced. Had the serum really worked? Could it have healed her this quickly, this completely? Or was it something else? The possibility scared him as much as it exhilarated him.

When they arrived at the hospital, Vance didn't even wait for the car to fully stop before he was out, heading toward the entrance. Alice followed closely behind, her steps as frantic as his. The sterile halls of the hospital seemed endless, each one leading them closer to the truth. Nurses glanced at them as they rushed past, but neither of them cared.

Finally, they reached the ward where Lily had been recovering. A few steps more, and there she was—just as Alice had said.

Lily was standing.

She was moving slowly, supported by a physical therapist and a nurse on either side of her, but she was upright, her legs bearing weight. Her face was a mixture of concentration and sheer amazement as she took shaky steps down the hallway. The look on her face as she spotted her parents made Vance's heart clench.

"Mom, Dad!" she called, her voice filled with a joy that made tears spring to Vance's eyes. "Look at me!"

Alice ran to her, throwing her arms around her daughter the moment the therapists paused to give them space. Lily stumbled a little under the embrace, but she was standing, her legs steadying after a moment.

"Oh my God, Lily," Alice sobbed, cradling her daughter. "I can't believe it... I can't..."

Vance stood frozen, watching the scene unfold. His mind reeled with the impossibility of it, yet there she was—his daughter, standing, walking. The emotions hit him like a tidal wave, and before he knew it, he was beside Alice, pulling them both into his arms.

"I told you, Dad," Lily said, her voice cracking as she looked up at him. "I told you I'd walk again."

Vance smiled through the tears welling in his eyes. He stroked her hair, the weight of everything he had done settling deep in his chest.

He had broken every rule, crossed every line. But for this—for this moment—he would do it all again.

The doctors stood at a distance, exchanging hushed whispers, their faces pale with confusion. None of them had an explanation. The scans they had taken just days before showed irreversible damage. But here she was, defying their predictions, doing the impossible.

"How... how did this happen?" one of the doctors finally approached, speaking cautiously, as if afraid to break the spell. "We were certain the damage to her spine was... unrepairable."

Alice shook her head, still holding Lily close. "I don't care how," she said, her voice thick with emotion. "It's a miracle. That's all I know."

Vance remained silent, his gaze locked on his daughter, his heart pounding in his chest. A miracle, Alice had said. Perhaps. But he knew what it really was. It wasn't luck or fate—it was science. It was Omega's blood.

Lily took a few more steps with the therapists, her strength still faltering but her resolve unshaken. She would need months of therapy, maybe years. But she was walking.

Vance couldn't stay in the moment any longer. He needed a second to breathe, to process. He excused himself, slipping out into the hallway, away from the excited chatter.

He had done it. He had succeeded.

But what now?

As he leaned against the cool wall outside the room, a flood of mixed emotions overtook him—relief, guilt, pride. He had played God, used something untested on his own daughter, and now—now she was walking. But how long would it last? Would there be side effects? And what if someone found out?

Shoving the thoughts aside, Vance closed his eyes for a moment. He had to keep this secret. For Lily's sake. For his family's sake.

And whatever the consequences... he would face them when they came.

For now, he would simply enjoy the miracle.

Chapter 7: Pressure Points

Vance sat in his office, staring out through the massive glass windows that framed the city skyline. The sun was just beginning to climb, casting long, golden rays across the buildings below. It was a breathtaking view, one that usually brought him a sense of peace. But not today. Today, his mind was a storm of conflicting thoughts.

His daughter, Lily, was walking again—a miraculous success. But beneath the triumph, an unsettling feeling gnawed at him. The serum he had created from Omega's blood had worked, but it was untested, unpredictable. And now, there were bigger things looming on the horizon.

A soft chime broke the silence, followed by a knock on his office door.

"Mr. Hadrian," his secretary's voice came through the intercom. "General Strayer is here for your appointment."

Vance exhaled sharply, pushing the weight of his thoughts aside. "Send her in."

The door opened, and General Sarah Strayer strode into the office with her usual commanding presence. Her uniform was immaculate, her expression as sharp and unyielding as ever. A woman of fierce reputation, Strayer had little patience for delays or excuses—especially not from someone on her payroll.

"General," Vance greeted her with a tight smile, rising from his chair. "Please, have a seat."

Strayer didn't return the smile. She walked briskly to the chair in front of his desk and sat down, folding her arms across her chest. Her eyes locked onto him with the intensity of someone who was not in the mood for pleasantries.

"I'll get right to it, Vance," she said, her tone cold and businesslike. "I'm here because we need to talk about the bio-weapons program—and why I've seen absolutely no progress on what you promised."

Vance steeled himself. He knew this conversation was coming, but that didn't make it any easier. "I assure you, General, I've had some breakthroughs recently that are going to change everything."

"Breakthroughs, huh?" Strayer raised an eyebrow. "Well, I'm glad to hear that. But the problem is, we've been waiting for these 'breakthroughs' for months now. And we're running out of time."

She leaned forward, her eyes narrowing. "You're supposed to be developing the next generation of soldiers. Weapons that we can use in times of war instead of human soldiers. I've seen nothing but reports and delays. What exactly are you working on, Vance?"

His jaw clenched. He wasn't about to tell her about the serum he'd developed for Lily—not yet. He needed more time. "I've been perfecting the integration process. The fusion of animal DNA is... complex. But as I said, I've made significant strides. I just need a little more time to finalize the testing."

Strayer's eyes flashed with impatience. "More time? We don't have more time. You were given a mandate—to create something that would prevent us from using humans and, in turn, save human lives. And what have you delivered so far? Nothing."

She stood up, her voice growing colder with every word. "I'll be frank with you, Vance. If you don't show me something concrete—something I can take back to my superiors—I'm recommending that we cancel all your contracts. Your funding will be pulled, and this entire operation will be shut down."

Vance felt his pulse quicken. He couldn't afford to lose this project. Not now. Not when he was so close. He took a deep breath, steadying himself.

"I understand your concerns, General," he said, choosing his words carefully. "But I assure you, what I'm working on is going to revolutionize everything. I'm on the cusp of something that will surpass all expectations. I just need a few more weeks to—"

"You have one week," Strayer interrupted, her tone final. "One week to show me something real, or I'm pulling the plug."

Her cold gaze bore into him for a moment longer before she turned on her heel and headed for the door. She paused just before exiting and glanced back at him.

"I'll be back next week, Hadrian. And I expect results. Do not disappoint me."

With that, she walked out, leaving Vance alone in the silence of his office, the weight of her ultimatum pressing down on him like a lead blanket.

Vance sat back down heavily in his chair, running a hand through his hair. He had to move fast. The serum he had developed for Lily was a success, but using it as the foundation for hybrid bio-weapons would be a different challenge altogether.

Still, he had no choice.

Vance looked over at the locked cabinet in the corner of his office. Behind the reinforced glass, the last few vials of Omega's blood sat in cold, sterile stasis, their blue hue glowing faintly under the soft light. They were the key to everything. He had known that since the moment he'd first seen Omega—majestic and terrifying, her body regenerating faster than any human or machine could react. Now, her blood was the only thing that could save his career—and his daughter.

But there was no way Reese, the so-called "ethics police," would ever go along with what he was about to do. Reese was brilliant, but his moral compass was unwavering. Vance, on the other hand, had no such luxury. His funding was on the line, his contract with the military hanging by a thread, and, more importantly, Lily's miracle had shown him that he was close. So close. He couldn't afford to lose it all now.

Vance stood, walked over to the cabinet, and unlocked it with trembling fingers. He pulled out the vials, staring at the swirling liquid inside. It was the answer. It had to be.

Without hesitation, he grabbed his lab coat and headed down to the lower levels of his building, where his laboratory lay hidden behind layers of security only he could bypass. The hallway lights flickered as he descended into the cold, sterile environment.

The lab was silent except for the soft hum of machinery. In the center of the room, he was taken aback to find not three, but four units lined up in a row, each one meticulously labeled. "Aquila, Lynxara, Titanax, and... Felonix?" he murmured, raising an eyebrow in curiosity at the last name. Felonix? The name struck him as odd, almost mythical, and he couldn't recall ever authorizing such a designation. He shrugged off the thought—there was no time to waste analyzing the labels. With a sense of determination surging through him, Vance decided he would proceed with the treatment for all four embryos, each containing an embryonic hybrid in deep freeze. They were early-stage experiments—fusions of animal and Kaiju DNA that Vance had been working on for months. So far, every attempt had resulted in failure. The two DNA strains always fought each other, breaking down the host organism within days. But now, with Omega's blood, he believed he could stabilize the fusion process.

He had to.

Approaching the cryo-chambers, Vance input the security codes, and the pods hissed as they began to thaw. He watched as frost melted away from the glass, revealing the shadowy figures of the embryos floating inside. They were no bigger than a grapefruit, each one representing a different animal's DNA mixed.

wasted no time. He placed the vials of Omega's blood onto the sterile lab tray and grabbed a syringe. Carefully, he extracted a precise amount of the serum, his hands steady despite the weight of what he was about to do.

"Here we go," he muttered to himself as he inserted the syringe into the first embryo.

The blood of Omega flowed into the tiny, undeveloped creature, disappearing into its form. Vance knew the properties of Omega's blood—its regenerative abilities, its extraordinary adaptability—would give these hybrids the stability they lacked. Omega's DNA would act as a bridge between the disparate animal and Kaiju genes, fusing them together in a way that would prevent rejection, mutation, or decay. It was the breakthrough he needed.

After injecting each of the four embryos with the serum, Vance activated the incubator. The machine whirred to life, its interior glowing softly as it began to simulate the conditions of a mother's womb—a controlled, safe environment where the hybrids could develop without external interference.

Vance wiped the sweat from his forehead and leaned back, watching the embryos slowly begin to respond. Their tiny forms started to twitch, small movements rippling through them as the serum worked its way into their cellular structure.

A mixture of excitement and anxiety gripped him. This was it. The hybrids were in the process of becoming something more, something stable. If it worked—when it worked—he would have results to show General Strayer. He would save his contracts, secure his funding, and, with that, continue perfecting his work with Lily.

Vance set the incubator's timer and secured the chamber. It would take time for the embryos to fully develop, but once they did, they would be ready for testing—ready to prove his theories correct.

As he left the lab, a small, dangerous smile crept across his face. He was playing with fire, yes, but for the first time in months, he felt in control. Omega's blood was his key to everything.

And soon, the world would see what he had created.

Chapter 8: Discovery and Suspicion

Reese entered the lab the next morning, still groggy from a restless night of sleep. The work surrounding Omega's abilities and how they could potentially revolutionize human medicine had consumed his thoughts for days. It was exciting, yet frustrating. Every hypothesis he had come up with had hit a roadblock. Applying a Kaiju's incredible regenerative properties to human biology was far more complicated than any of them could have imagined.

He tossed his bag on the counter and went about his usual routine—coffee, reviewing notes, checking the equipment. But something caught his attention almost immediately: the incubators were active.

His brow furrowed in confusion. That didn't make sense. The embryos—Aquila, Lynxara, Titanax, and Felonix—had been in stasis for months now. They weren't supposed to be touched. Not yet. He hurried over to the monitoring station, his fingers flying across the keyboard as he brought up the live data. His breath caught in his throat.

All four embryos were stable.

Not just stable—growing.

"What the—?" Reese muttered, his eyes widening as he checked the vital signs. Heart rates, oxygen levels, nutrient consumption—all were well within healthy ranges. His mind raced. This wasn't possible. How had they stabilized? They had spent months trying to prevent cellular rejection and DNA breakdown, and yet here were these four embryos, thriving.

A quick glance at the system logs told him something even more alarming. The incubators had been activated only hours ago, sometime in the dead of night. They'd gone from dormant to accelerated growth in an impossibly short period of time. And the most shocking part? They weren't just growing at a normal rate. They had expanded by weeks in mere hours. It was as though something had turbocharged their development.

"How?" he whispered to himself, feeling a pit forming in his stomach. He leaned closer to the display showing Aquila—an avian-like creature, its limbs extending in length and muscle density more rapidly than he'd ever thought possible.

He flicked to Lynxara next, a feline hybrid showing signs of early muscle coordination as it twitched within its chamber, its form already taking on a lithe, powerful structure.

Titanax, a colossal creature in the making, already displayed an early indication of bone plate formations, growing far larger and stronger than anything the data had suggested.

And then there was Felonix.

The mysterious embryo—the one he hadn't even planned on using until recently—was growing faster than the others. Its heartbeat was strong, and its form more fully developed, though the monitoring system struggled to categorize its genetic structure. It was almost as if Felonix was something altogether new.

"This is insane..." Reese breathed, staring at the timers on the system. They had been activated only a few hours ago, right around 3 AM. The timer logs were clear as day. Someone had done this deliberately.

"Vance," Reese whispered to himself. He couldn't think of anyone else with the clearance and ability to run these kinds of tests without alerting the rest of the team. But why? And what had he done to stabilize the embryos?

His mind raced, pieces of the puzzle beginning to align, though the picture was still blurry. Vance had been acting strange for weeks, almost avoiding direct conversations about progress. Could he have made a breakthrough and kept it secret?

Reese stared at the active chambers, his heart pounding. Something about this felt wrong. He couldn't shake the feeling that whatever had been done to these embryos had crossed an ethical line—a line Vance might be willing to step over in his desperation.

He took a deep breath, knowing he'd need to confront Vance, but he also couldn't ignore the scientific marvel happening right in front of him. Weeks of growth in mere hours. Stable, active embryos. This could change everything—if it didn't destroy them first.

Reese stormed down the corridor toward Vance's office, his mind racing with disbelief. The image of those incubators, active and humming with life, kept replaying in his mind. The hybrids had been stable, yes—but they were also growing exponentially faster than they should. He wasn't just shocked. He was angry.

When he reached Vance's office, he didn't bother to knock. He threw the door open, startling Vance, who was seated at his desk, casually sipping coffee while reading through a tablet.

"Care to explain what the hell is going on in the lab?" Reese snapped, his voice barely contained.

Vance didn't flinch. In fact, a smirk curled at the corner of his mouth. "I assume you're talking about the hybrids," he said, setting his tablet down with a slow, deliberate motion.

"You know exactly what I'm talking about," Reese shot back. "The embryos. They're alive. They're growing. That's not supposed to be possible. We agreed to wait until we had all the data before taking any action."

Vance leaned back in his chair, entirely too smug for Reese's liking. "What are you complaining about? This is exactly what we wanted. The hybrids are stable, growing at a rate far beyond our original projections. We've made progress."

"Progress?" Reese couldn't believe what he was hearing. "Vance, you went behind my back, activated the incubators, and injected them with something. You didn't even consult the team! How did you do it?"

Vance tilted his head, studying Reese for a moment, clearly enjoying holding the upper hand. "I'm not sure why you're so upset," he said smoothly. "You should be thanking me. I gave the project the push it needed."

"I'm not asking again, Vance. How did you do it?" Reese's voice was hard, his fists clenched at his sides.

Vance stared at him, the smirk fading slightly. He seemed to weigh his options before finally sighing, leaning forward in his chair. "Alright, fine. I'll tell you. But only because I'm tired of you breathing down my neck." He stood up and walked over to a locked cabinet on the far side of the room. From it, he retrieved a small vial—the last of the blood samples they had taken from Omega.

Reese's stomach dropped. "No..."

Vance nodded, holding the vial up to the light. "I used Omega's blood. Spliced it with the hybrids' DNA. That's what stabilized them. Her regenerative properties gave them the strength to survive the fusion of different animal genetics."

"You're insane," Reese said, stepping back, his heart racing. "You have no idea what Kaiju DNA is capable of. We don't know what kind of side effects this could have on the hybrids."

Vance's expression hardened, the smugness quickly replaced by something colder. "You're overreacting, Reese. It worked. That's what matters. The government's been breathing down my neck for months. They want results. They want weapons. And I've delivered. You should be thanking me for saving this project."

Reese shook his head, trying to keep his composure. "At what cost, Vance? You're messing with forces we barely understand. Kaiju DNA is dangerous. Unpredictable. We could be creating something far worse than we realize."

Vance's eyes narrowed. He stepped forward, his voice low and confrontational. "The government was tired of waiting. They wanted progress, not endless theories and delays. And if you've forgotten, this is my company. If you don't like how I'm running it, you're more than welcome to walk out that door."

Reese felt a surge of anger, but Vance wasn't done. He stepped closer, almost in Reese's face now.

"Besides," Vance continued, "it worked. In more ways than one."

Reese's brow furrowed in confusion. "What do you mean?"

Vance's smirk returned, though darker now. "Let's just say... I've already tested the regenerative properties myself. The hybrids aren't the only ones benefiting from Omega's blood."

Reese took a step back, realization dawning on him. "You tested it on yourself?"

Vance simply shrugged, his eyes gleaming with dangerous pride. "Why not? And let me tell you, Reese—it works. I'm fine. Better than fine, actually."

Reese stared at him, horror creeping into his thoughts. This was far worse than he had imagined. Vance had crossed a line that couldn't be uncrossed, and now he was throwing caution to the wind.

Reese stood in stunned silence, trying to process everything that had just happened with Vance. The hybrids, Omega's blood... it was all too much. But before he could even leave Vance's office, something else caught his attention—a soft knock at the door.

When Reese turned, his heart nearly stopped. There, standing in the doorway, was Lily.

Not in a wheelchair. Not bedridden. Standing.

"Hey, Dad," she said with a bright smile, as if this were the most normal thing in the world. "Just thought I'd stop by."

Reese's jaw dropped. "Lily?"

She was walking—walking—and not with the cautious, stilted movements of someone fresh out of physical therapy. She looked as though she had never had a problem in her life. Her steps were confident, her posture relaxed.

He turned back to Vance, and suddenly everything clicked. The hybrids, the blood, the breakthroughs... the regeneration.

It wasn't just the hybrids Vance had tested Omega's blood on.

"You..." Reese began, his voice hollow as the weight of realization hit him. "You used it on her, didn't you?"

Vance said nothing, only watching him with an expression of smug satisfaction. Reese's throat tightened. He didn't say another word. Instead, he turned on his heel and walked out of the office, unable to look at either of them. As he made his way down the corridor, his mind was a storm of thoughts—anger, betrayal, disbelief. Vance had gone too far, and now, it was clear that nothing was off-limits to him.

Reese marched straight to the lab, not even bothering to look back. Once there, he grabbed a duffel bag and started stuffing his personal effects into it, moving with a single-minded determination. He couldn't stay. Not after what Vance had done. There were lines you didn't cross, and Vance had bulldozed right over them.

The door to the lab creaked open. Reese didn't need to look up to know who it was.

"You're leaving?" Vance's voice was laced with disbelief. He leaned against the doorframe, crossing his arms. "After everything we've accomplished?"

Reese didn't stop packing. "I can't be part of this anymore."

Vance's expression darkened. "This? You mean progress? You're walking away from the most significant breakthrough in human history."

Reese zipped up his bag and finally looked at him. "This isn't progress, Vance. This is insanity. You injected your own daughter with Kaiju blood, and now you're playing god with these hybrids. We have no idea what the long-term effects could be. What if something goes wrong? What if you've created something you can't control?"

Vance pushed off the doorframe, stepping closer, his eyes gleaming with something unsettling. "What if everything goes right, Reese? What if this changes everything for the better? What we've done here could end disease, regenerate limbs, extend life! You're so focused on what could go wrong that you're blind to the possibilities."

"This isn't about possibilities!" Reese snapped. "This is about morality. Ethics. You're gambling with things you don't fully understand. And the fact that you don't even see that—"

"Spare me the lecture," Vance interrupted, his tone venomous. "You're always so high and mighty, aren't you? Always the one with the ethics and morals while I'm the one actually getting things done. The government doesn't want more delays, Reese. They want results. I gave them what they wanted."

"At what cost, Vance?" Reese shot back, his voice rising. "What happens when this all spirals out of control? When these hybrids grow into something we can't manage? Or when your daughter—"

Vance's face twisted, and Reese knew immediately he had struck a nerve. "Don't," Vance warned, his voice low and dangerous. "Don't you dare bring Lily into this."

Reese took a deep breath, trying to keep his cool. "Look, I get it. You did what you had to do for her. I would've done the same if it were my child. But this—this is different. What you're doing with the hybrids is wrong. You've lost sight of everything we set out to do."

Vance stepped closer, his expression dark and confrontational, almost daring Reese to push him further. There was something unsettling in his eyes—a flicker of rage, or maybe desperation. He seemed unhinged, teetering on the edge of something dangerous. "I haven't lost sight of anything," he said through gritted teeth. "You're just too scared to see the bigger picture. Too scared to embrace the future."

Reese felt a chill crawl up his spine. This wasn't the Vance he used to know. There was something different about him now—something... off. The way he stood, the way his eyes gleamed with a manic intensity.

"I can't be part of this," Reese said firmly, slinging the duffel bag over his shoulder. "This isn't science anymore. It's madness."

Vance scoffed, shaking his head. "Then leave. Go ahead. Walk away. But don't come crawling back when the rest of the world realizes what we've done here. You'll be remembered as a coward who couldn't see past his own fear."

Reese met his gaze, steady and unyielding. "I'd rather be a coward than a monster."

Vance's smirk faltered, replaced by a cold, furious glare. For a moment, it seemed like he might lunge at Reese—like the tension between them was about to explode into violence. But instead, Vance took a slow, deliberate step back.

"Get out," Vance said quietly, his voice dripping with barely restrained anger. "And don't come back."

Reese nodded, turning on his heel and walking out of the lab without another word. As he left, he felt a strange sense of relief, but it was overshadowed by the sinking realization that he was leaving Vance unchecked, heading down a path that could only lead to disaster.

The hybrids were growing. And with Vance at the helm, who knew what they would become.

After Reese stormed out of the lab, the tension lingered in the air like static before a storm. Vance watched the door close behind him, his expression cold and unyielding. Without hesitation, he reached over to the intercom, his finger hovering above the button before pressing it firmly.

"Security," he said, his voice carrying a darker, more commanding edge than usual. "Make sure Dr. Bennett leaves the building immediately. Deactivate all his clearances—access to the lab, office, everything."

The response was immediate. "Understood, sir."

Vance didn't feel bad about it. In fact, the decision gave him a strange sense of satisfaction. This is what power feels like, he thought. Not just authority over the building, but something more primal. It was deeper, sharper. He was in control now, not just of his research, but of something far greater.

He leaned on the cool metal desk in front of him, his mind replaying the confrontation with Reese. Who does he think he is? Vance thought, the anger still simmering beneath his skin. Reese had always been the cautious one, the hesitant one. But this wasn't a time for hesitation. They were on the verge of something world-changing, and Reese was too small-minded to see it.

Coward, Vance seethed. Reese's refusal to see the bigger picture felt like a betrayal. Here they were, standing on the edge of godhood, and Reese was too afraid to take the plunge.

Vance's thoughts grew darker as his frustration swelled. The world needed this. It needed someone like him—someone who wasn't afraid to break the rules to bring about real change. Why should he hold back? The hybrids were stable. Lily was walking again. Every move he made was justified, and now he was reaping the rewards. Reese was weak, afraid of consequences that might never come. He's obsolete now.

As Vance continued to stew in his thoughts, he suddenly became aware of a strange sensation in his hands. His palms were digging into the desk, the pressure steady. But it felt different. More solid. He glanced down at his fingers—and froze.

The metal beneath his hands was warped. His fingertips had pressed into the stainless steel surface, leaving deep indentations. For a second, Vance didn't understand what he was seeing. He blinked, lifting his fingers and inspecting the dents with a growing sense of awe.

A sinister grin slowly spread across his face.

The Kaiju blood—it hadn't just healed his thumb. It was doing something more. Something extraordinary.

He flexed his fingers experimentally, feeling the subtle surge of strength radiating through his hands. The desk, which should've been immovable beneath normal force, had given way to his touch like soft clay. His heart quickened in excitement. This was power. Real power. Not just control over his research, but over his own body. The Kaiju's gift had gone beyond healing—it was enhancing him, making him stronger.

Vance straightened up, still grinning as he marveled at the imprints he had left behind. *This is just the beginning.*

Before he could let the implications sink in further, a voice broke through his thoughts.

"Dad?" Lily's soft voice called from the doorway. "Are you ready to go home?"

Vance blinked, snapping back to reality. He turned to see his daughter standing in the lab doorway, looking as radiant and healthy as ever. Just seeing her there reminded him of why he had done all this in the first place. Lily. She was the reason he had crossed these lines, and she was proof that his methods worked.

He forced himself to relax, wiping the grin from his face and replacing it with a more gentle smile. "Yes, honey," he said, his voice still carrying that undercurrent of control. "Let's go home."

As he walked over to her, he couldn't help but glance back at the desk one last time, the twisted metal gleaming under the sterile lights. The power that surged through him was intoxicating, and the implications of what he could do with it were limitless.

Taking Lily's hand, he left the lab behind, a new sense of purpose swelling within him. The world was changing—and Vance Hadrian was going to be the one to shape it.

Chapter 9: Fanboy Fury

Reese trudged into the loft, feeling the weight of his decision to walk away from Vance's increasingly dangerous experiments still pressing down on him. His thoughts were a chaotic jumble of ethics, fear, and frustration as he dropped his keys on the counter and kicked off his shoes.

The TV was blaring from the living room, and Reese could see his brother, Blake, sprawled out on the couch, his eyes glued to the screen with a look of intense annoyance. It only took a glance for Reese to recognize what Blake was watching—Supernatural, the series finale. Oh no.

Reese sighed, already knowing what was coming. He made his way over to the couch and sat down next to Blake, who barely acknowledged him, too wrapped up in his growing displeasure.

"You've got to be kidding me," Blake muttered, arms crossed, scowling at the TV.

Reese looked at the screen just in time to see Dean Winchester dying—again. This time, it wasn't from a demon, an angel, or some eldritch horror, but by getting impaled on a rusty nail in a random barn fight.

"This is how they're ending it?" Blake practically shouted, his voice rising with disbelief. "DEAN gets taken out by a piece of rebar? After everything—the demons, the angels, God Himself—he dies from a rusty nail? Seriously?"

Reese chuckled. He had never been into the show like Blake was, but he could see the absurdity. "A little anticlimactic?" he teased.

"Anticlimactic?!" Blake snapped, sitting up straighter. "Dude, this is Supernatural—Dean's survived hell, literally. And now he's taken out by construction equipment? Where's the big heroic finale? Where's the epic send-off? I sat through fifteen years of demons and drama for this?"

Blake groaned and ranted on, not giving Reese a moment to respond. "And what about Sam? He looks like he walked off the set of This Is Us in the last montage. Like, what is happening? Why is he suddenly old, and why does he look like someone's uncle who coaches Little League?"

Reese couldn't help but laugh out loud. "I'm guessing you didn't like it, then?"

"I've read fanfiction that gave these characters a better send-off!" Blake threw his hands in the air in exasperation. "They spent 15 seasons building these guys up to be basically superheroes, and then they just... they just give up? I mean, come on! Dean deserved better. We deserved better. Even God was scared of these guys!"

Blake grabbed the remote and paused the episode. "Look at this," he said, pointing angrily at the frozen screen where Dean lay on a makeshift funeral pyre. "They're burning his body in some random woods. Where's the emotion? The legacy? Where's the damn closure?! It's like the writers just threw in the towel."

Reese smirked, leaning back into the cushions. "You think you could do better?"

Blake's eyes lit up, and he spun to face his brother, full of energy now. "Heck yes, I could! You know what they should've done? They should've had Dean and Sam go out together in a blaze of glory—maybe fighting Lucifer again or some other cosmic force—something big! And then, if they wanted to get all emotional and tragic, fine, have Dean die after saving the world one last time. But not like this. Not from some stupid nail."

Reese raised an eyebrow. "And Sam?"

Blake rolled his eyes. "Sam should've taken up the mantle, right? Like, he could've carried on the family legacy in some meaningful way. But nooo. Instead, we get Grandpa Sam in a weird montage, living the most boring life ever. It's like the writers forgot who these guys were."

Reese couldn't stop laughing now. "Yeah, you're not the only one who thinks that. I read reviews where people were saying the same thing. Everyone's mad about that nail. There's a petition somewhere to rewrite the ending."

Blake scoffed, "Good! Because if I was in charge, I'd have written an ending that would have people talking for years. Dean and Sam teaming up with Castiel and maybe even God to stop some final cataclysm, sacrificing themselves for the universe. That's how you do it."

"Well," Reese said, standing up to head toward the kitchen, "there's always the reboot."

Blake groaned dramatically, burying his face in his hands. "Don't even joke about that. They'll probably make it all about some random kids no one cares about, and the whole show will be a CW teen drama."

Reese shook his head, still laughing as he grabbed a drink from the fridge. For a moment, Blake's animated fanboy ranting distracted him from the darker thoughts swirling in his mind. But as the laughter faded, the reality of the situation with Vance slowly crept back in. He sat down again, feeling the weight return to his shoulders.

Blake wasn't done. Not by a long shot. As Reese returned to thecouch, he realized he didn't mind. For now, he'd let himself get lost in his brother's fury over a fictional world—it was a welcome escape from the chaos waiting for him back in reality. "You know what this reminds me of?" Blake said, pointing an accusatory finger at the TV. "The ending of Angel—remember that disaster? Angel on The CW? They spent five seasons building up the Wolfram & Hart stuff, Angel's redemption arc, and then it just—boom—cut to black in the middle of a fight. No closure. Just, 'We're fighting the apocalypse, and now you'll never know what happened!'" He waved his hands dramatically. "Like, what even was that?"

Reese smirked, realizing how much fun this was going to be. "Oh yeah, I remember that. Didn't they kill off Wes in the last ten minutes, like it was nothing? 'Hey, sorry about your life, man, but we gotta wrap this up, bye!'"

Blake groaned, gripping his hair in frustration. "Exactly! Wesley dies, and we're just supposed to be okay with it. No epic showdown for him, no redemption. They just end him, and we never even get to see if Angel actually wins or loses the fight. One minute, he's about to take on an entire army of demons, and the next minute—credits!"

Reese chuckled. "Yeah, that was pretty rough. But at least it wasn't as bad as this," he said, nodding toward the TV again. "At least Angel had, you know, actual stakes."

Blake threw his arms up. "Exactly! Thank you! You know it's bad when Angel's ending looks like Citizen Kane compared to this. I mean, what is the Supernatural writers' excuse? They had 15 seasons! They had time to figure this out!"

Reese leaned back, enjoying Blake's outrage. "Fifteen seasons of monsters and demons, and they give you a nail. That's something special right there."

Blake leaned forward, gesturing wildly. "It's not just the nail! It's the whole last episode. They spend half the episode on some random hunt like it's season two. And then suddenly Dean's dead, Sam's an old man, and Castiel doesn't even show up! What about the epic romance they were hinting at with Dean and Cas? They spent all this time teasing it, and then... nothing! This was worse than the ending of Angel, and I never thought I'd say that!"

Reese grinned and took a slow sip of his drink, pretending to think deeply about it. "You know," he said, setting the glass down, "at least Buffy ended well."

Blake whipped around to face him, his eyes going wide. "Oh, don't even get me started on Buffy! That stupid amulet—'Oh, Spike is a hero now! He gets to save everyone!'—what about Buffy?! She spent the whole show fighting, and then what? They blow up the Hellmouth, and she's like, 'Guess I'll go shopping now?'"

Reese couldn't stop laughing. "And don't forget about the Ubervamps," he added, egging Blake on. "One minute, they're the biggest threat to the entire world, and the next minute, they're cannon fodder."

Blake threw himself back into the couch, looking utterly defeated. "I swear, it's like these shows forget how to end themselves. Why even build a huge threat if you're just going to wave it away with a magical doohickey in the last ten minutes?"

Reese nodded seriously, still smiling. "Yeah, a lot of people felt like that. It felt rushed."

Blake pointed at him again. "Exactly! It was rushed. They throw in all this 'Potential Slayer' stuff at the last minute, and then—poof—now everyone's a Slayer. It's like the writers just said, 'We don't have time to explain this, let's just make everyone special and call it a day.'"

Reese was nearly crying from laughter now. "You really can't stand bad endings, huh?"

Blake crossed his arms and shook his head, looking genuinely hurt. "After all those years invested? No. They owe us better endings than this crap. And trust me, if I ever get to write something, I'm giving it a proper ending, something people will remember."

Reese finally managed to calm his laughter. "Well, you could definitely do better than that," he said, motioning toward the screen, where Sam was now tearfully looking at an old photograph.

Blake sighed heavily. "I could write a shopping list that would be better than this."

Blake was pacing the room like a man on a mission, his frustration building with every step. He whirled around to face Reese, hands on his hips, eyes wild. "If I ever see Joss Whedon," he announced with the gravitas of a general leading troops into battle, "I am punching him dead in the face."

Reese raised an eyebrow, amused but trying to stay serious. "And what would you say after that heroic punch?"

Blake jabbed a finger into the air as if delivering a final verdict. "That's for Angel, you hack! Ruining my childhood with your one-trick-pony nonsense!"

Reese couldn't hold back a laugh. "Seems a bit extreme. What did Whedon ever do to you, exactly?"

Blake scoffed, throwing his arms wide. "What did he do to me? Oh, let's start with his whole career! The man peaked with Buffy, got high on his own snarky fumes, and then just kept milking that same tired formula. Quirky banter? Check. Forced character death for shock value? Double check. Plot twists that feel like a personal attack? Don't even get me started."

Reese shook his head, grinning. "You're still mad about Justice League, aren't you?"

Blake stopped pacing long enough to point dramatically at his brother. "Exactly! He butchered it! Took Zack Snyder's epic and turned it into some Franken-Whedon disaster. What was that bloated mess of quips and bad CGI? And don't even get me started on the drama with Ray Fisher. He made the cast hate him!"

Reese nodded, intrigued. "Yeah, Ray Fisher definitely had issues. Didn't Gal Gadot get into it with him, too?"

"Oh, yeah!" Blake rolled his eyes. "Mr. 'I run Hollywood' allegedly threatened Wonder Woman herself. Like, dude thought he could tank her career! Meanwhile, the internet's been dragging him for years. And now, he's canceled harder than Firefly!"

Reese chuckled. "He probably won't be getting any big projects soon."

Blake let out a dramatic sigh of relief. "Good! The last thing we need is another Whedon-fied dumpster fire. Same formula, same smug dialogue. He's the human embodiment of copy-paste. Honestly, we should thank the universe if we never have to suffer through another 'Whedon project' again."

Reese was practically shaking with laughter by now. "So you're basically saying he's... retired by force?"

Blake grinned like a villain monologuing his victory. "For the sake of all that is holy in cinema—yes. Let him rest. In peace. And let someone else who can handle character arcs without turning them into a punchline take over."

Reese shook his head, amused. "You've really been holding onto this grudge, haven't you?"

Blake flopped back onto the couch dramatically, crossing his arms. "Hey, I just care about quality storytelling. Can't let the hacks ruin it for the rest of us."

The room finally settled down, Blake's righteous rant fading as the Supernatural credits rolled in the background. Blake, still shaking his head, glanced over at Reese. "So, enough about my vendetta against Whedon. How was your day?"

Reese let out a deep breath, his serious thoughts catching up with him. "Man, it's been... a lot."

Blake raised an eyebrow, leaning in. "Oh yeah? Spill it."

Reese glanced toward the kitchen, feeling the weight of the day. "It's Vance. And the hybrids. Something's really messed up, Blake."

Blake's playful expression fell, replaced with concern. "What do you mean? What's going on with Vance?"

Reese ran a hand through his hair and started pacing just like Blake had been. "You remember those hybrids? The ones we had in cryo?"

Blake nodded, sitting up straighter. "The ones that were supposed to be in deep freeze for... ever? Yeah."

Reese took a deep breath. "Well, they're not in cryo anymore. Vance pulled them out, injected them with something, and now they're growing—way too fast."

Blake blinked. "Wait, what? What did he inject them with?"

Reese hesitated for a second before answering. "Kaiju blood. Omega's blood."

Blake's eyes widened. "Are you kidding me? The Omega? The Queen Kaiju? He used that on the hybrids?"

Reese nodded grimly. "Yeah. And it worked. They're growing at an insane rate, their vitals are stable, and Vance is acting like this was his master plan all along. He's... changing, Blake."

Blake's face darkened. "What do you mean, 'changing'?"

Reese's pacing grew faster, his voice quieter. "When I tried to confront him, he was... off. More aggressive. Like he was daring me to challenge him. And I'm pretty sure he's been injecting himself with the Kaiju blood too."

Blake leaned forward, eyes wide. "Wait. You think Vance is using Kaiju DNA on himself?"

Reese stopped pacing, his expression grim. "I don't just think it. I know it. Lily showed up today—fully healed. I mean, completely. And Vance is acting like he's some kind of god now."

Blake paled. "Holy crap... this is way worse than I thought."

Reese nodded, rubbing his face in frustration. "I tried reasoning with him, but he's too far gone. He said the government wants results, and he's going to give them what they want—no matter the cost. He basically told me to leave if I wasn't on board."

Blake sat in stunned silence for a moment before leaning forward, his voice steady. "So what are you going to do?"

Reese let out a deep sigh. "I'm out, Blake. I packed up my stuff. I can't be part of this anymore."

Blake looked at his brother, his expression shifting to determination. "Then I guess it's up to us to stop him. Before he goes too far."

Vance stood in the dimly lit laboratory at GeneSys, watching the hybrids through the thick glass walls of their incubators. It had only taken three weeks—far faster than anyone had expected—for the creatures to grow to their current size. Each hybrid was now about half the size of a human, and the mutations had fused their genetic components in fascinating and terrifying ways.

The shark-eagle hybrid, Aquila, swam lazily in a water-filled tank, its sharp fins slicing through the liquid with a graceful yet predatory movement. Its eagle talons flexed, claws clicking against the tank's walls every so often, as if testing for weaknesses. Vance admired Aquila's sleek design—a perfect combination of air and sea.

Beside Aquila, Lynxara, a monstrous blend of lion and hyena, paced in her enclosure, her golden eyes glowing faintly in the low light. Her powerful muscles rippled under her spotted fur, and her sharp, hyena-like laugh echoed ominously in the sterile lab. There was something primal, almost sadistic, in her gaze. Vance felt a flicker of doubt about her control but shook it off. She would follow commands, he was sure of it.

Titanax was the most imposing. Part gorilla, part elephant, its hulking body dominated its reinforced steel cell. The creature's massive arms swung heavily, and its thick, grayish skin seemed impenetrable. Vance marveled at Titanax's sheer power, but he also knew that this hybrid's size made it a liability if not controlled properly. The thought sent a chill down his spine—if Titanax ever broke free, it would be a walking tank, unstoppable.

Lastly, there was Felonix, the least intimidating at first glance. A sleek cheetah, Felonix had the slim, agile body of a predator built for speed, but something about its piercing gaze made Vance wary. Its eyes gleamed with intelligence, far more than he was comfortable with. The way it watched him from its cell suggested that Felonix was sizing him up, calculating.

As Vance observed them, a thought nagged at the back of his mind. Control. These hybrids were designed to be weapons, but how could he ensure they remained loyal to him? These creatures were smart—too smart—and their primal instincts ran deep. What if one day, the training wasn't enough?

He glanced at the panel monitoring their vitals. Everything seemed stable, but Vance knew that wasn't enough. He needed something more—a way to ensure their obedience, no matter what. His eyes narrowed as he pondered his options.

"Perhaps... a failsafe," he muttered to himself. Some kind of implant, maybe? A neural chip that could disable or incapacitate them if they ever rebelled? Or maybe a chemical trigger, something that could be introduced into their bloodstream—an agent that would allow him to seize control of their nervous systems at a moment's notice.

Vance rubbed his chin, his mind racing with possibilities. Omega's blood had given the hybrids their accelerated growth and power, but it also carried unpredictable elements. What if he could isolate certain parts of that Kaiju DNA and combine it with technology? He had seen what happened when someone tampered with Omega's blood, and part of him wondered if he should follow in that path more directly.

His fingers tapped rhythmically against the control panel, a slow smile creeping across his face. The hybrids were evolving faster than anyone could have anticipated, but that only meant they would need him even more to guide them.

Vance paced back and forth in the dim light of the lab, his mind whirring with the possibilities. As he watched the hybrids—Aquila, Lynxara, Titanax, and Felonix—shift in their reinforced cells, he knew the key to controlling them wasn't just physical. Sure, their cages were strong, but these creatures were evolving faster than expected. It wouldn't be long before mere walls wouldn't contain them.

No, the real control had to come from within. Something in their biology. Something that would ensure their loyalty at the flip of a switch. A chemical trigger.

Vance stopped pacing and turned toward his computer terminal, his fingers flying across the keyboard as he scrolled through the data on Omega's blood. The Kaiju DNA was like nothing he'd ever seen—a cocktail of power, regeneration, and unpredictable potential. But deep within the data, he found it: a subtle, hidden marker in Omega's genetic code. It was like a lock—a small vulnerability buried inside the titanic strength.

If Vance could design a chemical compound that interfaced with that marker, he could build a biological "back door" into the hybrids' systems. With a single command, he could flood their systems with the compound, effectively seizing control of their bodies.

A grin spread across his face as the idea took root. He could implant the trigger directly into the hybrids, but that wasn't enough. There had to be no chance of failure. No room for error. He needed to hold the key to their obedience—literally.

He needed to be the trigger.

Vance sat down at his workstation, the glow of the monitors lighting up his face in a sinister hue. He began to map out the plan. The chemical compound would be a blend of Omega's DNA and a modified neurotoxin. Once injected into the hybrids, it would lie dormant, completely undetectable, unless activated. And the only person who could activate it... was him.

To do that, the trigger needed to be integrated into his own body. A failsafe that would ensure he could never lose control of the hybrids, no matter what. A small, surgically implanted device inside his bloodstream—one that could release the activation signal at will.

The idea was both terrifying and exhilarating. He'd seen what Kaiju DNA could do, but this—this was on another level. Vance began compiling the ingredients, running simulations, and refining the process. The trigger compound had to be perfect. It couldn't just control them; it needed to be absolute. No glitches, no malfunctions. It had to be part of them, as much as their DNA, and as much a part of him as his blood.

Hours passed as he worked feverishly, a man obsessed. The lab assistants had long since gone home, and the only sounds were the low hum of the equipment and the steady beeping of the hybrids' vitals. Finally, after what felt like days, Vance sat back, staring at the final formula glowing on the screen.

"This is it," he muttered to himself. The ultimate control.

He quickly arranged for the surgery, knowing there was no time to waste. The procedure was delicate—integrating the trigger into his own bloodstream required precision. But Vance had long since passed the point of caring about personal risk. He needed this control more than anything. Without it, the hybrids could turn on him, and all of his work, his legacy, would be for nothing.

Two days later, the surgery was complete.

Vance lay on a cold metal table, blinking the haze out of his eyes as he woke up. He could feel it—the implant, small, almost unnoticeable, pulsing faintly with energy in sync with his heartbeat. It was there, inside him, the key to his empire.

Slowly, he sat up, the room still spinning slightly from the anesthesia. His mind raced. He had done it. The hybrids were now bound to him in ways they couldn't even comprehend.

As he stood and looked at his reflection in the sterile lab mirror, Vance felt a surge of triumph wash over him. No matter how strong the hybrids grew, no matter how intelligent they became, he would always have control.

Always.

He looked back at the hybrids, now resting in their cells, unaware of the invisible leash tied to their very existence.

"Let's see how well you follow orders now," Vance whispered, a cruel smile curling at the edge of his lips.

Chapter 10: "Predator's Leash"

The sun hovered low over the horizon, casting a golden glow across the waters off the coast of Key West, Florida. Gentle waves lapped against the hull of Vance's private yacht, a sleek, black vessel sitting quietly about a half-mile from shore. Vance stood on the deck, his eyes hidden behind dark sunglasses, watching the scene unfold.

A group of swimmers, oblivious to the danger lurking just beneath the surface, splashed and laughed as they enjoyed the warmth of the Atlantic Ocean. Little did they know, just a few hundred feet away, Aquila—his prized hybrid, a monstrous fusion of shark and eagle—glided silently through the water, her bioluminescent eyes fixed on them.

Vance's heart pounded with anticipation. This was Aquila's first true test, a delicate balance of raw instinct and controlled obedience. He needed to see how close she could get to the swimmers without giving in to her predatory nature. Would the trigger he implanted inside her truly work?

He leaned against the railing of the yacht, holding a small tablet in his hands, which displayed Aquila's vitals, movements, and proximity to the swimmers. The data streamed in real-time, showing her heart rate accelerating as she moved toward the group. Her sleek, silver body, covered in faint, shimmering scales, cut through the water with deadly precision. The wings fused along her muscular sides fluttered, making small adjustments in the water's current as she glided effortlessly.

Closer.

Vance's pulse quickened as Aquila swam to within twenty feet of the nearest swimmer. A young woman, completely unaware of the monster beneath her, floated on her back, staring up at the bright blue sky. Her friends were further ahead, dunking each other in a game of water tag.

Vance narrowed his eyes, watching Aquila's body language closely. Her dorsal fin was now fully extended, slicing through the water like a blade, but she remained silent, her predatory instincts held at bay—for now. He could feel the tension building inside her, see it in the way her muscles coiled, ready to spring forward in an explosive attack. She was testing the limits of her restraint, as if weighing her instincts against the invisible command that had been implanted in her.

Ten feet.

Aquila circled the swimmers, her massive form casting a shadow beneath the water. Vance's thumb hovered over the activation switch on his tablet. The trigger was ready—his failsafe. But he wanted to push it just a little further, to see how close he could let Aquila get before the beast within her broke free.

The swimmers laughed, splashing each other, still blissfully unaware of their brush with death.

Five feet.

Aquila's eyes flared, a subtle glow from her bioluminescent pupils reflecting in the water as her instincts surged. Vance could feel it now, through the connection between him and the trigger—the bloodlust rising within her. Her heartbeat quickened, her muscles tensed, and in a split second, she turned sharply, angling toward the young woman floating on her back.

Vance's finger slammed down on the activation switch.

Instantly, a shockwave of control rippled through Aquila's nervous system, originating from the chemical trigger embedded deep within her DNA. Her body froze, muscles locking as the artificial command seized control of her motor functions. The predatory glow in her eyes dimmed, her instincts forcibly suppressed.

A few feet from the girl, Aquila halted, hovering in the water like a statue. The swimmers continued their fun, unaware of the apex predator mere inches from them.

Vance exhaled slowly, watching as Aquila's movements became more fluid again, but this time, they were precise, calculated—under his control. With the simple flick of his finger, he had transformed a lethal killing machine into an obedient tool. Aquila turned away from the swimmers, her sleek form retreating gracefully back into the depths, following the command to leave them unharmed.

The sense of power coursing through Vance was intoxicating. He had done it. He had tamed the untamable. Aquila, the perfect hybrid of air and sea, the ultimate predator, was completely at his command.

He lowered the tablet, the adrenaline still pulsing through his veins, and watched as Aquila surfaced briefly near the yacht, her massive head rising from the water. Her eyes, once filled with hunger, now looked at him with something closer to acknowledgment—a recognition of who held the leash.

Vance grinned.

"You did well," he whispered to himself, nodding in approval. "But this is just the beginning."

As Aquila sank back beneath the waves, Vance turned his gaze back toward the horizon. The sun was setting now, casting a deep orange glow over the water. The world had no idea what was coming. Soon, he would unleash more of the hybrids—Lynxara, Titanax, and Felonix—each with their own unique abilities, each bound to his will through the same chemical trigger that controlled Aquila.

But for now, he had proven his method worked. The test was a success.

Vance stepped away from the railing and headed back inside the yacht, his mind already racing with plans for the next phase of his grand design. The world's most dangerous creatures were now his weapons, and he held the keys to their power.

As the yacht's engines roared to life and pulled away from the coast, Vance couldn't help but smile at the thought of what he would do next. The hybrids were ready. The world was not.

Vance had nearly forgotten about General Sarah Strayer. Almost.

It had been months since their last conversation—a hurried and tense meeting in which she had granted him a week to show progress on his so-called hybrid project. A week. And though he had long since blown past that deadline, the General had not returned. At first, Vance assumed she had written him off, that she had more pressing matters to attend to. But in the back of his mind, he knew better. Sarah Strayer was not someone who simply forgot about promises.

And today, as the morning sun spilled through the windows of his GeneSys office, she was here to collect.

Vance was sitting behind his desk when the door slid open, and in walked General Strayer. Her entrance was as commanding as ever—her sharp green eyes scanning the room, her posture rigid, every movement deliberate. She wore her standard military uniform, perfectly pressed, her badges and insignia gleaming. Her Pomeranian, Kevin, trotted in alongside her, the small creature almost comically at odds with his owner's fierce demeanor.

"General Strayer," Vance greeted her with a smooth, almost saccharine tone. He stood and extended his hand. "You're looking well."

Sarah ignored his hand, her lips curling into a polite but cold smile. "Dr. Vance. I trust you haven't been sitting idle all this time?"

Vance chuckled, withdrawing his hand, unfazed by her brusqueness. "Idle? Me? Perish the thought, General. No, no... I've been very busy. I think you'll be pleased with the results."

Sarah arched an eyebrow, moving further into the room, her gaze not quite meeting his. She scanned the papers and digital models spread out on his desk—a map of DNA helixes, hybrid schematics, performance reports. "We'll see about that," she said, her voice level but carrying a weight of authority. "I'm not one to be strung along, Vance. You promised progress."

"Indeed," Vance replied, a glimmer of satisfaction in his eyes. "And I've delivered. I'd like to introduce you to someone."

Sarah tilted her head, a skeptical expression crossing her face.

Vance smiled, a grin that didn't quite reach his eyes. "Ah, General, I was hoping you'd ask. I've developed something truly groundbreaking—a chemical trigger. A kind of backdoor into their biological systems, if you will. It's embedded deep within them, allowing me to... guide their behavior. With just a touch of a button, I can control their actions—override those pesky instincts."

Sarah's expression remained neutral, but Vance could sense her calculating. "You've built yourself a safety net, then," she remarked, her tone almost amused. "But what happens if you're not around?"

Vance shrugged, his charm faltering for just a moment as a flash of mania lit his eyes. "That won't happen, General. I'm far too careful for that."

Sarah's eyes darkened as she studied the hybrids in their reinforced enclosures. Each one radiated raw power, the kind of strength that couldn't easily be tamed. Vance was walking her through his pride and joy, showing off the monstrous creatures he'd cobbled together, but her gut was tight with unease. These hybrids weren't just weapons—they were ticking time bombs.

And that unnerved her.

As Vance continued his explanation, something in his demeanor made her pulse quicken. It wasn't just the hybrids, but the way he spoke about them. There was a barely concealed mania beneath his charm, a deep-seated obsession that could spiral out of control at any moment.

"I have to say, Vance," Sarah said, her voice calm but cutting, "I'm not convinced. I've seen what happens when things like this are unleashed. You're talking about apex predators here—creatures designed to hunt and kill. You really think a chemical trigger will be enough to keep them in check?"

Vance's smirk widened, his eyes gleaming. "Oh, General, you underestimate me. I've accounted for everything. The chemical trigger isn't just a safeguard—it's built into their very biology. It's embedded at the cellular level, entwined with their DNA. As long as I control the trigger, they won't lay a claw or a tooth on anyone without my say-so."

Sarah crossed her arms, narrowing her gaze. "And just how did you manage that? How did you get the DNA to bond this way? Combining two entirely different species doesn't just work by snapping your fingers. It's a biological nightmare."

For the first time, Vance hesitated. It was brief, barely a flicker of uncertainty, but Sarah caught it. The cornered look in his eyes.

"Well, General," he began, that smooth voice of his losing some of its sheen, "let's just say... I had a little help. The DNA sequencing was tricky, yes, but once we acquired the right material, it was surprisingly cooperative."

Sarah's heart skipped a beat. "What material?" she asked, her tone sharp and deadly serious.

Vance's smile returned, but it was different now—more predatory. "Omega's blood."

Sarah froze, her breath catching in her throat. For a moment, she didn't even hear the hum of the lab's machinery or the shifting of the hybrids behind her. All she heard was the ringing silence after those two words: Omega's blood.

"You what?" Her voice was dangerously quiet, but beneath that calm exterior, a storm was brewing.

Vance leaned against one of the lab tables, almost casual, as though what he'd just admitted was no big deal. "We had access to some of the Kaiju's remains after Omega's little rampage in New York. Once we extracted the blood samples, it was a simple matter of splicing. Omega's

DNA has a unique quality—remarkably adaptable. It integrated into the hybrids with ease."

Sarah's fists clenched at her sides, her entire body rigid with fury. "You used Omega's blood? You took DNA from a Kaiju we could barely contain—let alone control—and you spliced it into your little Frankensteins? Are you out of your goddamn mind, Vance?"

His smirk faltered at the edge of her rage. "General, I—"

"Do you have any idea what you've done?" she snapped, cutting him off. Her voice was rising, trembling with fury. "Omega is one of the most dangerous creatures we've ever encountered. We barely survived her first appearance, and you thought it was a good idea to use her DNA? For hybrids?"

"Sarah, calm down," Vance said, his voice taking on a more defensive tone. "You're overreacting. These hybrids aren't Omega. They're smaller, more contained, and I've built in safeguards—"

"Safeguards?" she interrupted, her eyes blazing. "You think a chemical trigger is a safeguard against that?" She pointed toward the cells, where the hybrids paced and growled. "Vance, you can't control them. Not forever. No one can. You've spliced together apex predators and given them the DNA of a Kaiju that nearly wiped out an entire city!"

Vance opened his mouth to protest, but Sarah wasn't done. She stepped closer, her voice dropping into a furious whisper. "You've put us all in danger. Do you even realize what could happen if one of these things breaks free? If they start to mutate or—"

"They won't mutate," Vance insisted, standing up straighter, his own voice growing colder. "I've accounted for—"

"Shut it, Vance." The command was sharp and final. "This project is over. As of right now, I'm shutting you down."

Vance blinked, his confident demeanor faltering for the first time. "You... what?"

"You heard me," Sarah said, her voice laced with steel. "I'm ordering this project shut down immediately. These hybrids—these abominations—will be destroyed."

Vance's face twitched. The charming mask he wore so well began to crack, his eyes narrowing with something darker. "General, you can't just shut me down. We're on the verge of something unprecedented. These hybrids could be the key to stopping human lives from being wasted on the battlefield."

"I want to stop death," Sarah said, her tone unwavering. "Not create more of it. And that's exactly what you've done here. You've built a ticking time bomb, Vance. I won't risk the lives of innocent people because you decided to play God."

Vance's smile had completely vanished now. He took a step forward, his voice lowering into something more insidious. "You think you can just waltz in here and take control of my research? You have no idea what you're shutting down. These hybrids... they're the future, General."

"They're a disaster waiting to happen," Sarah shot back. "And I won't let them loose on the world. This is over."

Her words hung in the air like a death sentence. Vance stared at her, his face twitching with suppressed rage, but she didn't flinch. Sarah Strayer was not someone to be intimidated.

Vance's eyes flickered to the hybrids in their cells, then back to Sarah. "You're making a mistake."

"No, Vance," she said, her voice ice-cold. "The mistake was letting you get this far."

Without another word, she turned on her heel and began walking toward the exit, her heart still racing, her mind calculating the next steps. She would make the call to shut GeneSys Labs down—destroy the hybrids before they could be unleashed.

But as she left, she could feel Vance's eyes burning into her back, a cold, seething fury simmering just beneath the surface.

And somehow, Sarah knew this wasn't the end of it.

Vance sat in his office, fuming, his fingers drumming impatiently against the cold surface of his desk. The tension in the room was palpable, his mind spiraling into darker thoughts. *Who does she think she is?* The nerve of General Strayer to waltz in here, full of her arrogance, and demand the shutdown of his work—his hybrids—just like that. He glared at the screen in front of him, watching the old footage of the Kaiju Task Force's battle against Omega.

The monstrous creature loomed on the screen, tearing apart everything in its path—ships, buildings, lives. The footage was grainy, full of static and chaos, but it was all too familiar. He had watched this battle countless times. Watched as Omega unleashed her fury, watched as the Kaiju Task Force scrambled to fight her off. *They had no idea what they were up against,* he thought bitterly. *No idea of the scale of power they were dealing with.*

But no one shut down her project, did they? The Kaiju Task Force had been given every chance to prove themselves, no matter how many lives were put on the line. How many soldiers had died in that battle? How many more would have fallen if Alpha hadn't been able to kill Omega? And now she had the gall to tell him that *his* creations, *his* meticulously engineered hybrids, were too dangerous? Too uncontrollable?

Hypocrites, the lot of them.

Vance clenched his fists, his eyes narrowing as the footage looped again—Omega ripping through a battleship like it was made of paper, her bioluminescent scales glowing ominously in the night. And yet, there they were—the soldiers, the Task Force, throwing themselves at her in some noble but futile effort to save lives.

If they had had his hybrids, man-sized or not, maybe they wouldn't have had to risk human lives in that battle. Maybe Omega wouldn't have left such a trail of destruction. His hybrids would have been faster, stronger, more adaptable. A perfect force to challenge the Kaiju. But no, the General didn't see that. She was too blinded by her self-righteousness, too trapped in her narrow-minded thinking to see the future he was trying to build.

On the desk before him, a holographic image flickered to life—a figure clad in sleek, metallic armor. But this wasn't just any armor. It was a prototype, a new design Vance had been working on in secret. The Valkyrie suits had been effective in their time, sure, but they were limited. This, however... this was something else entirely. The armor was more predatory, more streamlined, more lethal. Its name hovered above the image in faint digital letters: Iron Wraith.

He leaned back in his chair, eyes fixed on the hologram. This would be his ultimate weapon, his answer to Strayer's arrogance and the world's ignorance. If they had had a battalion of these... of his Iron Wraiths, perhaps the outcome of that battle would have been different. Perhaps there wouldn't have been so much death.

"I'll show her," Vance muttered, his voice low and dangerous. "I'll show them all."

His thoughts were a maelstrom of bitterness and anger, swirling with images of what could have been. The hybrids would have saved them, he thought. They were the next step in evolution, the perfect soldiers—untiring, unflinching, unstoppable. But Strayer couldn't see it. She was too fixated on the past, too bound by conventional thinking to understand what he was trying to achieve. She didn't get it.

Vance's mind flashed back to the moment she had stormed out of his lab, her words still ringing in his ears: "This project is over. I'm shutting you down."

"Not if I shut you down first," Vance hissed through clenched teeth, his bitterness hardening into a resolve as cold as steel.

He wouldn't let her destroy everything. She thought she could simply walk in here, throw her weight around, and dismantle years of his work? She thought she could kill his creations, his hybrids—his children? No. He wouldn't allow it. He had put too much into this. Too much time, too much energy, too much of himself.

Vance's eyes shifted back to the Iron Wraith hologram. This suit, this predatory armor, was just the beginning. If General Strayer wanted a war, he'd give her one. Not just with his hybrids, but with everything he had. He would unleash the full might of his creations, and then, when she saw what they could do—when the world saw—she'd have no choice but to acknowledge his brilliance. His genius.

"They'll see," he muttered, a manic gleam in his eyes. "They'll all see."

He'd make sure of it.

Vance leaned forward, the hologram reflecting in his cold, calculating gaze. He could already envision it—the Iron Wraith leading an army of hybrids, cutting down any Kaiju that dared to rise. His creations would dominate the battlefield, and he would be the one holding the leash. No one would be able to stop him. Not Strayer, not the Task Force, not anyone.

He'd show her.

He'd show them all.

Chapter 11: Sunday Brunch & Strange Waters

Blake, Reese, and Norah sat around the small kitchen island in Blake and Reese's loft, lazily picking at breakfast. The sun was shining through the large windows, giving the room a warm, lazy Sunday morning vibe. Norah, dressed sharply as always, had stopped by unannounced, which wasn't uncommon.

"Tesla's really been keeping me busy, but someone's gotta save the future, right?" Norah said, her voice dripping with playful arrogance as she swirled her cup of coffee.

"Wow, tell me more about how you're single-handedly revolutionizing technology," Blake deadpanned between bites of scrambled eggs.

"Yeah, it's a real shame you're stuck doing groundbreaking work while the rest of us mere mortals eat cereal and waste oxygen," Reese chimed in sarcastically, his mouth full.

Norah grinned smugly, leaning back in her chair. "You should both take notes. Maybe one day you'll rise to my level. Oh, and by the way, you are coming to church, right? Or do I have to drag your lazy butts out of this loft myself?"

Blake raised an eyebrow. "Church? I don't remember signing up for that."

"Because you didn't," Norah shot back. "But it's Sunday, and someone has to make sure you two don't devolve into complete heathens. Reese, I'm talking to you."

Reese threw his hands up in mock innocence. "Why am I getting singled out here? Blake's the one who tried to set off fireworks in the parking lot last Christmas."

"Hey! I was making the service more memorable," Blake said defensively, grinning. "You're welcome, by the way."

Norah rolled her eyes, biting back a laugh. "Sure, Blake, because pyrotechnics are exactly what Pastor Jenkins was going for when he talked about peace on Earth."

In the background, the news droned on from the TV, half-forgotten while they bantered. The anchor's voice was calm as images of a military base flashed on screen. Something about strange occurrences happening in the Arctic. The anchor's words began to filter through the conversation.

"...military personnel stationed at Fort Asgard, a remote Arctic base, have reported strange creatures in the water near their location. Several reports indicate sightings of large, dark shapes moving beneath the ice. In addition, communication disruptions and unexpected power surges have been occurring in the area. Officials are investigating the source of these disturbances but have yet to release a formal statement..."

Reese froze mid-bite, his fork hovering inches from his mouth. "Wait... what was that?"

He grabbed the remote and quickly rewound the segment. The three of them went silent as they listened to the report again, this time with full attention.

"Strange creatures... communication disruptions... power surges..." Reese repeated, narrowing his eyes at the TV. "That doesn't sound good."

Blake leaned back in his chair, throwing a grin at his brother. "You thinking what I'm thinking? Sounds like we've got a Kaiju sighting on our hands."

Norah scoffed, waving a dismissive hand. "Oh, please. People see strange things in the Arctic all the time. Shadows, seals, floating chunks of ice. You know, normal stuff. And we haven't had any reports of rift activity since Omega."

Reese didn't look convinced. "But the power surges? That's not normal. It's exactly what we've seen before—just before things go sideways."

Blake shrugged. "Could just be the Northern Lights messing with the electrical grid. Or... it could be a giant sea monster ready to pop up and smash the place to bits."

Norah gave him a look. "You're not helping."

"I wasn't trying to." Blake grinned.

"Look, I know we've been on lazy alert since Omega, but don't start jumping at shadows," Norah said, her voice firm. "No rift, no Kaiju. End of story."

Reese frowned, still staring at the screen. "Maybe, but we should at least keep an eye on it. If something's out there, we don't want to get caught with our pants down."

Blake leaned in with a teasing smirk. "I'm just saying, if this is Kaiju-related, you owe me a Tesla. You know, for all the trouble I'm going to go through saving the world again."

Norah rolled her eyes but smiled. "Deal. But it's not a Kaiju, Blake. You're just looking for an excuse to avoid church."

Blake winked. "Guilty as charged."

As they finished their breakfast, the loft was filled with a mix of sarcasm and laughter, but Reese's eyes kept flicking back to the TV. Something about that report gnawed at him, a sense of unease creeping in. He couldn't shake the feeling that they might be seeing the start of something big.

Something they weren't prepared for.

The drive to church was, as always, a lively one—mostly because Blake couldn't stop talking.

"I'm telling you, it could be Kaiju. Think about it. Strange sightings? Power surges? Arctic? It's like Kaiju 101. And if it is, we're not even remotely prepared. We don't have our mechs, no Valkyrie suits, nada. They've got everything locked away tighter than Fort Knox, and the military is crawling all over that place. We'd be toast if anything popped up."

Norah, sitting shotgun, sighed and rubbed her temples. "Blake, for the last time, there is no Kaiju. It's the Arctic—there are always strange things happening up there. It's probably a whale or a giant squid or whatever eats penguins these days."

"Squid eat penguins now?" Blake said with mock horror. "Why didn't anyone tell me?!"

Reese, in the driver's seat, stayed silent, his eyes focused on the road ahead. The report had clearly rattled him, but he wasn't saying a word. Not yet, at least.

Blake leaned forward between the front seats, still babbling. "No, seriously though. What if? We'd be caught with our pants down! I mean, picture it—us, the mighty Kaiju Task Force, reduced to civilians because the suits are locked up. I'd have to fend off a Kaiju with a spork from the church picnic."

Norah rolled her eyes, keeping her eyes forward. "I'm sure your spork skills will come in handy if we ever face a radioactive burger. Until then, maybe try enjoying the Sunday air?"

Blake shrugged. "I'm just saying. We've faced weirder things. And I still think it's unfair they took our Valkyrie suits. You know how many times I had to sneak out to the garage just to look at mine? It was like having your favorite toy put in a time-out for no reason."

Norah groaned, giving him a side glance. "You're being ridiculous. We've gone months without Kaiju sightings. There's no reason to think this is anything more than Arctic hysteria. You've been reading too many conspiracy forums."

"I call it staying informed," Blake said, folding his arms. "You call it paranoia."

Reese glanced at Blake in the rearview mirror, still quiet, but Blake caught the look. "See? Reese is thinking it too. You're just in denial."

Norah turned and raised an eyebrow at Reese. "Reese, seriously? Back me up here."

Reese's eyes flickered toward her briefly, then back to the road. He didn't say a word.

Blake grinned smugly. "See? Silent Reese speaks volumes. He's with me."

Norah threw her hands up in defeat. "Unbelievable. It's like talking to a brick wall with you two."

As they pulled into the church parking lot, Blake was still chattering about all the potential Kaiju-related disasters that could happen, while Norah just shook her head in amusement.

They got out of the car and were immediately greeted by familiar faces: Dr. Heather Isabelle, now just called "Heather" among friends, waved at them from the entrance of the church, along with their grandmother, Becky Stetser, and their mother, Jessica Bennett.

Blake stepped out of the car and sighed dramatically. "Ah, church. The one place Kaiju can't reach us."

Norah elbowed him in the ribs. "Watch it. We're here now. Don't embarrass us."

"I make no promises," Blake muttered, straightening his jacket.

As they walked up, their mom, Jessica, smiled brightly at them. "Well, well, look who finally decided to show up. Got some good news for you guys—your dad's home. He's inside waiting."

Reese's eyes widened. "Dad's back from the road? How long's he been home?"

"Just this morning," Jessica said. "He's been gone a while, so I'm sure he'll be thrilled to see you all."

"That's great," Blake said, smiling. "I'll make sure to fill him in on all the Kaiju rumors. You know, so he's prepared in case anything crawls out of the ocean while we're singing hymns."

Norah groaned again. "Can you please let that go for, like, ten minutes?"

Blake smirked. "I'm just saying... better safe than sorry."

They made their way into the church, Heather walking alongside Reese with a knowing smile. "You okay? You've been quiet."

Reese nodded, but his mind was still on the news report. "Yeah, just... thinking. I'll tell you about it later."

Heather gave him a curious look but didn't press. She knew when Reese had something on his mind, it was better to let him work through it.

Inside the church, they spotted their dad, David Bennett, sitting near the front, waving them over with a big grin. Blake and Reese both smiled as they made their way down the aisle, with Norah in tow, nudging Blake in the ribs again.

"Don't even think about bringing up Kaiju in front of Dad," she whispered.

Blake grinned. "Too late. It's already happening."

Norah shook her head, resigned to the chaos. It was just another Sunday morning with the Bennett siblings.

The sermon was a classic, one that always drew a few extra "Amens" from the congregation. Today's focus was on Daniel and the lions' den, a story the preacher told with such fire and passion that even Blake, usually prone to drifting off into daydreams about Kaiju, was fully attentive.

"Daniel," the preacher began, his voice rising with each word, "was thrown into the lions' den. He faced a certain death. Hungry, savage lions, with teeth like swords, claws like daggers. Yet what happened? Did he tremble? Did he cry out in fear?"

The congregation murmured, "No, he did not."

"No, he did not!" the preacher echoed, slamming his fist on the pulpit for emphasis. "He stood firm in his faith. He knew that God had the power to deliver him from the jaws of death. And so, he was spared! The lions, fierce as they were, did not lay a single paw on him!"

A collective "Amen" filled the room, followed by a wave of hallelujahs.

The preacher leaned forward, voice lowering for dramatic effect. "Brothers and sisters, we all face our own lions' dens. They might not be the beasts of the wild, but they are the trials of this life. Fear, doubt, failure—they roar at us, they threaten to devour us. But like Daniel, we must stand firm. For God will shut the mouths of our lions and deliver us."

Blake leaned over to Reese and whispered, "You think if I got thrown in with a Kaiju, my faith would shut their mouths?"

Reese suppressed a grin and elbowed Blake in the ribs, whispering back, "Let's hope we never have to find out."

Norah gave them both a look that said, Behave, but even she had to hide a smirk.

The sermon wrapped up with a resounding call to trust in God's protection, and the Bennetts found themselves walking out of the church with a renewed sense of peace. Little did they know, their own lions' den was waiting just around the corner, though theirs wouldn't be filled with lions—but something far more monstrous.

After the service, they headed out to the church courtyard, where their dad, David Bennett, was already sitting on a bench with his trucker cap tilted low and his arms crossed over his chest, waiting for his kids with a wide grin on his face.

"There they are!" David called out, standing up and opening his arms. "My crew! Y'all look like you've been behaving yourselves."

"Mostly," Reese said with a grin, stepping forward for a hug.

Norah hugged him next, shaking her head. "We're lucky we got Blake to stay quiet through most of the sermon."

Blake, of course, was next, dramatically throwing himself into his dad's arms. "It was touch and go there for a minute, Dad. The lions were hungry. They almost got me."

David chuckled and gave him a firm pat on the back. "I'm sure you gave them indigestion. Good to see you all. Now, what's been going on? Catch me up."

The siblings sat down on the nearby benches, with their dad in the middle, while their mom, Jessica, chatted with their grandmother Becky by the church doors. It didn't take long for the conversation to shift into full Bennett-family mode: full of jokes, banter, and, of course, Blake being Blake.

"So, Norah," David began, "still running things at Tesla? Got those electric cars flyin' yet?"

Norah grinned. "Not flying yet, but we're close. Working on some new tech, though. It's top secret."

Blake leaned forward, eyes wide. "Top secret? Or government secret? You can tell us. We won't spill. What are you making? Jetpacks? Kaiju-repelling force fields?"

Norah rolled her eyes. "It's a new charging system for EVs. Not as exciting as Kaiju stuff, sorry."

Blake waved it off. "Hey, anything could be Kaiju-related if you try hard enough."

Reese smirked. "Are you gonna connect everything to Kaiju today?"

Blake didn't miss a beat. "Of course. Especially since we might be on the verge of a new Kaiju event!"

David raised an eyebrow. "Oh boy, here we go. What's this now?"

Blake puffed up his chest like a kid who just found buried treasure. "So, this morning, on the news, they were talking about strange sightings at a military base in the Arctic. Weird power surges, creatures in the water, the whole nine yards. And I'm telling you, Dad, this could be Kaiju. The signs are all there."

David chuckled, giving him a look. "Strange creatures in the Arctic? Son, that's probably just a walrus having a bad hair day."

Norah snorted. "Thank you!"

Blake crossed his arms, undeterred. "Laugh all you want, but you weren't there when Omega showed up. These things come out of nowhere, and when they do, you wish you'd listened to me. Next thing you know, we'll have a giant igloo monster stomping around, and we'll be stuck without any of our mechs."

Reese finally chimed in, a slight grin on his face. "Yeah, because when I think Arctic monsters, I think 'giant igloo.'"

"I'm just saying," Blake continued, now getting more animated, "it could be anything. We're sitting ducks right now. No Valkyrie suits, no Task Force, nothing. What if it is Kaiju? What then? We're just gonna throw snowballs at it?"

David laughed out loud, clapping Blake on the shoulder. "You've always had a wild imagination, son. Maybe that's what the military's missing—more creative solutions like yours."

Blake raised a finger as if making a profound point. "Exactly! Creativity. That's how we beat these things. Also, mechs. But creativity first."

Norah sighed, shaking her head. "You've officially lost it."

Blake shrugged. "Maybe. But when a Kaiju shows up at our doorstep, you'll be glad I was prepared."

Their dad chuckled, leaning back. "Well, as long as you've got it all figured out, I'll sleep better at night."

Blake nodded, dead serious. "You should, Dad. You really should."

Reese, still thinking about the news report from earlier, remained quiet. He wasn't convinced Blake was right, but something about it gnawed at him. Maybe it wasn't Kaiju—but there was definitely something strange going on up north. Something they might have to face sooner than any of them expected.

And just like that, the lions' den was already beginning to take shape.

As Blake enthusiastically cornered Pastor Jenkins by the refreshment table, rattling off everything from Kaiju theories to the controversial ending of Supernatural, David Bennett caught sight of Reese, who had been quiet all morning. Unlike his siblings, who seemed to take everything in stride, Reese had a heavy air about him. Something was weighing on his mind.

David, always perceptive when it came to his kids, gently placed a hand on Reese's shoulder. "Walk with me, son."

Reese gave a small nod, glancing back at Blake. "Good luck to Pastor Jenkins. He's in for a long one."

David chuckled. "Poor guy doesn't know what's about to hit him."

As they strolled toward the back of the churchyard, Norah was chatting with her kids, and Blake's animated voice carried on in the distance. "Look, Pastor, if you didn't like the Supernatural finale, I get it. But let's be real—Chuck as the villain was genius. Plus, there's no way Sam could've kept hunting forever! And don't get me started on how Kaiju would've fit right in as the next big bad after Lucifer. I'm telling you, it would've blown people's minds!"

Pastor Jenkins, Ever the patient soul, David tried to interject, but Blake was on a roll. "Seriously though, Pastor, do you think God ever took a look at those Winchester boys and thought, 'Wow, I really made them go through it, huh?'"

David and Reese smiled at Blake's ramblings, but once they were far enough away from the others, David turned to his son, his expression serious. "What's on your mind, Reese?"

Reese sighed, running a hand through his hair. "It's Vance. He's been working on something... something dangerous."

David raised an eyebrow. "Dangerous how?"

Reese glanced around, making sure they were still out of earshot. "Vance is creating hybrids. Not just any hybrids, Dad. These things—he's mixing Kaiju DNA. And... he used Omega's blood."

David's face stiffened at the mention of Omega. "He what?"

"I know, it sounds crazy. But he's got these things, Dad. They're human-sized for now, but they're unstable, unpredictable. I don't think he can control them. And what if these 'strange creatures' being sighted in the Arctic are connected? What if they're Vance's hybrids?"

David fell silent for a moment, his jaw tightening. His son had no idea just how close his concerns were to the truth, and it weighed heavily on David's heart. For two years, he'd kept his identity as Alpha—a Kaiju Task Force operative—hidden from his children, wanting to protect them from the burdens that came with that knowledge. And now, seeing Reese so troubled, he felt the pull to reveal the truth more than ever. But he resisted.

If they knew he was Alpha, it would change everything—how they looked at him, how they trusted him. They needed him to be their father, not some larger-than-life hero.

"Reese," David said carefully, choosing his words, "you're right to be concerned. Vance... he's always been a wildcard, even back in the day. But you've got something Vance doesn't."

Reese looked at him, confused. "What's that?"

"Your heart," David said simply. "Vance might have his science and his hybrids, but you have something more powerful—your instincts, your conscience. You know what's right, and you're not afraid to stand up for it. That's why you're worried, because you care about the bigger picture, about people. Vance doesn't."

Reese sighed. "I just wish I could talk to Alpha... get his advice. He always seemed to know what to do."

David felt a pang of guilt. If only Reese knew.

"I understand," David said softly, swallowing the urge to reveal the truth. "But you don't need Alpha to tell you what to do. You already know. Trust yourself, Reese. You've got the same instincts he does."

Reese looked down, wrestling with the weight of it all. "I'm just afraid I'll make the wrong decision, that I'll let something slip through the cracks, and it'll be too late to stop it."

David put his hand on Reese's shoulder, gripping it firmly. "Son, making hard decisions is part of being a leader. You won't always know the right answer right away. But if you do what you know is right, you'll come through it stronger. And you're not alone. You've got your brother, your sister, your family. We're all in this together."

Reese's expression softened slightly. "Yeah... I guess you're right."

David smiled warmly, though the internal struggle still raged within him. For now, he'd keep his secret. But watching Reese wrestle with these challenges, he wondered how long he could withhold the truth.

"For now," David said, "let's pray about it. Sometimes, when we don't have all the answers, it's best to ask the One who does."

Reese nodded, and the two of them bowed their heads. David placed his hand on Reese's back and prayed quietly. "Lord, we ask for Your wisdom and Your guidance. We're facing things we don't understand, but we know You see the bigger picture. Help Reese, help us all, to walk in faith and make the right choices. Keep us safe and protect us from whatever dangers lie ahead."

As they finished, Reese took a deep breath, feeling a little lighter. "Thanks, Dad. I needed that."

David smiled, but inside, the weight of his secret remained. For now, he'd trust Reese to navigate this without knowing the truth. But the day would come when he'd have to reveal himself as Alpha—and when it did, everything would change.

Chapter 12: Strange Reports and Stranger Powers

Reese sat at his desk, staring at his computer screen, an amused smirk creeping onto his face. The latest batch of military reports had just come in—strange sightings off the coast of Alaska, mysterious ripples in the water, strange lights under the ice in the Arctic, and even whispers of shadowy creatures lurking in Africa. His eyes scanned the lines, but his brain kept drifting to one thought: Blake would be losing his mind over this.

He leaned back in his chair, stretching his arms and cracking his knuckles. "Great," he muttered to himself. "I'm starting to sound like Blake, the cryptid king."

He could practically hear his brother's voice in his head: "See, Reese, this is exactly what I've been saying! Strange creatures? Shadowy shapes? That's textbook Kaiju!"

Reese chuckled under his breath, imagining Blake in full-on cryptozoologist mode, complete with his collection of blurry Bigfoot photos, his Gamera posters, and a stack of conspiracy books taller than he was. "Next thing you know," Reese muttered to himself, "I'll be out in the middle of the woods with a flashlight, waiting for Mothman to say hi."

But despite the humor, something nagged at him. These reports felt... different. The details were too precise, too frequent. And after everything Vance had told him about the hybrids—and the unsettling possibility that they were out there, somehow connected to these sightings—he couldn't just sit back and do nothing.

Reese leaned forward, tapping away at his keyboard, discreetly pulling up satellite imagery from the Arctic Circle. The images showed strange disturbances in the water, massive shapes moving beneath the ice, and cracks spreading like spiderwebs across glaciers. Definitely not normal.

"Just great," he muttered, glancing at a grainy image of what looked like a massive shadow near the surface. "Blake's gonna have a field day if he sees this. I'm practically a cryptozoologist now."

He shook his head, smiling slightly as he began cross-referencing the reports with the satellite data. For all his jokes, a small part of him felt the thrill of the chase. Maybe Blake had been onto something all along. Maybe there were things out there, things people weren't ready to believe.

Meanwhile, back at GeneSys Labs, Vance paced in front of his workstation, his eyes darting between multiple holographic screens displaying the latest data from his hybrids. The creatures, now fully grown and humanoid in form, were showing new signs of evolution—and not in ways Vance had expected.

Omega's blood had done something to them.

The hybrids, once mere genetic experiments designed for control, were now exhibiting strange new abilities. Their bodies were changing, adapting, growing stronger by the day. And their intelligence... it was as if they were learning, observing, becoming more aware.

Vance stood in the dimly lit lab, staring intently at the array of holographic screens surrounding him. The glow from the monitors reflected off his glasses as he swiped through the data, reviewing the latest reports on his hybrids. The creatures were advancing faster than even he had anticipated, their powers evolving at an unprecedented rate.

He paused at the first chart: Aquila, the shark-eagle hybrid, a monster that looked like it had leapt straight out of a nightmare. Its eyes gleamed with a predatory, intelligent focus. Aquila had quickly become one of his most dangerous creations.

Abilities:

Storm Flight: Aquila could summon violent storm clouds as it soared through the sky. It was like watching a force of nature as it moved with incredible speed, tearing through the heavens. The clouds followed it like a loyal pack, and with a beat of its wings, it could summon gale-force winds to disorient anything—or anyone—in its path.

Electro-Shock Fins: The metallic fins along its back charged with electricity, enabling Aquila to shoot powerful lightning bolts at its targets. It could weaponize the very storm it created, striking down enemies with precision lightning strikes. The last test had fried every drone Vance sent into the storm, much to his satisfaction.

Talon Strike: Its talons, sharp enough to shred through steel, made it a menace both in the air and on land. Vance had watched it rip through reinforced metal dummies like they were tissue paper. Those talons were perfect for grabbing prey—or for tearing through a city's infrastructure if necessary.

Tidal Scream: Aquila's most terrifying ability, though, was its sonic blast. When it opened its shark-like jaws, it could release a deafening roar that created tidal waves near water or air-pressure shockwaves in the sky. This ability had proven to be a game-changer in Vance's simulations. Aquila could level entire fleets with a single scream.

Vance swiped to the next chart, studying Lynxara, the lion-hyena hybrid. It was an apex predator, driven by its savage instincts and hunger for dominance.

Sonic Roar: Like Aquila's Tidal Scream, Lynxara could unleash a devastating roar, but this one was lower, guttural, and focused. It created sonic shockwaves that toppled buildings and disoriented anyone within range. The roar wasn't just loud—it was destructive, shaking the very ground beneath its feet.

Pack Leader: Vance had discovered that Lynxara possessed a natural ability to summon smaller scavenger creatures—hybrids or mutated wildlife from the surrounding areas. In battle, Lynxara could overwhelm opponents not just with its raw power but also with sheer numbers, directing these creatures with a predator's instinct.

Regenerative Endurance: Much like its Omega lineage, Lynxara had a near-instantaneous healing factor. Injuries that would kill other beasts were mere scratches to it, and it regenerated so quickly that even in the heat of battle, it was impossible to weaken.

Predator's Frenzy: But what truly set Lynxara apart was its bloodlust. Once it got a taste of its opponent's blood, it entered a berserk state, increasing its speed, strength, and aggression. During a recent test, it had decimated an entire simulation environment after tasting a single drop of blood from one of the hybrid assistants.

"Fascinating," Vance murmured, staring at the screen, his mind already racing with possibilities. Lynxara was a beast of strategy and raw savagery, one of his most versatile creations.

Next was Titanax, the gorilla-elephant hybrid, towering above the others. It was a hulking brute, designed to bring down the most fortified defenses with ease.

Tusks of Destruction: The tusks were infused with a metallic alloy derived from Omega's blood, allowing Titanax to conduct powerful energy blasts. In one test, the creature had skewered a tank with ease, sending a surge of energy that obliterated the vehicle from the inside out.

Trunk Slam: Its trunk was not just a massive appendage—it was a weapon. Titanax could swing it like a battering ram, smashing through steel and concrete with a single strike. When it hit the ground, the resulting shockwave sent vehicles and rubble flying in all directions.

Primal Roar: Titanax's roar was another weapon in its arsenal, a deafening bellow that disoriented anyone caught in its radius. The sound waves it emitted were strong enough to knock over structures and send even the most battle-hardened soldiers running for cover.

Regenerative Healing: And, like the others, Titanax had the gift of rapid healing. Thanks to Omega's blood, it could recover from even the most grievous injuries in a matter of minutes. Its size, strength, and endurance made it nearly unstoppable.

Vance looked up at the glass where Titanax stood, breathing heavily, its tusks scraping the ground as it moved. It was a juggernaut, capable of wreaking untold destruction. He swiped to the final chart: Felonix, the cheetah—not a hybrid but a wonderful surprise—the fastest of them all.

Super Speed: Felonix could reach speeds up to Mach 3, moving so fast it became nearly invisible to the naked eye. Vance had watched in awe as Felonix tore through a field of obstacles, dismantling them one by one before any of them had the chance to react.

Energy Claws: Its claws, like Titanax's tusks, could emit electrical surges, capable of ripping through reinforced steel and conducting powerful energy blasts that destabilized buildings and vehicles. Felonix was both fast and deadly.

Cloak of Shadows: And, as if its speed wasn't enough, Felonix could phase out of visible light, becoming practically invisible. It could stalk its prey without being seen, striking only when it was ready.

Enhanced Reflexes: With reflexes heightened to superhuman levels, Felonix was nearly impossible to hit. It dodged attacks with ease, weaving through bullets and energy blasts as if they were moving in slow motion.

Vance grinned. Each hybrid was a masterpiece, each one more deadly and more unpredictable than the last. Together, they were the ultimate weapons—living, breathing instruments of destruction.

But Vance knew that controlling them was becoming increasingly difficult. Their intelligence was growing, and they were becoming more aware of their own powers. For now, they obeyed him, but the day would come when his control over them would be tested.

He shut off the screens and stared out at the four beasts standing behind the reinforced glass. Omega's blood had changed them in ways he hadn't foreseen, but it had also made them more powerful than anything the world had ever seen.

Vance leaned back in his chair, his fingers drumming thoughtfully against the cold metal desk. The data was promising—no, better than promising. It was exceptional. His hybrids were fully operational, their powers exceeding every expectation. They were ready for real-world tests. He knew it was time to take them out into the field.

But it had to be done quietly. The world couldn't know, not yet. These missions had to be covert, executed with precision and complete discretion. No one could know about the hybrids—not until Vance was ready to reveal them on his own terms. And so, the first set of missions was planned.

The night was quiet, the moon barely casting a glow over the desert sands of North Africa. A terrorist cell had established a compound far from any populated area, using the cover of darkness to smuggle weapons and organize strikes against governments across the region. Intelligence agencies had been watching, but no one had the means to stop them—until now.

Vance's first test was simple: a silent takedown.

Aquila, the shark-eagle hybrid, was deployed under the cover of a gathering storm, its massive wings effortlessly slicing through the desert winds. With a single beat of those wings, it could whip up gusts strong enough to mask its presence. As it hovered above the compound, its Electro-Shock Fins crackled with energy. In the blink of an eye, bolts of lightning struck the power grid, frying every generator in the compound.

Without electricity, the entire base went dark, leaving the terrorists vulnerable. Aquila swooped in silently, using its Talon Strike to rip through communication towers and equipment. The operation was over in minutes, and no one had ever seen what hit them. By the time the authorities arrived, the place was a graveyard of destroyed weaponry and silent structures, but not a single body lay on the ground.

Mission one: flawless.

Vance couldn't hide his grin as he reviewed the footage. The success of the mission only emboldened him. Next came a mission closer to home—an anonymous tip about a gang-run operation smuggling illegal arms into the heart of a U.S. city.

This time, Vance unleashed Felonix. The cheetah hybrid darted through the streets, barely a blur to anyone who might've been watching. It moved so fast, it appeared as little more than a trick of the light. With its Super Speed, it dismantled the operation in a matter of seconds, disarming every criminal, sabotaging the smuggled weapons, and even sabotaging the getaway vehicles before anyone knew what had happened. By the time the gang members realized what was happening, Felonix was long gone, invisible thanks to its Cloak of Shadows.

Another perfect strike.

But it was the next mission where Vance felt the true power of his creations—and their value to his long-term plans. The world was holding its breath as tensions escalated between Iran and Israel. Intelligence suggested that a missile strike was imminent. No one had concrete proof, but if it happened, it could spark a regional war that would ripple across the globe.

Vance knew he couldn't allow that. But instead of waiting for the missiles to hit, he sent Titanax on a covert mission deep into the heart of the desert, where the missile launch site had been hidden.

The sheer size of the gorilla-elephant hybrid made it seem impossible to keep such a creature undetected, but the darkness of the desert, combined with Titanax's immense strength, made it the perfect candidate for the job. With its Primal Roar, Titanax disoriented the launch crew, sending them fleeing into the night and leaving the facility vulnerable.

As the first missile took flight, Titanax's massive form lunged upward, using its Tusks of Destruction to strike the missile mid-air, diverting it into the empty desert before it could reach its target. The resulting explosion was swallowed by the night, far away from any population center.

Titanax didn't stop there. With its Trunk Slam, it decimated the entire launch site, flattening the complex with a few well-placed blows. The missile program was obliterated, and Titanax slipped away into the night, unseen and unstoppable.

The Israeli government had no idea how close they'd come to devastation. The world remained blissfully unaware of the creatures that had saved them from the brink of war.

Vance couldn't have been more pleased. Every mission had been executed flawlessly, without a single hitch. No lives had been lost, and none of the hybrids had been seen. To the world, these events were nothing more than inexplicable incidents—mysterious accidents, natural phenomena, freak coincidences. But Vance knew better.

His hybrids were the future of warfare, the perfect soldiers.

As he looked over the charts from each mission, he felt a sense of immense satisfaction. The data showed perfect obedience. Each creature had followed his commands to the letter, with no deviation. Aquila's lightning strikes had been flawless, Felonix's super speed unrivaled, and Titanax's brute strength had torn through steel and concrete like it was nothing. Even Lynxara, who had been sent on a separate mission to neutralize a heavily fortified cartel base in South America, had accomplished its goal with terrifying precision. The cartel's leaders had never stood a chance against Lynxara's Sonic Roar and overwhelming Predator's Frenzy.

Yet, as Vance sat back, basking in his success, he missed the subtle signs that something was changing.

Back in their containment units, the hybrids paced restlessly. Aquila's eyes flickered with intelligence as it watched the lab's automated drones fly overhead. Lynxara growled low, a sound that reverberated through the lab, though Vance didn't seem to notice. Even Titanax, the most obedient of the hybrids, showed signs of unease, its massive form shifting in its reinforced enclosure.

Vance had dismissed the slight changes in behavior as nothing more than post-mission energy, but if he had been paying closer attention, he might've noticed the way Felonix's eyes lingered on the lab door as if contemplating an escape. Or how Lynxara's claws tapped rhythmically against the floor, a subconscious act of rebellion. Aquila's wings twitched, as though testing the boundaries of the containment field.

They were growing restless.

They were growing tired of their invisible leash.

For now, Vance's control held. But beneath the surface, the hybrids were evolving—becoming more than just tools for his use. And if Vance wasn't careful, he might soon discover just how dangerous his creations could become when they were no longer content with being controlled.

For now, the leash remained tight.

But for how long?

Vance paced back and forth in the cold, sterile lab, his eyes twitching with irritation. The news broadcast from earlier still replayed in his mind, the smug face of General Sarah Strayer haunting him. She'd been the one to recommend his program, to greenlight the hybrid experiments, only to later shut it down when she deemed it "too dangerous." Too dangerous? What did she know about danger? She hadn't been in the lab, hadn't seen the potential, the power. And now, she'd gone on national television, gloating about her decision.

"How dare she?" Vance muttered through clenched teeth, hands shaking as they gripped the edge of his desk. He slammed his fists down, sending papers and test tubes scattering across the lab floor.

For four hours straight, Vance had been in an unrelenting rage. His once meticulous workbench was now a mess of shattered glass, spilled chemicals, and torn reports. This wasn't like him. Vance had always been precise, calculated, and calm under pressure. But lately, things were changing. He was changing.

His temper flared at the slightest inconvenience. If a calculation was off, he'd fly into a rage. If the hybrids didn't respond perfectly to a command, he'd lash out, throwing equipment, shouting until his throat was raw. His staff had learned to stay clear of him when he was in one of his moods. Even Alice, his wife, had distanced herself, growing tired of his constant mood swings and obsessive work habits.

Vance barely noticed her absence anymore. He had been staying at the lab for days at a time, justifying it with the excuse that there was too much to do, too much to monitor. But deep down, there was something else. He didn't want to be around anyone. Not Alice, not his staff, not even himself. Something inside him felt... off. More than just anger. It was a gnawing sense of hunger, a lust for power that grew stronger with each passing day.

What Vance didn't realize was that Omega's blood wasn't just changing his hybrids. It was changing him too.

Meanwhile, across town, Reese was wrestling with his own concerns. He had been piecing together reports of strange sightings and unexplained events that seemed... unnatural. Creatures spotted where they shouldn't be. Things no one could explain. He'd always teased Blake about his cryptozoology obsession, but now Reese felt like he was the one diving into a rabbit hole of conspiracy theories.

He shook his head, letting out a small chuckle. "I feel like Blake right now," he muttered to himself. "Next thing I know, I'll be chasing after Bigfoot."

But this wasn't a joke. The more he learned, the more uneasy he became. These creatures—whatever they were—weren't just cryptids or legends. There was something bigger at play, and Reese couldn't shake the feeling that Vance was somehow behind it all. The hybrid program, the shutdown, Vance's growing paranoia... it all fit together, but the pieces weren't quite clear yet.

Reese knew he needed to share what he'd found with Blake and Norah. He couldn't keep this to himself any longer. If Vance was experimenting with creatures, and these hybrids were involved, they had to know. It wasn't safe to keep this under wraps. They needed to be ready.

Pulling out his phone, Reese dialed Norah's number. It rang twice before she picked up, her voice warm but cautious. "Reese? Everything okay?"

"Yeah... well, no," Reese said, rubbing his temple. "Listen, can you meet me at Blake and my loft? I've got some stuff I need to talk to you about. It's important. Really important."

There was a brief pause on the other end of the line before Norah spoke again, this time with a hint of concern. "What's going on, Reese? You sound... off."

Reese sighed. "I'll explain everything when you get here. Just—just trust me, okay?"

"Okay," Norah agreed, though the worry in her voice was unmistakable. "I'll be there soon."

As Reese hung up the phone, he took a deep breath. He could hear Blake in the other room, excitedly rambling about Kaiju to Pastor Jenkins, who had stopped by for a visit. Reese couldn't help but grin at his younger brother's enthusiasm. Blake had been on a Supernatural binge lately, and his obsession with Kaiju had reached peak levels of intensity.

"No, Pastor, I'm telling you, if Dean Winchester had just one Kaiju on his side, they could've taken out Lucifer so much easier. Like, seriously! Just imagine—Zephyrus swoops in, massive lightning strike, game over for all the demons!" Blake was gesturing wildly, his voice growing more animated by the second.

Pastor Jenkins nodded politely, clearly overwhelmed but too kind to cut Blake off. "That does sound... interesting, Blake."

"Interesting? It's genius!" Blake declared. "I should write a fanfic about this. Supernatural meets Kaiju! It'll break the internet, Pastor, mark my words!"

Reese snorted a laugh, despite the heaviness weighing on him. Even in the middle of everything, Blake's boundless energy was contagious. But tonight wasn't the time for Kaiju fan theories. Tonight, they needed to focus on the real monsters lurking in the shadows—the ones Vance was playing with.

As Reese sat down, waiting for Norah, he couldn't help but wonder—would they be ready for what was coming?

And would Vance?

Back in the lab, Vance stared at his reflection in the mirrored glass of the containment unit. The hybrids were safely locked inside, but as he gazed at his own face, he barely recognized the man looking back at him. His eyes were bloodshot, his skin pale, and dark circles lay under his eyes from too many sleepless nights.

It's General Strayer's fault, he thought, his hands trembling with rage again. *She did this. She's the reason my work's being shut down. She's the one holding me back.*

His lips curled into a sneer, and without thinking, he slammed his fist into the glass. His knuckles split open, but he didn't even feel the pain. All he could see was her—her smug face, her dismissive attitude, her complete ignorance of what he had been trying to achieve. She would pay for this. They all would.

Vance didn't know it yet, but the blood of Omega was coursing through his veins, warping his mind, feeding his growing hunger for power. The hybrids weren't the only ones evolving. He was becoming something else. Something darker.

But for now, all he could focus on was his rage—and the need for revenge.

Chapter 13: The Tables Have Turned

Reese, Blake, and Norah sat at the table, with a stack of blurry satellite images spread out before him. He stared at the pictures, frowning, as his siblings joined him. Norah, ever the composed one, settled into a chair across from Reese, while Blake dropped into the seat next to him, eyes gleaming with mischief.

"All right," Reese began, his tone serious, "I know this is going to sound crazy, but you guys need to see this." He tapped the pile of images with his finger, sliding a few toward Norah and Blake.

Norah leaned in, studying the grainy photos with a critical eye, but Blake? Blake just grinned. "Wait, wait, wait," he said, holding up one of the pictures and squinting at the barely discernible outline of... something. "Reese... is this... blurry creature footage?" Blake's voice was full of barely contained laughter.

Reese sighed, already regretting this. "Yeah, I know. It's not exactly National Geographic quality, but—"

"Blurry creatures," Blake repeated, biting his lip to keep from laughing. "You've been making fun of me for years—years—about my cryptozoology stuff. And now here you are, the proud owner of blurry creature images." He slapped the table, laughing. "Oh, this is rich! This is too good! I mean, do you want me to break out my old notebooks and theories too? Maybe you've finally seen Bigfoot!"

Reese shot him a look. "Blake, come on. This is serious."

Blake wiped a tear from his eye. "Oh, it's serious, all right! Look at these pictures! I can't tell if that's a Kaiju or just an overgrown possum caught on a bad day."

Norah, trying to keep a straight face, cleared her throat. "Blake, let's focus." But even she couldn't suppress a small smile. "Reese wouldn't bring this to us unless it was important."

"Thank you, Norah," Reese said, giving her a grateful nod before turning to Blake. "And no, it's not a possum. Look, I've been doing some digging, and these sightings… they line up with some of the locations where Vance was known to have been on vacation."

Blake's smile faded slightly, but the playful glint in his eye remained. "Oh, so now we're blaming Vance? Next, you'll tell me Vance's hybrids are out there knocking over trash cans and eating stray cats."

"Blake, I'm serious!" Reese snapped, pushing another photo toward him. "Look at this one. Whatever that is, it's not normal. And it's not random. It's been spotted near old military testing grounds, abandoned facilities—all places where Vance had connections. You don't think that's a coincidence, do you?"

Blake picked up the photo, his brow furrowing as he inspected it more closely. "Okay, okay. I'm listening now. But I still reserve the right to make fun of you later."

"Of course you do," Norah said dryly. "But for now, let's focus on what this means. If Vance is involved in this, we need to figure out what he's up to."

Reese nodded. "Exactly. I don't know if it's Vance's hybrids, or if it's something worse. But these creatures… they're not normal. They're not Kaiju like Omega, but they're something. And if Vance is behind this, we need to stop him before things get out of hand."

Blake leaned back in his chair, rubbing his chin thoughtfully. "You know, part of me hopes it's just a bunch of wild animals that somehow mutated into blurry monsters. But then again, Vance has always been a bit of a mad scientist. This would be so on-brand for him."

"Vance's experiments were shut down," Norah said, flipping through a few more of the satellite images. "But if he's found a way to continue them in secret, that could explain all of this. Still, even if it's related to his work, that doesn't mean it's something we can just walk in and stop."

"Right," Reese agreed. "That's where we hit a wall. If it's Vance, we need evidence. We need proof. And right now, all I've got is a bunch of..."

"Blurry creature photos," Blake finished for him with a smirk.

Reese shot him a look. "Yes, fine. Blurry creature photos. But you're the expert in weird, unexplainable stuff. You've seen Kaiju before. What do you think?"

Blake gave the photos one last look, then shrugged. "Honestly? Could be anything. Mutated hybrids, escaped government experiments, maybe even some alien pets that got loose—who knows? But whatever it is, we're not exactly equipped to handle it right now."

Blake's humor disappeared as reality set in. "You guys remember the Valkyrie suits? We used those to take down Omega. But guess what? They're locked up tighter than Fort Knox. Even if these blurry creatures are Kaiju-adjacent, we're gonna need those suits, and they're under heavy guard."

"Not to mention," Norah added, "we don't even know if Vance is actually behind this. It could be something entirely different—some rogue military project, another experiment gone wrong, or worse—something we don't even know about yet."

Reese sat back, frustrated. "So what? We're just supposed to sit here and do nothing? We've got creatures out there wreaking havoc, and we don't have a way to stop them?"

Blake scratched his head, thinking. "Well, we could always, you know, break into the base, steal the suits back, go all Mission: Impossible on this thing..."

Norah gave him a flat look. "Blake, that's insane."

"Is it, though? I mean, we've faced down Kaiju, fought in mech suits the size of buildings, and you're telling me this is where we draw the line on insanity?"

Reese chuckled despite himself. "He's got a point."

Norah sighed, rubbing her temples. "Okay, let's say, hypothetically, we could get the suits. How would we even do that without getting caught? The government isn't exactly going to hand them over."

Reese leaned back in his chair, his serious expression a sharp contrast to Blake's usual grin. "First things first," he said, glancing between his siblings. "We need proof. Blurry images alone won't cut it. Norah and I will check out Vance's lab and see what we can dig up—something concrete."

Blake, still holding one of the satellite images up like it was a prized piece of art, wiggled his eyebrows. "And what about me? Do I get to break into a secret lab too? Or should I keep hunting blurry possums?"

Reese rolled his eyes. "No, you get the glamorous job of talking to Heather. See if she can put us in contact with the General."

Blake immediately groaned, dropping the photo back onto the table. "Oh, great. Because Heather is going to totally go for that. 'Hey, Heather, got a few blurry pictures here of maybe-possibly creatures—could you do us a solid and call up the General? No biggie, just a potential global threat.' Yeah, she's gonna love that."

Norah snorted. "Well, that's where you come in, Mr. Charm. Use that Blake magic. Flash her the smile. Maybe tell a few of your ridiculous jokes."

Blake narrowed his eyes at her. "First of all, my jokes are legendary—thank you very much. Second, Heather is a scientist, not some starstruck fan of the Blake Charm. She's going to want hard evidence, not my killer one-liners."

Reese smirked. "She'll need something before she goes to the General, that's for sure. But we don't have much else right now. So unless you want to suit up and join us in some high-tech stealth action, your best bet is convincing her."

Blake sighed dramatically, throwing his hands up in defeat. "Fine, fine. I'll give it a shot. But when she shuts me down, don't come crying to me. This Blake Charm has limits, you know."

Norah leaned forward, her voice mock-serious. "Oh, no. Don't tell us the great Blake Bennet has limits! What happened to the guy who swore he could talk his way out of anything?"

Blake put a hand over his heart, playing along. "Hey, I never said anything. I said most things. I'm not a miracle worker—just an expert in the fine art of persuasion."

Reese shook his head, laughing under his breath. "Well, work your art, Picasso. We need Heather on board. And who knows? Maybe this time your smooth talk will actually come in handy."

Blake grabbed a handful of the blurry photos, holding them up triumphantly. "Oh, trust me, I'm about to dazzle her with the mystery of the universe right here. These photos scream, trust me, I know what I'm talking about."

Norah grinned, standing up. "Good luck with that, Mr. Smooth. Me and Reese will be sneaking around a high-tech lab, risking our lives, while you—"

"Get rejected by a scientist. Yeah, I got it," Blake finished for her. "Don't worry, I'll bring my A-game. She won't know what hit her."

As Blake headed toward the door, Reese called out, "Remember, we need her to take us seriously. No jokes about Bigfoot, okay?"

Blake raised a hand without turning around. "I make no promises. Bigfoot is always on the table."

They watched him exit the loft, and seconds later, his voice echoed from the hallway. "Hey, Heather! Guess who's calling you with something super important—no, no, it's not about cryptids this time, I swear—well, maybe kind of..."

Norah facepalmed. "He's hopeless."

Reese chuckled. "He'll figure it out. Or at least, he'll amuse her enough to get us some time. In the meantime, we've got our own problem to handle."

Norah turned to face him, her expression serious. "Yeah. How exactly are we going to sneak into a high-tech lab? This isn't like a walk in the park. Vance's lab is under constant surveillance, and he's got all kinds of security measures in place."

Reese crossed his arms, thinking. "We're going to have to get creative. Vance isn't going to leave anything important just lying around. We'll need a distraction to slip in unnoticed."

Norah raised an eyebrow. "Oh, so we're just going full heist movie now? Should we plan an elaborate scheme with gadgets and fake mustaches?"

Reese smirked. "Not quite. But we do need to figure out a way to blend in. We can't just waltz in through the front door."

Norah folded her arms, pacing around the room. "There's gotta be a way to bypass the main security systems. Maybe we could pose as contractors or something? Maintenance workers?"

Reese nodded. "That could work. If we can create a plausible enough cover, we might be able to slip in without raising any alarms. Vance's focus is probably on the lab work itself, not the people maintaining the facility."

Norah paused, thinking it over. "Alright. So, we get in posing as contractors. Then what? We need access to his restricted areas. And we can't afford to trip any alarms."

Reese pulled out a small device from his pocket and held it up. "I've been working on something that might help with that. It's a signal jammer—temporary, short-range. It won't take down the whole system, but it might give us a few minutes to move through any secured doors without tripping the alarms."

Norah smiled, impressed. "You've been busy."

Reese grinned. "Hey, I like to be prepared."

She nodded, feeling more confident. "Alright. Let's figure out the rest of the plan. We get in, use the jammer to bypass the secured areas, and find whatever Vance has been working on. If he's behind these hybrids, we need to know what we're dealing with."

"Exactly," Reese agreed. "And we'll need to move fast. We can't afford to get caught snooping around in his lab."

Chapter 14: "Blurry Evidence and Big Promises"

Blake strutted into Heather Isabelle's lab like he was auditioning for a spy movie—except his swagger was more comedy than cool. Heather, engrossed in her work, didn't even glance up as he dramatically slid into the room. Typical.

"Heather!" Blake said, raising his hands like he was about to make a grand proclamation. "I come bearing... well, blurry photos. But they're important blurry photos!"

Without looking up, Heather sighed. "Blake, if I have to look at one more blurry picture of swamp gas and call it a creature, I'm locking you in a cage with Kevin," she deadpanned, referring to General Strayer's Pomeranian.

"Whoa, whoa," Blake waved his hands in mock surrender. "That fluffball is vicious, but this time it's not swamp gas. No, this is big. Kaiju-big."

Heather finally raised an eyebrow, spinning her chair around to face him. "Kaiju-big? Are you sure you're not just blowing up an image of your lunch again?"

"Rude," Blake said, holding up a folder. He slapped it down on the table like it contained top-secret documents. In reality, it was just a bunch of smudgy, low-res images. "Feast your eyes on this!"

Heather glanced down, then back up at him, unimpressed. "Blake... this looks like Bigfoot took a selfie with a potato."

"Hey! That potato happens to be Vance's possible mutant hybrids, okay? Maybe even creatures he's been cooking up in his lab!" Blake leaned in, lowering his voice like he was delivering a classified secret. "Reese thinks he's up to no good, and these... fine, artistically blurry photos might be the key to proving it."

Heather blinked at him, clearly trying to contain her sarcasm. "Blake. These are smudges. You want me to go to General Strayer with smudges? Do you want to be the laughingstock of the entire operation? Again?"

Blake dramatically clutched his heart, pretending to be wounded. "Smudges? You wound me, Heather. These are mystery creatures. Potential evidence. Could even be Kaiju-level threats!"

She gave him a deadpan stare. "Blake, it could also be a large cat with bad posture. I can't go to the General with blurry photos of someone's lost house cat."

"Lost house cat?" Blake chuckled. "Now, that is an interesting take, but trust me, these are no tabby cats. Reese thinks Vance is up to something big, and these mystery creatures are part of it. We just need a little meeting with General Strayer to put this whole thing together."

Heather put down the photos and rubbed her temples. "So, let me get this straight—you want me to go to General Strayer, the most no-nonsense person on the planet, and show her these smudges as evidence of a world-ending conspiracy?"

Blake flashed his most charming smile. "Exactly! But hey, once we get something more solid, you'll see. I just need you to get us in front of the General, and we'll take it from there."

Heather crossed her arms. "And how, exactly, are you planning on getting this 'solid' proof? More blurry photos? Maybe catch Bigfoot on video this time?"

"Funny," Blake said, smirking. "No, Reese and Norah are on that. They're scoping out Vance's lair of doom as we speak. I just need you to do what you do best: work your magic and get us an audience with the General. I promise you, solid proof is on the way."

Heather stared at him, then slowly nodded. "Okay, Blake. I'll talk to her. But if you bring me one more smudge, I'm sending you to live with Kevin. Forever."

Blake gave a mock salute. "You got it! No more smudges. Scout's honor."

As he swaggered out the door, Heather called after him, "Blake! I'm serious. No more fuzzy nonsense!"

"Smudges?" Blake called back. "Never heard of 'em!"

Once he was outside, he pulled out his phone and dialed Norah. "Alright, we're in. Heather's going to talk to the General, and we just need to break into Vance's lair without getting mauled by his freaky science pets. Easy peasy."

Norah's voice came through, flat and unimpressed. "Blake, just get home and stop saying things like 'easy peasy' before I change my mind about helping."

"Always with the attitude!" Blake grinned as he headed off. "Just wait 'til you hear about my next idea—Operation Sneaky Sneak."

In the dark recesses of Vance's lab, the hybrids stirred. Titanax, the massive gorilla-elephant hybrid, was pacing its containment cell, its tusks occasionally sparking against the metallic walls. The creature's trunk slammed the ground in frustration, sending minor tremors throughout the facility. There was an unsettling shift in the air, something almost tangible. Titanax wasn't alone in its restlessness. The others—Aquila, Lynxara, and Felonix—were testing their containment cells more aggressively than usual, pushing at the energy barriers that restrained them.

Something was changing inside them. A raw, primal urge was bubbling to the surface. And soon, it was going to explode.

Outside, Reese and Norah moved with careful precision through the shadowed alley leading to the lab's hidden entrance. Reese crouched low behind a ventilation duct, his heart pounding against his ribs. They had managed to avoid the patrols so far, but the high-tech lab's security was no joke. The cameras, motion sensors, and armed guards were enough to make Reese wonder if they should have waited for Blake to bring them more than just blurry photos and charm.

"We can't screw this up," Reese whispered, his voice barely audible over the sound of distant machinery.

Norah, crouching next to him, shot him a smirk. "Don't worry, Reese. I've got us covered." She reached into her jacket and pulled out a small, sleek device.

"What's that?" Reese asked, eyes narrowing.

Norah handed it over to him. "Put this around your neck."

Reese did as instructed, pulling the necklace over his head. The moment it settled on his neck, the device activated, projecting a shimmering, black mask over his face, hiding his identity completely. His eyes widened beneath the mask.

"This... is awesome!" Reese whispered, his voice now distorted by the mask's filter. He grinned beneath the projection. "You're turning me into Blake. Do I get his terrible jokes too?"

Norah rolled her eyes but couldn't hide a small smile. "Please, spare me the Blake impression. This is serious. We can't afford to be seen by any of Vance's security systems. If anyone reviews the footage, they'll have no idea it's us." With that, she activated her own mask, which immediately concealed her features with a sleek, dark visage.

Reese examined himself, turning his head slightly. "This is some high-tech stealth gear, Norah. I feel like I should be off hunting cryptids with Blake now. Next thing you know, I'll be chasing blurry creatures and making bad puns."

"Focus, Reese," Norah said, though her voice held a hint of amusement. "This isn't a game."

They moved swiftly and silently toward the entrance, scanning for any last-minute patrols. Norah expertly disabled the nearby security lock, and the door slid open with a faint hiss.

Once inside, the dimly lit hallways of Vance's lab stretched out before them. The sterile scent of chemicals and machinery filled the air, making Reese's skin crawl. They moved cautiously, their footsteps muffled by the specialized boots Norah had outfitted them with. Each step brought them closer to the heart of the lab, where Vance's secret experiments were housed.

As they reached the central corridor leading to Vance's private lab, the sound of footsteps echoed nearby. Norah grabbed Reese's arm and yanked him into the shadows of a storage room, her breath held. They crouched low behind several stacked crates, listening.

A group of lab technicians was finishing up for the night, laughing and chatting as they walked down the corridor. One of them stopped by the lab entrance, checking some final readings on a console. Reese felt his pulse quicken. If they were caught now, all their planning would be for nothing.

Norah nudged Reese, and he glanced at her. She gestured toward the technicians, as if to say, Be patient. Wait for them to leave. Reese nodded, keeping his breathing steady.

After what felt like an eternity, the last of the staff members finally packed up and left, the lab's lights dimming as the automatic lockdown sequence began. The building was now mostly empty, save for a skeleton crew working in other parts of the facility.

"Alright," Norah whispered, her voice barely audible. "Now's our chance."

They crept out from their hiding place and approached Vance's lab door. Norah worked her magic again, bypassing the security lock with ease. As the door slid open, they slipped inside. The sterile, metallic interior of the lab greeted them—computers, equipment, and various vials of Omega's blood lining the counters.

But it was the containment cells on the far side of the room that grabbed their attention.

Reese's breath caught in his throat as he saw them—the hybrids, including the monstrous Titanax, pacing and testing their boundaries. The faint hum of the containment fields buzzed through the air. Each hybrid seemed agitated, their eyes glowing faintly, muscles tensing with a violent energy.

Norah stepped forward, eyes scanning the monitors. "Something's wrong with them," she muttered. "They're getting more aggressive, and they're trying to break free."

Reese could only nod, his eyes fixed on the towering figure of Titanax as the creature slammed a tusk into the energy barrier, causing sparks to fly.

Reese stared wide-eyed at the hybrids, their agitation growing with every minute. Titanax, especially, seemed ready to tear through its containment field. The massive hybrid's muscles rippled, its tusks scraping against the energy barrier that sparked and hummed in protest.

"We need proof. Photos—clear ones this time," Reese muttered, pulling out his new Tesla Kaiju-proof phone. The sleek device, designed to withstand even the electromagnetic pulse of a Kaiju, powered up instantly. He glanced over at Norah, who already had her phone out, snapping photos like she was a tourist in front of the Eiffel Tower.

Norah flashed a proud smile as she adjusted the phone's settings. "You know, I had a hand in designing these bad boys. Virtually indestructible, EMP resistant, and the camera? 4K, with Kaiju motion tracking. It's a masterpiece, Reese. You can thank me later."

Reese chuckled. "Kaiju-proof phones. What next, Norah? Kaiju-proof toasters?"

"Hey, I'm just saying," she quipped, continuing to snap photos. "These might be the best things I've ever made."

But as they took more pictures, the hybrids became noticeably more agitated. Titanax let out a low, rumbling growl, its trunk swinging wildly. The other hybrids—Lynxara, with its sleek feline build, and Aquila, the bird-like monstrosity—began pacing faster, their eyes glowing an eerie blue as they pressed against their containment cells. Felonix, the most feral-looking of the bunch, bared its fangs, snarling at the invisible barrier keeping it trapped.

"Uh, Norah?" Reese said, slowly lowering his phone. "I think we're ticking them off."

Norah glanced up from her screen, finally noticing the increasing hostility in the room. "You think?"

"We should get out of here before they—"

A loud bang echoed through the lab as Titanax slammed its tusk into the containment field again, sending a spray of sparks through the air. Reese jumped, and Norah grabbed his arm, yanking him toward the door.

"Go, go, go!" she hissed, her voice filled with urgency.

They quickly exited the lab, slipping back into the shadows of the hallway. The tension in the air felt thick as they hurried down the corridor, their hearts racing. Norah locked the door behind them, and they quietly made their way out of the building.

Inside the lab, the hybrids continued to test the limits of their containment cells. Titanax, driven by a primal instinct that even Vance could no longer control, pressed harder and harder against the energy barrier. The constant resistance, the glowing heat of the invisible wall, was driving it into a frenzy.

And then, with a deafening crack, it happened.

Titanax's tusk pierced through the containment field, shattering it like glass. The energy dispersed in a violent explosion of sparks and electricity. With a roar that shook the lab to its foundations, Titanax stepped forward, free at last.

The other hybrids followed suit, the failure of one containment cell creating a chain reaction. Lynxara, its sleek form a blur of motion, leapt through the collapsing energy barrier, its glowing eyes reflecting pure, unbridled rage. Aquila, the massive avian-shark hybrid, flapped its wings with a power that sent equipment flying across the room, smashing into walls and shattering windows. Felonix, with a terrifying snarl, clawed its way out, ripping through the remaining containment mechanisms with ease.

The lab was in chaos.

Titanax rampaged through the room, its massive form crashing into walls, sending machinery flying like toys. Alarms blared, but the few remaining staff members had already fled the facility. Sparks flew as containment equipment exploded, and the hybrids tore through everything in sight.

Aquila screeched, its wings unfurling as it smashed through the ceiling, sending chunks of metal and concrete raining down. Lynxara darted through the wreckage, its claws leaving deep gouges in the lab's walls as it sought an escape route. Felonix followed, its growl rumbling through the lab like thunder.

Titanax, however, was the most destructive. The enormous hybrid rammed through walls, smashing through doorways as if they were made of paper. In moments, the facility was nothing more than a shattered ruin, and Titanax led the charge outside.

The hybrids made their way to the coastline, a short distance from the lab. The ocean roared ahead of them, vast and untamed. Titanax let out another bellowing roar, one that echoed across the horizon, before it plunged into the water. The others followed, disappearing beneath the waves with terrifying grace, leaving destruction and chaos in their wake.

The ocean swallowed them, hiding them from view. But even as they disappeared into the depths, the world would soon learn that they were no longer bound by Vance's control—or by any leash at all.

The hybrids were free.

Chapter 15: The Blood of Omega

The ocean stretched out before them, dark and endless. Beneath the surface, the hybrids swam with terrifying speed and precision, their monstrous forms cutting through the water like shadows. The farther they went from the coastline, the deeper and colder the water became. Yet, for creatures like Titanax and its kin, the icy depths were a welcome refuge.

They had escaped.

After hours of relentless swimming, the hybrids found a remote chain of islands, hidden from human eyes by a thick wall of mist and jagged cliffs. The islands were uncharted, a forgotten remnant of the world—untouched by modern civilization. The largest of the islands had deep caves carved into its rocky shores, perfect for hiding. Here, among the blackened stones and storm-battered shores, the hybrids made their new home.

But something was wrong. As they settled into the dark, damp caves, each of them could feel it—a burning sensation, coursing through their veins. It wasn't just the rush of freedom or the thrill of survival. No, this was something deeper. Something primal.

The blood of Omega was inside them, and it was changing them.

Titanax, always the leader, took the largest cave for itself. Its tusks scraped against the rock as it moved inside, its massive form casting long shadows against the jagged walls. It tried to rest, but the pulsing heat in its body grew stronger. The blood of Omega—the ancient queen of the ocean—had mixed with its own.

At first, Titanax thought it was pain. But then it realized—this was evolution. Omega's blood was accelerating its mutation.

It began slowly, with a surge of pressure in Titanax's bones and muscles. Its skin rippled and cracked, its tusks elongating into brutal, sharpened spears. With a sickening crunch, its body began to grow. Muscle and sinew stretched, bones lengthened, and Titanax roared as its body swelled to an incredible 40 feet in height. The once-massive hybrid now dwarfed everything around it, its thick hide hardening into something impenetrable, lined with jagged spikes along its spine.

Titanax's eyes burned brighter, glowing a deep blue as the mutation continued. The blood of Omega was transforming it into something more—something that could challenge the queen herself. It stood, the ground beneath it shaking with the weight of its colossal form, and let out a thunderous roar that echoed through the caves, shaking the very earth.

But Titanax wasn't the only one.

Lynxara, the sleek feline hybrid, had curled itself into a corner of a smaller cave, its glowing eyes half-closed in a state of restless agitation. The blood of Omega surged through its veins, too, spreading its influence like wildfire. Lynxara's body began to ripple, its lean form filling with newfound strength. Muscles bulged beneath its fur, stretching the skin as it grew to 30 feet in height.

Its claws extended, gleaming like blades, while a thick, spiked mane erupted along its back. Lynxara's once-graceful movements were now laced with brutal power, each step resonating with predatory force. Its eyes, now glowing with an eerie light, scanned the cave for threats, its tail lashing as if ready to strike.

The blood of Omega had turned Lynxara into a beast even more deadly than before.

Aquila, the shark-eagle hybrid, perched on the jagged edges of a cliff overlooking the ocean. Its wings were tucked close to its body, but the mutation hit it suddenly—like a bolt of lightning. Its spine cracked, sending a sharp jolt of pain through its body as its wings exploded outward, expanding into a massive wingspan that stretched the width of the cave.

Its beak elongated, curving into a serrated, deadly point, while its talons grew even sharper, capable of tearing through metal with ease. Aquila's body swelled, its muscles bulging as it grew to 30 feet in height. The blood of Omega coursed through it, amplifying its strength, transforming it into a creature that could summon hurricanes with a single beat of its wings.

Aquila let out a screech, its piercing cry cutting through the night, as it scanned the horizon with its glowing eyes—hungry, ready to hunt.

Felonix, the most feral of the hybrids, paced back and forth in its cave, snarling as the mutation took hold. The blood of Omega tore through it like wildfire, igniting its primal instincts. Its fangs grew longer, dripping with venom, as its muscles expanded, pushing against its skin. Felonix's back erupted with jagged spikes, sharp and deadly, while its claws scraped against the stone, leaving deep gouges in the rock.

At 30 feet tall, Felonix was now a nightmare—a creature of pure aggression, with no hesitation to kill. Its glowing red eyes blazed with malevolence as it prowled the cave, its venom-laced fangs gleaming in the dim light.

The blood of Omega had done its work. Felonix was now more monster than hybrid.

The hybrids, now mutated far beyond their original forms, stood taller, stronger, and deadlier than ever before. The blood of Omega had reshaped them, turning them into true apex predators. In the quiet of the mist-shrouded island, they waited, hidden from the world. But they would not stay hidden for long.

The sky above Vance's lab was choked with the thick, acrid smoke of destruction. Vance's car rolled to a stop just outside the perimeter, and his heart sank at the sight before him. Half of the building had been obliterated—twisted metal, shattered glass, and charred debris littered the ground. Military trucks and FBI vehicles surrounded the facility, their flashing lights casting an eerie glow against the backdrop of devastation.

As Vance stepped out of the car, his mind raced. He knew what had happened. Titanax. The hybrids. They had broken free. But now, he needed to control the narrative, to keep everything under wraps, just as he always had.

"Mr. Vance!" a voice called out to him. It was his press officer, Jack Freeling, rushing over with a phone in one hand and a frantic look on his face. "We're trying to spin it, but it's not looking good."

Vance's eyes narrowed. "What exactly are you telling them?"

Freeling swallowed nervously, his eyes darting toward a group of military personnel nearby. "We've issued a statement saying there was a lab room explosion. Faulty equipment, gas leak—something to cover it up. But, uh… the military's not buying it."

Vance clenched his jaw. "And why the hell not?"

Before Freeling could answer, a voice cut through the air—sharp and commanding.

"Vance."

General Sarah Strayer stood at the edge of the wreckage, her arms crossed and her face set in a deep scowl. Her dark hair was pulled back into a tight bun, and her sharp eyes were locked on Vance as she approached, flanked by a group of military personnel. Her Pomeranian, Kevin, was conspicuously absent—this was no time for casual conversation.

"General Strayer," Vance said, his voice icy. He forced a smile, but it didn't reach his eyes.

She didn't bother with pleasantries. "You want to explain to me why half your facility is in ruins and why it looks like something broke out of this building?"

Vance's heart skipped a beat, but he remained calm. He had rehearsed this. He had always been good under pressure. "It was an accident. Some equipment in one of the experimental labs malfunctioned. There was a gas leak, which triggered an explosion. It's been contained, and—"

"Enough," Sarah snapped, cutting him off. Her eyes narrowed as she took a step closer, her voice dropping to a dangerous level. "This doesn't look like a gas explosion, Vance. This looks like a containment breach. The kind where something inside your lab broke out."

Vance met her gaze, refusing to back down. "You're mistaken, General. It was an accident. The hybrids were destroyed, as per the order."

Sarah's eyes blazed with fury, and she stepped even closer, her face inches from his. "Don't lie to me, Vance. Those hybrids were supposed to be neutralized. We both know what was in that lab. Don't play games with me. Did you even destroy them, or is this your mess?"

Vance felt the tension in the air thicken. His press officer was hovering nervously in the background, while the military and FBI agents stood watching the confrontation. Vance swallowed the urge to lash out but kept his voice steady, cool. "Of course, they were destroyed. I followed orders. This was an accident, nothing more."

Sarah wasn't buying it. She took another step forward, her voice lowering to a near growl. "I know what a containment breach looks like. You've lost control, haven't you? What the snark were you doing in there, Vance? Playing God again? Those creatures were supposed to be terminated."

Vance clenched his fists. He could feel the anger rising inside him, but he knew better than to explode. Instead, he shifted the blame, his voice turning venomous.

Vance clenched his fists so hard his knuckles turned white. His heart pounded in his chest, the searing heat of his anger rising to a boiling point. He was done playing nice. General Strayer had pushed him too far.

"You know what, Strayer?!" Vance snapped, stepping forward. "This is all your fault! My project, my life's work—shut down because of you and your paranoid superiors! You killed it! You ruined everything!"

Sarah paused mid-stride, turning back to face him with a cold, hardened expression. "I did what had to be done, Vance. Those things were too dangerous to be left alive. You were reckless, and you refused to see it."

Vance's jaw tightened as a dangerous gleam flickered in his eyes. "Reckless? You don't know the first thing about what I was trying to achieve! You had no right to shut me down! I was this close to breaking new ground—creating something the world has never seen! And you threw it all away because you couldn't handle a little risk!"

Sarah's lips curled into a thin, bitter smile. "I did the right thing, and you know it. Letting those hybrids roam around like some kind of twisted science experiment? It was a disaster waiting to happen. You lost control, Vance. And I wasn't about to let you bring that catastrophe down on everyone else."

"They were destroyed!" Vance shouted, his voice cracking with fury. "Just like you wanted. They're gone, Strayer. You got your way!"

Sarah's eyes narrowed, her tone sharp as a blade. "You're damn right I got my way. And if I hadn't stepped in when I did, we'd be dealing with far more than a blown-up lab right now. Those hybrids were a threat—your threat. And it's over now."

Vance's breath was ragged, fury clawing at his insides. He wanted to scream at her, to make her understand what she had taken from him, but he knew it was pointless. She would never see things his way. She had never understood what he was capable of.

"I'll be taking full control of the building from here on out," Sarah said, her voice calm but authoritative. "The military will oversee everything. You won't be allowed inside until we figure out what really happened."

Vance's eyes widened in disbelief. "You can't do this!" he shouted. "This is my lab! My research!"

"It's already done," Sarah said flatly, turning away. "Effective immediately, you're out. I suggest you get your affairs in order and leave."

Vance felt the ground slip from under him, a sinking weight of helplessness mixed with a storm of rage. His voice trembled with anger. "You have no right! This is—"

But Sarah wasn't listening anymore. She walked away, leaving Vance standing alone in the wreckage of what had once been his empire, her decision final.

The soldiers began to move in, setting up barricades, locking down entrances, and corralling the remaining lab staff away. Vance stood frozen, watching his world collapse around him, powerless to stop it.

The burning fury in his chest flared into a white-hot rage.

Hours later, Vance stormed into his home, slamming the door shut behind him. His house was a pristine facade, hidden in the upscale neighborhoods where people assumed nothing out of the ordinary happened. But in the basement, behind a series of reinforced steel doors and biometric locks, was his real sanctuary: his secret lab.

He descended the stairs two at a time, his mind racing with bitter thoughts, each one darker than the last. He swore under his breath, his hands shaking with rage as he keyed in the code to unlock the lab's entrance. The door slid open with a hiss, revealing the dimly lit room where his most classified experiments had taken shape. Rows of computer screens flickered with data, and various prototype devices were scattered across the workbenches.

But Vance's eyes were drawn to one corner of the room, where a large metallic containment unit stood sealed. Inside was his secret project—something he had been working on in the shadows, even while the hybrids were his public obsession. She thinks she destroyed my work, he thought, his lip curling into a snarl. She has no idea what I've been building.

He stormed over to the containment unit, his fingers trembling with a combination of fury and anticipation as he keyed in the access code. The doors hissed open, revealing the contents inside: a sleek, unfinished device—a weapon, though it looked far more advanced than anything the military had ever dreamed of.

"This will make her pay," Vance muttered to himself, his eyes glinting with the madness of a man pushed to the edge. "She thinks she can take everything from me? She thinks she can destroy my life's work and walk away?"

His hands moved quickly, his fingers flying over the keyboard as he activated the systems. The machine hummed to life, glowing softly with the power of untapped potential.

"She's the one who started this war," Vance whispered, a twisted grin spreading across his face. "And I'll be the one who ends it."

Each keystroke, each wire he connected, each piece of the puzzle falling into place fueled his vengeful fire. The anger coursed through him like a fever, making his blood run hot, sharpening his focus. His thoughts were consumed by one goal—revenge.

General Sarah Strayer had humiliated him, stolen his work, and stripped him of his power. But she underestimated him. She thought cutting off his lab access would be the end of him. She thought she could control the situation.

Vance's laughter echoed through the cold, sterile lab. "She'll see," he murmured. "They'll all see."

Chapter 16: Dismissed

Blake, Reese, and Norah walked through the government building, their footsteps echoing down the sterile, fluorescent-lit hallway. The cold, corporate vibe was a stark contrast to their usual chaos.

"Seriously, is it a rule for government buildings to feel this soulless?" Reese muttered, shoving his hands in his pockets. "I'm pretty sure I saw a cactus back there that gave up on life."

Norah smirked, glancing at the blank walls. "A cactus would be the most personality this place has seen in years."

Blake grinned. "Maybe we'll get lucky and find a fern in the General's office. It's got to be a jungle in there, right?"

As they approached General Sarah Strayer's office, the humor fell away, replaced by the weight of the task ahead. They were about to confront the highest-ranking military officer they knew, and it wasn't just about Vance—they needed to convince her that the Kaiju Task Force was essential. Blake pushed open the heavy oak door without knocking, marching into the room with the kind of confidence only reckless adventurers could muster.

"General Strayer," Blake greeted, flashing a quick smile. "You're looking as cheerful as ever. Maybe we caught you at a bad time?"

General Sarah Strayer didn't bother to look up right away. She sat behind her desk, flipping through reports with the calm of someone who had better things to do. Her office was just as spartan as the rest of the building—no fern in sight.

"What do you want?" Sarah's tone was clipped, not in the mood for banter.

Reese sauntered over and dropped a folder on her desk, his grin irrepressible. "Oh, nothing major. Just proof that our good friend Vance is still playing with fire—and, you know, creating hybrid monsters."

Blake leaned on the back of a chair, arms crossed. "We figured you'd want a heads-up, you know, before another Omega-sized problem explodes on your doorstep."

Norah nodded. "You're welcome, by the way, for the casual world-saving we've been doing."

Sarah's eyes narrowed as she scanned the files and photos they'd gathered from Vance's secret lab. "You think I don't know about Vance's experiments?" Her voice was steady, but there was an edge of irritation. "The hybrids were destroyed, as ordered."

Blake raised an eyebrow. "Funny, because the evidence we found says otherwise. It's like Vance missed that memo."

"We're just saying," Norah chimed in, "if you're relying on 'trust me, they're all gone,' you might want to double-check."

Sarah closed the file, setting it down as if she had already made her decision. "The situation is under control. Vance is being watched. If he steps out of line, we'll handle it."

Blake's jaw tightened. "And what if he's already out of line? You can't just sit on this. We've seen what he's capable of, and if he's not stopped, it's going to be another disaster."

Sarah leaned forward, eyes sharp and unyielding. "I understand your concerns. Believe me, I do. But the military has it covered. I appreciate what you did for this country—for the world—when you took Omega down. But this? This isn't something for you to worry about anymore."

Reese scoffed. "So you're telling us to just kick back, relax, and trust that everything's peachy? Yeah, because that always works out great."

"I'm telling you to stand down," Sarah replied, her tone firm but not without a hint of respect. "The Task Force isn't being reinstated. We don't need it. And right now, I've got bigger problems than rumors about a mad scientist."

Blake stared at her, disbelief clear on his face. "You really think Vance is just going to stop? That he won't try something worse?"

Norah shook her head, her sarcasm fading into real frustration. "Look, we've all been through hell to keep things from spiraling out of control. You can't just sweep this under the rug."

Sarah's expression softened, if only slightly. "I'm not dismissing what you did. Omega, the Kaiju—you stopped something no one else could. But right now, we've got systems in place, people in charge. This isn't for you to handle."

Blake clenched his fists, biting back the argument that was on the tip of his tongue. He knew Sarah wasn't an enemy, but her dismissal stung. They had earned their place in this fight, hadn't they?

Reese, always the first to break the tension, threw his hands up. "Alright, fine. But when Vance's next monstrosity kicks down your door, don't say we didn't warn you."

Norah gave a half-hearted salute. "We'll just be over here, sipping coffee, waiting for the apocalypse. Again."

Sarah stood, signaling that the conversation was over. "You're dismissed. Go live your lives. The military will take care of this."

Blake shot her a final look, nodding stiffly. "If you say so."

As they walked out of the office, the door clicking shut behind them, Reese let out a low whistle. "Well, that went about as well as a Kaiju at a dinner party."

As Reese, Norah, and Blake walked out of the government building, the crisp evening air hit them, offering a momentary relief from the stifling tension that had filled Sarah Strayer's office. The trio moved in silence, each lost in their own thoughts. The streetlights flickered on as they headed toward the parking lot.

"Well, that was a colossal waste of time," Reese muttered, shoving his hands into his jacket pockets. "She acted like we were trying to sell her some conspiracy theory."

Blake's jaw clenched as he opened the door to his car. "She's got blinders on. Vance is up to something. I can feel it."

Norah rolled her eyes, leaning against the hood. "Yeah, well, her 'no big deal' approach is gonna bite her in the ass soon. And when it does, we'll be the ones cleaning up the mess. Again."

Blake sighed, glancing back at the imposing government building. "We'll figure it out. Somehow."

They piled into the car, their conversation fading into the distance as they drove off, the government building looming quietly in their rearview mirror.

Back inside General Strayer's office, the dim light from her desk lamp cast long shadows across the room. Sarah exhaled slowly, massaging her temples. The kids' concerns were not entirely misplaced.

The shadows shifted behind her, and a low voice interrupted her thoughts. "You're letting them off easy."

Sarah didn't jump or react; she simply turned, mildly surprised but not entirely caught off guard. From the far corner of her office, a figure stepped forward, shrouded in darkness. Alpha emerged from the shadows, his imposing figure like something out of a comic book. His tactical suit, a blend of black and gray, made him seem more like a myth than a man.

She smirked, leaning back in her chair. "You know, if you keep lurking around like that, I'm going to start calling you Batman."

Alpha's lips twitched in the slightest hint of amusement. "You can call me whatever you want, General. But the kids aren't wrong. Vance didn't just walk away from his experiments."

Sarah sighed, standing up and walking to the window, peering out at the darkening sky. "I'm not an idiot, Alpha. I know those hybrids weren't all destroyed. The pictures they brought in are proof enough that something's still out there. But Blake and his crew are too impulsive. I can't have them running around stirring up trouble."

Alpha crossed his arms, his voice calm but firm. "They did help stop Omega."

Sarah turned to face him, her expression softening slightly. "I appreciate what they've done for the country—hell, the world. But this is different. We're dealing with something that might go deeper than just a few hybrids running loose."

She paused for a moment, then locked eyes with Alpha. "I need you to do what you do best. Quietly. Vance's lab is still operational, even if it's officially shut down. I want you to get in there, find out what he's really up to, and report back. But leave Blake and the others out of this. The last thing I need is them playing hero and getting in over their heads."

Sarah paced back and forth in her office, her brow furrowed as she spoke to Alpha, who stood silent in the shadows. "We've got a bigger problem than Vance," she began, her voice tight with frustration. "You remember the cleanup after Omega's last attack? The President's been breathing down my neck ever since. Turns out, some of Omega's blood got into the ecosystem during the fight. It wasn't just a containment breach—it's a biological disaster waiting to happen."

She stopped pacing, crossing her arms as she turned to face Alpha. "The scientists have been working around the clock, analyzing samples, running tests. What they've found is... disturbing. Omega's blood isn't just radioactive—it's transformative. It has the potential to mutate living organisms, and not just minor changes either. We're talking about accelerated evolution, mutations that could turn regular wildlife into something far more dangerous. The President's terrified that we're on the brink of another Kaiju outbreak, and I can't say I blame him."

Her voice dropped, and she glanced out the window as if the threat could be lurking just outside. "We're already seeing early signs in some of the wildlife near the impact zones—nothing too extreme yet, but it's only a matter of time. If even one mutated creature starts to grow or develop powers similar to Omega's, we could be looking at another wave of Kaiju. I need you to keep an eye on this while you dig into Vance's work. If his research overlaps with what's happening out there, it could explain a hell of a lot more than just those hybrids."

Alpha nodded, his eyes narrowing slightly. "Understood. I'll be in and out before they even know I'm gone."

Within seconds, he vanished, disappearing into the darkness of the office, leaving Sarah alone with her thoughts once more. She let out a long breath, the weight of the situation settling back onto her shoulders.

Later that night, the full moon hung low in the sky as Alpha slipped through the city streets, his movements silent and deliberate. He blended into the shadows with practiced ease, the only sound being the faint rustle of his tactical suit as he maneuvered through alleyways and onto rooftops.

Vance's lab, located in an inconspicuous industrial district, loomed ahead. Alpha moved like a shadow through the perimeter of Vance's lab, his every movement precise and calculated. The military presence was heavy, soldiers patrolling the grounds with precision, but they were no match for Alpha's stealth. He slipped past the guards with ease, blending into the darkness between their flashlights and the cold steel of the building. The few cameras that still functioned after the explosion had been strategically disabled, and within minutes, Alpha was inside, navigating the remnants of Vance's lab like a ghost. His training kicked in—no wasted movement, no unnecessary noise.

Inside, the place was a mess of scorched walls and debris, but Vance's main terminal was still intact. Alpha hacked into the computer with practiced ease, bypassing the usual security measures. Files and documents flashed across the screen—schematics, research logs, project updates—but there was nothing new. Most of it detailed the hybrid projects they were already aware of, confirming the existence of the experiments Blake, Reese, and Norah had uncovered. But just as Alpha was about to call it, one recently deleted file caught his eye: Iron Wraith. It was encrypted, locked behind layers of security, and stubbornly refused to open.

Alpha's fingers flew across the keyboard, attempting to crack it, but the encryption held firm. Time was running short; he could feel the presence of guards moving closer. With no other choice, Alpha copied the encrypted file to his suit's hard drive, securing it for later. Whatever Iron Wraith was, it was important enough for Vance to erase it, and that meant it was worth bringing back to Sarah. As he slipped back out into the night, his mind raced, already planning how to decrypt the file and uncover what Vance had been hiding. Something about this was bigger than the hybrids, and Alpha was determined to find out what.

Chapter 17: Global Devastation

Sydney, Australia—sun-drenched, vibrant, and alive. The city's iconic skyline gleamed under a cloudless sky, with the magnificent Sydney Opera House and the towering Sydney Harbour Bridge standing proudly above the bustling waters of the harbor. Ferries cut through the sparkling blue, carrying commuters and tourists alike, while beaches teemed with surfers and sunbathers. Cafes were buzzing with the morning rush as people chatted over coffee, their laughter blending with the city's familiar soundtrack of traffic, seagulls, and distant construction.

But the peace was shattered in an instant. A high-pitched screech echoed from the ocean depths, and suddenly, the water near the harbor churned violently. Emerging from the surf was a nightmarish creature—a fusion of an eagle and a great white shark, its massive wings stretching out wide, shadowing the city below. Aquila had arrived. Her talons, sharp as steel, sliced through buildings as she swooped down, tearing apart structures with terrifying ease. People ran in terror, but there was no escaping her wrath. She dove from the sky with terrifying speed, snatching fleeing civilians in her beak and devouring them whole, her blood-soaked wings beating against the sky. The once-beautiful harbor was awash with chaos, boats capsizing, and bodies sinking into the water as Aquila's predatory rampage continued. In less than an hour, Sydney lay in ruins—buildings crumbled, smoke rising into the air, and streets littered with debris and the dead. Without warning, Aquila screeched one final time before vanishing back into the ocean, leaving behind a city broken beyond recognition. The death toll was staggering—over 12,000 lives lost in the destruction.

Across the globe, chaos reigned once more as Titanax, a towering behemoth covered in thick, spiked armor, stormed through Johannesburg, South Africa. The city's vibrant streets and towering skyscrapers stood no chance against the sheer force of the beast. With each thundering step, Titanax sent shockwaves through the earth, crumbling buildings as if they were made of sand. His long tail leveled entire blocks and crushed anything in its path—people, cars, buses. The scent of smoke and blood filled the air as the ground opened in massive cracks beneath his weight. Panicked citizens fled in every direction, but Titanax's carnage was indiscriminate. Military forces arrived too late, their weapons barely scratching the surface of the beast's armored hide. In less than two hours, Johannesburg was reduced to smoldering rubble, the landscape unrecognizable. The death toll surpassed 20,000, and then, as quickly as he had come, Titanax vanished, his colossal form fading into the horizon.

In the United Kingdom, Lynxara, a ferocious lion-hyena kaiju with the agility of a lynx, descended upon Manchester with lethal precision. She leaped from building to building, her claws raking through concrete and glass like paper. Civilians screamed in terror as she hunted them down, her predatory instincts in full control. Unlike the brute force of Titanax, Lynxara's assault was swift, silent, and methodical. She pounced on fleeing crowds, picking off survivors one by one, her gleaming eyes filled with cold hunger. Fighter jets scrambled in the sky, but Lynxara was too fast, weaving between them with deadly grace before tearing them apart mid-air. Her roar reverberated across the city, leaving a trail of shattered lives and buildings behind her. Manchester had been crippled in less than an hour, the bodies of 15,000 civilians strewn across the city. Without a trace, Lynxara disappeared into the night sky, leaving behind only destruction.

Meanwhile, in Brazil, the rainforest seemed to shake as Felonix, a feline-beast kaiju, tore through Rio de Janeiro. His massive paws left fiery craters in the earth as he ran through the city, setting everything ablaze. Skyscrapers fell like dominoes, consumed by flames as Felonix bellowed with rage, his roar igniting trees, buildings, and anything in his path. The carnage was relentless as the kaiju hunted the people of Rio. The famous Christ the Redeemer statue crumbled under the force of his claws, reduced to nothing but burning rubble. Screams of terror filled the air as Rio's citizens tried in vain to escape the inferno. By the time Felonix disappeared back into the jungle, more than 18,000 lives had been lost, the city left smoldering and broken.

In just one day, four of the world's greatest cities were turned to graveyards. The death toll was catastrophic, with nearly 65,000 people perishing in the kaiju attacks. And the terrifying part? No one knew if the monsters would return—or where they would strike next.

Chapter 18: The World is on Fire

The television flickered with scenes of devastation. Footage from Sydney, Johannesburg, Manchester, and Rio de Janeiro played on a loop—cities in ruins, smoldering wreckage, and screams frozen in time. Norah's living room, typically a sanctuary of warmth and calm, was now heavy with dread. Her kids played quietly in the background, blissfully unaware of the chaos unraveling outside their small world. The faint sounds of her husband on a work call drifted in from the kitchen, his voice steady, completely detached from the horrors flashing across the screen.

Reese slouched on the couch, legs propped up on the coffee table, his eyes locked on the news but his expression one of grim sarcasm. "Well, if we weren't completely in the poop box before, we are now. These things make Vance's lab hybrids look like toddlers on a sugar rush."

Blake, sitting cross-legged on the floor, tossed a popcorn kernel into his mouth. "Yeah, but toddlers can be pretty scary. Ever see one with a sharpie and a clean wall? Nightmare fuel." He grinned, trying to lighten the mood. "But for real, we're talking full-scale apocalypse here. Like… real-life 'Kaiju: The Reckoning' edition."

Norah shot them both a look, arms crossed as she leaned against the wall. "This isn't a joke, Blake. These new kaiju aren't just hybrids. They're apex predators. And they're systematically tearing apart entire cities. We can't just sit here and do nothing." Her tone was serious, but the exasperation in her voice had a trace of amusement—like a tired mom scolding her kids for the umpteenth time. "Also, you're getting popcorn on my floor."

Blake glanced down at the small pile of popcorn surrounding him and gave a half-hearted shrug. "Collateral damage. My bad."

"Focus," Norah said, though she cracked a small smile. "We have to do something. The General doesn't think we're needed—fine. But the world's falling apart, and I'm not going to wait for permission while kaiju stomp through more cities. We need to act, reinstated or not."

Reese raised an eyebrow. "Okay, so we're just going rogue? I mean, sure, what's the worst that could happen? Besides, you know, us getting eaten alive by giant monsters?"

Blake leaned back on his hands, grinning. "Maybe they'll find me too stringy. I've been told I'm more of a lean-protein kind of guy."

Norah rolled her eyes, but there was a spark of determination behind her tired expression. "I'm serious. I don't care what Sarah thinks—we have to take matters into our own hands. We can't let these things burn the world down while we twiddle our thumbs."

Blake gave a dramatic sigh. "Alright, fine. But if we're doing this, can we at least get some cool outfits? You know, maybe a cape? I always wanted to do the whole superhero look."

"Yeah, sure," Reese cut in dryly. "Right after we save the planet from four kaiju, I'll pick you up a cape. Might even throw in a matching mask. But seriously," his voice dropped its usual sarcastic tone for a moment, "Norah's right. We can't just sit here."

The news anchor's voice droned on in the background, listing the rapidly climbing death tolls. Each number was a punch to the gut, a reminder of the stakes. Blake sighed again, this time without the humor. "Okay, so we do it. We stop these things. We save the world." He paused, looking between Norah and Reese. "But we do it our way. No General, no orders. Just us. The question is... how?"

Norah took a deep breath, glancing at her kids playing on the floor, unaware of the storm outside. "I don't know yet," she admitted. "But we've faced impossible odds before. We'll figure it out."

Reese nodded, his sarcastic demeanor giving way to grim determination. "Yeah, well, we'd better. Because right now, the world's going down in flames, and we're all out of time."

Blake tossed another kernel of popcorn in the air and caught it with his mouth. "So, capes or no capes?"

Norah shook her head, smiling despite herself. "No capes."

Reese leaned back in his chair, tapping his fingers against the table as he stared at the news feed flashing images of the destroyed cities. "You know," he said, breaking the silence, "we're not getting anywhere by just sitting here. If the General won't let us back in, why don't we take matters into our own hands? We've still got the skills, the experience, and Norah's nifty tech." He glanced at Norah with a smirk. "Why don't we just break into the Task Force building ourselves?"

Reese grinned, leaning forward with a gleam in his eye. "And while we're at it, why not suit up in the Valkyrie gear and go take care of these kaiju ourselves? Who needs permission when you've got badass tech?"

Blake leaned back on the couch, spinning a pen between his fingers. "So, let me get this straight. We're breaking into a government building, swarming with military personnel, armed guards, and top-notch security systems... and our master plan is to 'sneak in' like we're in some kind of spy movie?"

Norah shot him a deadpan look. "Yes, Blake. That's exactly the plan. Unless you have a better one?"

Blake grinned and leaned forward, lowering his voice dramatically. "Well, I was thinking... maybe we just bribe the guards. I mean, everyone loves pizza, right? We roll up with a couple of large pepperonis, say, 'Hey, we're just here for a security check,' and boom, they let us in. No fuss, no alarms, just us and a cheesy good time."

Reese snorted. "Yeah, Blake. I'm sure pizza delivery is exactly how top-secret government operations get infiltrated. Solid plan."

Blake shrugged, still grinning. "I mean, it's worth a shot. I've heard people do crazy things for pizza."

Norah sighed, pulling out her sleek metal case again. "Lucky for us, we don't need pizza. I've got something better." She opened the case, revealing the shiny gadgets inside, glistening under the living room light.

Blake's eyes widened like a kid in a candy store. "Whoa, what do we have here? Tesla tech? And I thought the coolest thing they made was an electric car. Guess I was wrong."

"Yeah," Norah said, ignoring his sarcasm. "Tesla's been working on some experimental gear. This little device here," she pointed to a small disk-like gadget, "can knock out all electrical systems in a fifty-yard radius. No cameras, no alarms. We'll be ghosts."

Blake's jaw dropped in mock disbelief. "Hold on a second. You're telling me you've had this James Bond tech sitting around and didn't think to tell us sooner? I could've used one of these during the last Thanksgiving dinner with Aunt Lori."

Norah rolled her eyes. "It's a prototype, Blake. And I don't think knocking out your aunt's Wi-Fi would've stopped her from asking about your love life."

"Fair point," Blake admitted. "But I bet it would've shut down her Alexa—small victories."

Reese stepped closer, examining the other gadgets in the case. "What's this one do? Makes us invisible or something?"

"Actually, yeah," Norah said with a grin, holding up a wristband with glowing blue circuits. "It's called the Phase Shifter. It distorts light around the wearer, rendering them practically invisible. But it only works for about sixty seconds before needing a ten-minute recharge."

Blake raised an eyebrow. "Sixty seconds? Not exactly a lot of time for breaking into a building. What are we supposed to do, run in like The Flash?"

"Well, unless you have superspeed, we're going to have to plan our moves very carefully," Norah said, handing the wristbands to both of them. "We're not going in to fight."

Reese snorted, strapping the wristband onto his arm. "So we're going in blind, with a fifty-yard EMP and invisibility for about as long as it takes Blake to come up with a bad joke. Awesome."

Blake gave a mock bow. "Why, thank you. I pride myself on my efficiency."

Norah shook her head, half-amused, half-annoyed. "Look, this is the best shot we've got. The General won't reinstate us, but that doesn't mean we can sit back and watch the world burn. These new kaiju are way more destructive than what we dealt with with Omega, and we can't afford to wait for permission."

Blake nodded, his humor fading just a bit as he leaned forward. "You're right. This isn't about us anymore."

Reese looked between them, a smirk still on his face but with a glint of seriousness in his eyes. "Alright, I'm in. But when this all goes wrong, just remember, I was the one who wanted to stay home and not get shot."

Blake patted Reese on the back. "Don't worry, buddy. If you get shot, I'll make sure to tell your story to the world. Maybe turn it into a Hollywood blockbuster. I'm thinking Chris Hemsworth could play you."

Reese rolled his eyes. "Yeah, right. Like Hemsworth could pull off my charm."

Norah strapped her own wristband on, a determined look in her eyes. "Alright, guys, focus. We leave tonight. Midnight, when the guard shift changes. We'll use the EMP to knock out the security systems, phase through the building, get the suits, and get out."

Blake grinned. "Piece of cake. Just like breaking into Area 51, except with fewer memes."

Norah gave him a look. "Let's hope it's that easy."

Blake clapped his hands together. "Alright, team! Let's do this. One stealthy government break-in coming up. And if all else fails, we'll fall back on Plan Pizza."

Chapter 19: The Infiltration

The New York Harbor was veiled in thick mist, with faint lights from the city skyline flickering through the fog, casting ghostly shadows over the choppy waters. Looming ahead was the Kaiju Task Force headquarters, a monolithic structure built on the harbor's edge, imposing and bristling with military presence. It looked less like a building now and more like a fortress, its once-open arms now guarded as if it were expecting an invasion. Foghorns wailed in the distance, accompanied by the low hum of naval ships patrolling the perimeter as Reese and Norah's sleek, three-person submersible slid silently beneath the waves like a shark hunting in the deep.

Inside the sub, Norah stared at the sonar screen, the rhythmic ping of the radar capturing the zigzagging patrol boats on the surface above. "Jeez, they've beefed up security big time," she muttered, narrowing her eyes at the map. "There are more guards here than there were fans at the last Tesla launch."

Reese, lounging in the cramped cockpit like he was on a leisurely Sunday drive, shot her a glance. "You know, I miss when our Tuesday nights involved pizza and Netflix, not breaking into military bases."

Norah smirked, her fingers dancing over the controls. "Yeah, I miss the days when giant monsters weren't trying to turn our planet into their personal wrestling ring. Simpler times."

As they ventured deeper into the harbor, the eerie glow of defense grids and the skeletons of old wrecks lit up the water around them. Mines floated ominously, guarding the submerged approach like sentinels from a forgotten era. "Wow," Norah muttered, eyes wide. "They really don't want us back, huh?"

Reese leaned forward, squinting at the black shapes of drones weaving through the water like mechanical sharks.

Reese grinned, rubbing his hands together. "Yeah, well, lucky for us, you've got Tesla's greatest hits at your fingertips. Your little stealth tech better work, or else we're going to be fish food."

Norah smirked. "Oh, it'll work. We're ghosts in this thing. No sonar, no radar. Not even a footprint in the water. Thank me for that later."

Their plan was nothing short of insanity. The Task Force building was fortified like a nuclear bunker, and walking through the front door was about as smart as trying to pet a kaiju. Instead, they were taking the back door—an old maintenance tunnel that had been forgotten when the building was redesigned. Their sub, equipped with cutting-edge tech, would slip through the defenses like a thief in the night.

"Alright," Reese said, sitting up straight, his eyes gleaming with mischief. "Here's the plan: we pop up through the old waste disposal tunnel, take out any stragglers, and then—bam!—we disable the security grid. Easy peasy."

"Piece of cake," Norah replied, the massive building looming ahead, growing ever larger in their viewports. "We'll just waltz right into the most guarded facility on the planet like it's a Sunday brunch."

Blake, lounging lazily in the back, finally spoke up. "No biggie, guys. It's not like the fate of the world depends on this or anything. Just another Tuesday, right?" He flashed a grin. "And hey, if we get caught, at least we'll have front-row seats to the kaiju apocalypse. Silver linings."

As the sleek, silent sub navigated past the network of defense grids and underwater mines, the tension in the cockpit was palpable. Norah, focused on the screen, adjusted the controls with surgical precision, making sure they stayed beneath the detection field. The old waste disposal tunnel was just ahead, an ancient relic forgotten when the Task

Force HQ was redesigned, and it would be their ticket inside. Reese, always the one to break the silence, leaned forward.

"Tell me again why the military's defense system looks like it was designed by someone who watched Jaws too many times? We're not swimming with sharks here."

Norah didn't glance up, keeping her eyes on the sonar. "Because, genius, we are the sharks. Now, unless you've suddenly learned to breathe underwater, let me focus before we trip a defense grid and blow up."

Blake, lounging in the back like this was a casual ride through a theme park, piped up. "You know, it's moments like these that make me realize we're either the dumbest people on the planet, or we just really, really love breaking into places we used to work at." He leaned forward. "Also, when this is over, I'm voting for a pizza night."

The sub quietly docked inside the waste disposal tunnel. With a soft hiss, the hatch opened, and they slipped into the shadowy tunnel. The faint sound of guards above echoed through the grates. Norah led the way, crouched low, holding up her hand for silence.

"Alright, listen up," Blake whispered, a rare moment of seriousness sneaking into his voice. "The soldiers? They're just doing their jobs. So if we run into any, let's not go all Die Hard on them, okay? We gotta take them out, but in the most gentle way possible." He grinned. "Think, like... ninja ballerinas. Subtle, elegant, mildly terrifying."

Norah rolled her eyes but smirked, pulling out a gadget that looked like a high-tech paintball gun and handed one to Reese and Blake. "Here, ninja ballerina, use this. It'll knock them out in seconds. Aim, shoot, boom—they're out cold."

Reese examined the gadget, skeptical. "So, you're telling me this thing won't, I don't know, explode their brains or something?"

Norah shrugged. "Worst case scenario? They wake up with a killer hangover. No brain explosions."

They crept through the dimly lit maintenance corridor, moving toward the hangar bay. Every step was cautious, the hum of security cameras whirring above them. Norah paused at a control panel, pulling out a small hacking tool and starting to bypass the first set of security systems.

"Two cameras down, three alarms disabled," she muttered, her fingers flying across the keys. "We're ghosts."

"Maybe you are," Blake whispered, peering down the hallway. "I'm more like a slightly noticeable breeze, you know? Cool, subtle, but definitely there."

Reese chuckled, but his attention snapped to movement up ahead. "We got company."

A guard was making his rounds, slowly approaching their position. Blake raised his paintball gadget and, with a quiet pop, shot the guard in the neck. The soldier blinked, wobbled for a second, then collapsed into a heap.

"That," Blake said, holstering the gadget with a satisfied grin, "was way too easy. It's like a Nerf gun for grown-ups."

They dragged the guard into a storage room and continued. Along the way, they encountered two more soldiers—one near the entrance to the hangar bay and another patrolling the corridor. Each time, Blake, Reese, or Norah dispatched them with the paintball gadgets, leaving the soldiers snoozing peacefully in their wake.

As they reached the final security checkpoint before the hangar, Norah paused to hack into the last system. "Almost there," she whispered. "Once we're in, we can access the Valkyrie suits."

Reese peeked through the door window, where the gleaming mechs stood tall, waiting for their pilots. "Man, I missed these things. I feel like we're in a sci-fi movie. Only with less explosions... so far."

Blake nudged him, smirking. "Don't jinx it, bro. I'm still hoping for pizza night."

As the trio slipped into the hangar bay, the massive Valkyrie suits stood tall, looming over them like mechanical titans ready for war. The lights in the hangar flickered briefly, casting shadows over the pink-and-black, red-and-white, and green-and-silver armor. Each suit was unique, meticulously designed, and every time they saw them, it was still a breathtaking sight.

Reese whistled low, looking up at his red-and-white suit with a smirk. "I mean, these things never get old. Like, I'm basically a Power Ranger. Only cooler. Way cooler."

Norah, already fiddling with the control panel to lock the hangar doors, shot him a look. "Cooler, sure. But also more dangerous. This is serious, Reese. These suits are the only thing standing between us and a bunch of kaiju that want to rip the planet apart."

Blake, standing in front of his green-and-silver suit, grinned like a kid at Christmas. "Yeah, yeah, serious. But you gotta admit, they're kinda beautiful, right? Like, if robots could win beauty pageants, mine would take the crown. Look at those sleek lines! I mean, come on, I'm basically piloting the love child of a Transformer and Iron Man."

Norah rolled her eyes, though a hint of a smile played on her lips. "Focus, Blake. Without a full team of scientists, it's going to take us forever to get these suits up and running."

Reese clapped his hands together, grinning. "Oh, you mean we can't just flip a switch and call it a day? What a shocker."

Norah ignored his sarcasm and moved to the control panel, locking all entrances to the hangar. "There. That should buy us some time. Now let's get to work. We have to suit up first before we can power these beasts."

Blake threw a dramatic salute, still wearing his grin. "Yes, Captain Serious. Ready for duty!"

They headed toward the lockers, donning their battle suits. Norah's was sleek and practical, matching her Valkyrie in shades of pink and black, with reinforced plates for agility and durability. Reese's suit was bold, with accents of red and white, designed for speed and power. Blake's green-and-silver suit had a futuristic edge, looking almost like something out of a sci-fi comic, and he reveled in the aesthetic.

"Every time I put this thing on, I feel like a superhero," Blake mused, adjusting his helmet. "Which is a shame, because I'm still just me. The superhero part comes when we get these bad boys online."

Reese grinned. "Yeah, except this superhero gig involves us doing the work of 30 scientists just to get these things moving."

With their battle suits on, they moved toward the towering Valkyries. Norah tapped into the first console, her fingers flying across the controls. "Normally, it'd take a whole team to power these things up. We're running on skeleton crew—just us. So, don't expect this to be quick."

Blake leaned over, watching her work. "Yeah, but we've got you. And you're basically a one-woman science team, so I'm not too worried."

Reese shrugged, activating his suit's interface. "Right, because a three-person skeleton crew breaking into a government facility to hijack multi-billion-dollar mech suits is totally the recipe for success."

As the suits hummed to life, Blake furrowed his brow. "Wait... once we're in the suits, how exactly are we getting out? I mean, we're kind of inside the most guarded building on the planet."

Reese raised an eyebrow. "We probably won't get out without the military noticing. We're a little hard to miss, bro."

Norah finished up her work on the control panel and turned to them, all business. "There's an ocean-side door at the far end of the hangar. Once we're in the suits, I'll flood the bay, and we'll swim out. They'll know we took the suits, but we don't have any other choice."

Blake blinked. "Wait, wait. You're telling me we're going to take these multimillion-dollar pieces of hardware and just... swim out of here?"

Reese chuckled, strapping himself into the cockpit of his Valkyrie. "Oh yeah. Just a casual swim in the Atlantic. Nothing to see here."

Blake sighed, but his grin returned. "Well, at least we're going out in style." He slid into his cockpit, the controls lighting up around him. "Let's just hope the kaiju don't mind that we're fashionably late."

Norah, already securing her own Valkyrie, spoke over the comms. "Ready or not, we're doing this. Get strapped in. Once the bay floods, there's no going back."

Chapter 20: "Beneath the Waves"

It was the kind of day that felt perfect. The Miami sun was blazing in a cloudless sky, casting golden rays down on the crowded beach. College students filled the shoreline, laughing, dancing, and throwing back drinks as music blared from portable speakers. Beach volleyball games were in full swing, with teams diving into the sand to spike the ball, while others played frisbee along the water's edge, cheering each other on. Children built sandcastles near the surf, their laughter ringing out over the chatter of vacationers.

The beach was alive—a perfect snapshot of summer bliss.

Dave Hogan, the most popular late-night talk show host on television, was on vacation with his family, finally taking a break from the relentless grind of showbiz. He stretched out on a beach chair, sunglasses perched on his nose, and an oversized straw hat shielding his face from the sun. He could hear his wife, Lori, and their three kids—Mason, who was 11; Piper, 8; and Max, 5—splashing around in the shallow waves, their voices carrying over the music. It felt good to relax for once—no scripts, no cameras, just the sound of the ocean and the laughter of his family.

Dave sipped his iced lemonade and sighed contentedly. "This is the life," he muttered to himself, sinking deeper into the chair. It was a far cry from the chaos of his show, where every moment was packed with celebrity interviews and sketches. Here, on the beach, life was simple and easy.

Suddenly, amidst the joy and carefree atmosphere, there was a shift. Far out in the ocean, a shadow began to rise beneath the surface, but no one noticed. Not at first.

A group of swimmers, about fifty yards from the shore, were playfully splashing in the deeper water. One girl, laughing with her friends, suddenly paused, a strange feeling settling over her. Something wasn't right. She treaded water, her eyes scanning the waves, but saw nothing out of the ordinary. Then, without warning, the surface of the water exploded.

Aquila, the shark-eagle hybrid, emerged in a burst of spray and foam. Her massive form was a terrifying combination of sleek predator and winged menace—her body the size of a great white, but with the wings of an enormous eagle. Her dark eyes gleamed as her massive jaws snapped shut around the nearest swimmer, a young man, pulling him under in an instant.

The screams began.

For a moment, the beach froze, everyone caught in disbelief. Then chaos erupted. People on the shore screamed as they saw blood pool in the water, and the frenzied splashing of swimmers trying to escape turned into a full-blown panic. Some sprinted toward the beach, desperate to reach safety, while others were too frozen in terror to move.

Dave Hogan sat up sharply in his chair, his heart pounding. "Lori! Kids!" he yelled, frantically scanning the water. His family was still near the shore, but he could see the fear in their faces as they watched the horrific scene unfold.

Aquila lunged again, her wings flapping as she dove through the water like a torpedo. Her razor-sharp teeth slashed through another swimmer, blood spraying into the air as people tried to pull themselves onto nearby floaties and boats. The water turned red as more bodies disappeared beneath the surface, their screams drowned out by the pounding surf and Aquila's screeches.

A man on a paddleboard was the next target. He tried desperately to paddle away, his arms shaking from fear and exertion, but Aquila was too fast. She soared over him, her shadow casting doom before she came down, talons gripping the board and dragging him under. The board snapped like kindling, his screams disappearing beneath the waves.

Dave jumped to his feet, his heart hammering in his chest. "LORI, GET THE KIDS OUT OF THE WATER!" he bellowed, sprinting toward the shore. The beach was now a scene of pure pandemonium—people were abandoning their beach towels, running for their lives. Coolers were overturned, radios smashed, and sand flew in every direction as hundreds of people stampeded up the shore, desperate to get away from the water.

Lori Hogan was already rushing toward the beach, grabbing Piper by the hand while Mason and Max clung to her legs, their faces pale with terror. "Dave!" she shouted, her voice shaking. "What the heck is happening?!"

"It's a kaiju from the water—just move!" Dave yelled back, grabbing Max in his arms as they bolted toward the sand dunes. Behind them, Aquila let out a piercing screech that cut through the air like a knife. The monster's wings flapped, sending waves crashing toward the shore, knocking over swimmers who were just moments from reaching safety.

A lifeguard blew his whistle and tried to calm the crowd, but there was no calming the panic that had taken hold. A woman tripped over a beach chair and was nearly trampled before someone grabbed her hand and pulled her to her feet. A young boy clutched a floaty in the shallow water, crying for his parents as Aquila circled ominously overhead.

Then the creature struck again.

Aquila surged toward the beach, her wings outstretched as she grabbed another swimmer by the legs and yanked them under, the water churning violently. The surface turned a deep crimson, and the sound of bones snapping beneath the water was sickeningly loud.

Dave's breath came in ragged gasps as he, Lori, and the kids reached the safety of the sand dunes. He turned around, panting, as they huddled together, eyes wide in horror. They watched as Aquila tore through the beachgoers, picking them off one by one, like a predator toying with its prey.

"Oh my God," Lori whispered, her arms wrapped tightly around the kids. "Dave, what is that thing?"

"I don't know, but we need to get out of here." Dave scanned the area, looking for any way out, but the entire beach was chaos. People were running in all directions, trying to find safety from the creature that had turned their peaceful day at the beach into a nightmare.

Aquila circled once more before diving back into the ocean, disappearing beneath the waves as quickly as she had emerged. The waters grew still again, but no one dared to move.

The attack had lasted only minutes, but it felt like hours.

Dave hugged his family tight, his heart still racing. "We need to get off this beach. Now."

Lori nodded, her face pale but determined. "Let's go."

The beach was in utter chaos, a scene from a nightmare. Screams echoed down the shoreline as Aquila continued her rampage, ripping through the crowds with deadly precision. She tore into emergency vehicles, snapping fire trucks like toys, and lunged at fleeing beachgoers, dragging some beneath the waves while others tried in vain to escape.

Dave Hogan held his family close, his heart pounding in his chest as he tried to guide them up the beach, away from the carnage. His wife Lori clutched Piper and Max, her face pale with terror, while Mason ran close behind, eyes wide and darting around for any sign of safety.

Suddenly, a loud boom echoed across the sky, like thunder but sharper, more immediate. The sound rattled the air, causing everyone on the beach—those still alive, at least—to pause and look up. Dave,

Lori, and the kids froze mid-step, their heads snapping toward the source of the noise.

High above, cutting through the sky like a streak of fire, a massive red-and-black Valkyrie suit descended at breakneck speed. It was moving so fast that the sonic boom from its flight path reverberated across the beach, shaking the ground beneath them.

Dave's heart skipped a beat. He knew exactly who that was.

"It's... Alpha," he breathed, his voice filled with awe and disbelief.

The Valkyrie suit, standing 25 feet tall, was a mechanical marvel. Its sleek red-and-black armor gleamed in the sun, and its powerful limbs moved with the precision and grace of a seasoned warrior. Dave had seen Alpha countless times on television, in news reports, and in viral videos. But seeing it in person—here, now, flying through the sky to confront the monstrous Aquila—was something else entirely.

Dave, the cool and collected late-night host, was having a full-blown fanboy moment.

"Holy crap, Lori! It's Alpha! The Alpha!" he shouted, pointing up at the sky like an excited kid. "This is insane! I can't believe I'm seeing this in person! Oh my, look at that thing!"

Lori, still pale but trying to hold it together, shook her head, trying to focus on getting the kids to safety. "Dave, we need to get out of here! We don't have time to—"

Before she could finish, the red-and-black Valkyrie suit slammed full force into Aquila's massive chest with a deafening crash. The impact knocked the 30-foot-tall Kaiju backward, her screech of rage echoing across the beach as she stumbled, talons digging deep into the sand to steady herself.

The collision sent shockwaves through the beach, knocking over beach chairs, umbrellas, and coolers. The force of the attack even caused some of the emergency vehicles Aquila had been destroying to flip over.

Dave's eyes went wide as Alpha, the 25-foot-tall Valkyrie suit, rose to its full height, standing between the beachgoers and the rampaging creature. The suit's pilot must have had nerves of steel—Alpha exuded an air of total confidence as it squared off against the Kaiju.

For a moment, the beach fell eerily quiet, the only sound the crashing of the waves as Aquila shook herself off and glared at Alpha with burning eyes. The beast let out a furious screech, spreading her massive wings as if to challenge the Valkyrie suit. Blood dripped from her talons, her teeth snapping in anger.

"This... is... amazing," Dave whispered, his jaw slack as he watched the showdown unfold. "Alpha vs. Aquila. Are you kidding me? This is the coolest thing ever!"

Even Mason, Piper, and Max were staring in awe, momentarily forgetting their fear as they watched the towering mech and Kaiju face off like something out of a blockbuster movie.

Aquila lunged forward with terrifying speed, her wings outstretched as she slashed at Alpha with her talons. But Alpha was faster. The Valkyrie suit dodged the attack and countered with a devastating punch to Aquila's side, sending the beast stumbling backward once more. The ground shook with each of their movements, like two titans locked in battle.

Alpha's fists glowed with energy as it prepared for another strike, its hydraulic systems whirring as the suit powered up. Aquila screeched again, enraged, and lashed out with her beak, trying to take a chunk out of the Valkyrie suit's armor.

The sight was overwhelming—this clash of titans happening right before their eyes. But Dave knew it couldn't last. No matter how thrilling it was, they were still in danger.

"We gotta go!" Lori shouted, snapping Dave out of his awestruck state. "Now, Dave!"

"Right! Right!" Dave shook his head, trying to refocus. He grabbed Mason's hand, and Lori scooped up Max while pulling Piper close. "Let's get to the city! Come on!"

They took off, running up the beach as fast as they could, away from the battle. Behind them, the sounds of Alpha and Aquila's clash echoed in the distance—metal against talon, roars of rage, and the crash of waves. But Dave couldn't help but glance back one last time, unable to fully tear himself away from the spectacle of it all.

As they reached the edge of the beach and sprinted toward the safety of the city, Dave muttered to himself, a grin spreading across his face despite the chaos.

"I can't wait to talk about this on the show."

Lori shot him a look. "Really, Dave?"

He shrugged. "What? It's gonna make killer ratings!"

And with that, the Hogan family fled into the city, leaving the battle of titans behind—but the memory of the showdown between Alpha and Aquila burned into their minds forever.

The battle between Alpha and Aquila was a whirlwind of destruction, with each clash more devastating than the last. Aquila, the shark-eagle hybrid, was a terrifying sight: her massive shark body and razor-sharp teeth combined with the powerful wings of an eagle, allowing her to swoop and dive with deadly precision. Her two thick arms and clawed feet ripped into the sand, and every swipe sent a cloud of debris flying as she tore through the beach.

Alpha stood his ground, red-and-black armor gleaming under the Miami sun like a superhero with a jetpack and no chill. It dodged Aquila's brutal strikes with smooth, mechanical grace, each of its moves a blend of brute force and high-tech precision. The pilot, David Bennet, inside the suit, was calm, but the suit itself was all business. Energy crackled from its fists as it landed a hard punch right to Aquila's side, causing her to screech and stagger back like a shark that just realized it bit into a jet ski.

But Aquila wasn't backing down. Letting out a roar that was half eagle, half angry lawnmower, she lunged at Alpha, her massive jaws snapping for a piece of that high-tech armor. Alpha, in what can only be described as a suit-pilot's version of "nope," spun out of her reach, its cannons firing off rapid bursts of energy. Sparks flew as the blasts hit Aquila, but the hybrid Kaiju powered through, slashing at Alpha's legs like a toddler having a meltdown at the beach.

It was chaos, plain and simple. Sand flew, energy beams lit up the sky, and the ground shook with every punch, kick, and claw swipe. Alpha delivered a devastating punch to Aquila's chest, sending a shockwave through the sand. For a moment, it looked like Aquila might be down for good. She crashed into the ocean's edge, wings twitching, her sharky face gasping for air as if she had just been punched in the gills.

Alpha raised an arm, ready to finish things off. But before it could land the final blow, Aquila did something unexpected. Instead of another furious screech, she let out a low, rumbling call—the kind of sound that makes you wonder if something big is about to happen. And spoiler alert: something big was about to happen.

The ocean responded to her call.

Suddenly, there were massive footsteps coming from the water, and before anyone could even process the new threat, two colossal shapes emerged from the waves. First came Lynxara, a lion-hyena hybrid that looked like she'd been hitting the gym and the battlefield for years. At 30 feet tall, she was all muscle, fur, and sharp teeth. Her mane was a mix of jagged fur and scales, and she strolled onto the beach like she owned it.

Then came Titanax, the elephant-gorilla hybrid. At 40 feet tall, this guy was all about size and power. His enormous body, covered in thick fur and hide, looked like it could bench press skyscrapers. With tusks that looked sharp enough to take down a building, he stomped onto the beach, shaking the earth beneath him.

Aquila, now flanked by her equally monstrous friends, rose to her feet, giving Alpha the kind of look that said, "This fight isn't over yet."

Alpha's pilot, David Bennet, scanned the newcomers, probably wondering if they had packed enough ammo for three Kaiju instead of just one. The heads-up display (HUD) lit up like a Christmas tree with warnings. Three Kaiju. On a beach. This was starting to look like the worst beach day ever.

Meanwhile, back in New York, things were finally getting interesting. Inside the underground hangar, the kids—Blake, Norah, and Reese—were powering up their own Valkyrie suits.

As Norah finished powering up her Valkyrie suit and the hangar bay finally flooded with ocean water, a sudden alert flashed on her HUD. Her suit was programmed to scan for any news reports about Kaiju activity, and sure enough, something had triggered it. She furrowed her brow and clicked on the alert, bringing up a live news feed. The urgent report showed the chaos unfolding in Miami: buildings crumbling, people running for their lives, and, of course, three giant Kaiju smashing everything in sight.

"Oh great," she muttered, catching the sight of Alpha desperately fighting off the trio of Kaiju. "Guys, we've got a problem."

Reese and Blake, already suited up, turned toward her, their suits gleaming in the dim light of the submerged hangar.

"What's up?" Reese asked, his voice calm but tense.

"Miami's under attack. Alpha's getting swarmed by not one, but three Kaiju. They're ripping the place apart," Norah replied, her voice tight with urgency. "He's not going to last much longer without backup."

Reese sighed, cracking his knuckles inside his suit. "So, we're heading to Miami then."

Blake, on the other hand, grinned like he was about to suggest they go grab ice cream. "Well, what are we waiting for? Punch it!"

With a single command, the jets on their Valkyrie suits roared to life, sending bubbles and a wake of white water rushing around them. The ocean-side door had fully opened, and in an instant, they blasted off through the water, leaving the hangar behind and slicing through the ocean at top speed.

As the three Valkyrie suits blasted out of the flooded hangar bay at an astonishing speed, the military scrambled into a frenzy. Radar screens lit up, alarms blared, and soldiers rushed to their stations, trying to make sense of what was happening. The massive mechs cut through the ocean with blazing jets, leaving white water and turbulence in their wake. Officers barked orders, trying to establish communication or track their trajectory, but the suits moved too fast for anyone to keep up.

"What the heck?" a stunned commander muttered, watching as the enormous figures disappeared from the radar, heading straight for the chaos in Miami. The base was in full panic mode.

Blake's voice crackled through the comms. "So, uh, anyone else think this is gonna mess up my tan? Because I'm not going back to that beach looking like a prune."

"Seriously, Blake?" Reese groaned. "We're heading into a Kaiju war zone, and you're worried about your tan?"

"I mean, yeah," Blake shot back, laughing. "It's Miami! If we don't save the city and look good doing it, what's the point?"

Norah rolled her eyes. "Blake, focus. Alpha needs us to back him up, not crack jokes."

"Hey, jokes are how I stay focused. That, and imagining how awesome it's going to be when I punch that shark-eagle thing right in the beak... Or whatever sharks have instead of beaks. Jaws? Whatever, I'm punching it."

Reese chuckled despite himself. "You might get your chance sooner than you think."

As the three of them sped through the ocean, the distant glow of Miami's skyline came into view, flickering against the darkening sky. But it wasn't the usual twinkling city lights; it was a mix of fires, sparks from collapsing buildings, and flashes of energy from Alpha's suit as it engaged the Kaiju trio.

But it wasn't the city that had Blake going into full fanboy mode—it was the epic battle unfolding right in front of them.

"Guys! Oh my god, guys! Look at Alpha!" Blake's voice crackled through the comms, practically vibrating with excitement. "He's going full-on kaiju-slaying beast mode! Did you see that punch? Oh man, he just took Lynxara by the mane and—wait, hold up, did he just body-slam Titanax?!"

Norah, trying to stay focused, muttered, "Blake, calm down."

But Blake was unstoppable. "Calm down? Norah, are you seeing this? Alpha is single-handedly handling three massive kaiju! That's like...like...a superhero fighting a Godzilla, King Kong, and, uh, Lionzilla mash-up! This is the coolest thing I've ever seen in my life! Oh man, this is like watching every action movie at once."

Reese, ever the sarcastic one, cut in. "You do realize we're about to join that fight, right? Try not to pass out from excitement before we get there."

Blake scoffed. "Pass out? Dude, I'm about to live my best life! Look at Alpha! He just drop-kicked Aquila into a building! Oh man, that's a ten-pointer in my book." He threw his arms up inside his Valkyrie suit, grinning ear to ear, practically bouncing in his seat. "I'm gonna get that move framed. Alpha vs. Three Kaiju—this is history, people! Somebody better be recording this."

As they zoomed closer to the city, they could see Alpha throwing punches, blocking attacks, and using all kinds of advanced tech to keep the three kaiju at bay. Even outnumbered, Alpha was holding his ground—slamming Titanax into a pile of rubble, dodging Aquila's sharp claws, and landing energy-charged hits on Lynxara's snarling face.

"Look at him go! My man's got moves like nobody's business. This is the ultimate kaiju showdown!" Blake's voice was full of admiration. "He's like...he's like the John Wick of giant robots! But bigger. And cooler. And with lasers!"

Norah and Reese exchanged glances inside their suits. They both knew this was serious—Alpha needed backup, and Miami was in ruins—but Blake's fanboy enthusiasm was contagious. Reese couldn't help but grin. "Okay, Blake, let's see if you can bring that energy when we jump into the ring. You ready to rumble, or are you just gonna sit on the sidelines with popcorn?"

Blake pumped his fist. "Popcorn? Nah, I'm bringing the main course!"

With that, the jets on their suits roared to life, sending them flying toward Miami at breakneck speed. Blake's excitement was at an all-time high, and he couldn't wait to dive into the battle alongside his hero, Alpha.

Chapter 21: "Kaiju Mayhem: Enter the Valkyries!"

The fight between Alpha and the three Kaiju was reaching a fever pitch. The city of Miami lay in ruins around them, smoke rising from shattered buildings and debris scattered across the streets. Alpha had been holding his own against the terrifying trio—Aquila, Lynxara, and Titanax—but it was starting to show. David Bennett, piloting the powerful Valkyrie suit Alpha, could feel the wear on both himself and the machine. His movements were slowing, and every blow he delivered seemed to take a little longer to recover from.

Titanax, the massive elephant-gorilla hybrid, roared as he landed a bone-shaking punch right into Alpha's chest. The impact sent a shockwave through the ground, and Alpha staggered backward. David gritted his teeth, already preparing to block the next blow, but Titanax was relentless. With a bellow, he charged forward, ready to deliver a third strike that could very well cripple the Valkyrie suit.

Just as Titanax's arm swung down, the ocean behind them erupted in a massive geyser of water, and out from the depths came three glowing figures—Valkyrie suits rocketing toward the battle. In a flash, they shot across the sky, landing with a thunderous boom right between the Kaiju and Alpha. Blake, Norah, and Reese had arrived.

Blake, of course, made an entrance. He landed in the classic superhero pose, one knee to the ground, fist firmly planted, head dramatically down. As he straightened up, his eyes lit up with excitement.

Blake grinned, looking over at Alpha like a kid trying to impress their idol. "Did you see that, Alpha? How'd I do? On a scale of one to 'totally awesome,' I'm thinking solid eleven!"

Before David could respond, Aquila, still enraged from her earlier fight with Alpha, let loose a blast of energy from her mouth. The beam smashed into Blake, sending him flying back, crashing into a ruined car with a loud thud.

"Ow, ow! Okay, definitely a twelve," Blake groaned from the ground, rubbing his backside. "I just made a kaiju-shaped butt imprint in this car. That's gotta be a record or something."

David's voice crackled across the comms, low and gravelly—just like the Batman impersonation Blake always teased him about. "What are you kids doing here?" His tone was sharp, but there was an undercurrent of relief.

Blake, struggling to his feet, gave a lopsided grin. "Saving your butt, obviously. What does it look like?"

David sighed, though it was more amused than annoyed. "You got knocked on your butt by a Kaiju, Blake. Not exactly a grand entrance."

"Hey, in my defense," Blake started, "that was a tactical fall. A strategy, if you will. Keeps 'em guessing."

Reese's voice cut in, dry as always. "Yeah, Blake, I'm sure you meant to do that. Real tactical."

Norah, ever the practical one, shook her head inside her suit. "Can we focus, please? We've got three Kaiju about to turn Miami into an all-you-can-eat destruction buffet."

David chuckled softly. "Glad you three made it. I was wondering how long I could keep these things entertained."

Blake, still buzzing with excitement despite the literal Kaiju chaos surrounding them, couldn't contain himself. "Are you kidding? You were crushing it! Dude, you drop-kicked Titanax. I saw it! You're like...the ultimate Kaiju-fighting ninja warrior! I'm getting that on a t-shirt. 'Alpha: Kaiju Drop-Kicker.' I'll send you one."

David smirked behind his visor. "I'll pass, but thanks. Now, how about we take these things down before they tear up the whole city?"

Blake, ever the jokester, saluted dramatically. "Aye-aye, captain. Let's show them what happens when you mess with Team Awesome!"

Norah sighed. "We are not calling ourselves Team Awesome."

"Team Kaiju Crushers?" Reese suggested with a shrug.

"How about 'Focus on the Battle Before We All Die?'" David interrupted, his tone deadpan.

Blake laughed, his hands already moving over the controls. "You're the boss. But seriously, can we take a moment to appreciate how cool this is? Three Kaiju. Miami. The ocean. It's like a monster movie, but we're the stars! Oh man, I'm gonna need a selfie with Titanax after this."

"Blake!" Norah snapped.

"Right, right, battle first. Photos later. Let's do this!"

Just as Reese prepared to make his move against Aquila, a blur of motion shot past him with terrifying speed. His HUD blinked red with a proximity warning, but before he could react, the massive form of Felonix skidded to a stop right in front of him. Standing at a towering 30 feet, the Kaiju cheetah snarled, baring rows of sharp teeth as its yellow and black-spotted fur shimmered under the Miami sun.

Felonix let out a guttural roar, its eyes glowing with intense energy. Reese caught a glimpse of Felonix's glowing eyes and the crackling energy coursing through its body. Something about these hybrids seemed off—more powerful, more volatile than before. Dodging another lightning-fast strike, Reese activated his suit's scanners, trying to make sense of the changes. His eyes widened as the data came through, confirming his suspicions. "Guys, it's the blood!" Reese shouted over the comms, blocking a swipe from Felonix. "The blood from Omega—it must've further mutated these hybrids. They've absorbed her energy and evolved into something even more dangerous! And judging by the fact that I'm staring down a 30-foot supercharged cheetah, they've definitely picked up some new tricks."

Blake, already hyped up on adrenaline, responded with a hint of excitement. "Oh man! This just got even better! We're basically fighting super Kaiju! Dibs on the one with wings!"

Norah rolled her eyes inside her suit. "Blake, focus. We've got four Kaiju and four Valkyrie suits. Let's spread out and take them down. Alpha, you handle Titanax. We'll take the others."

David, already in the thick of it with Titanax, grunted as he dodged a crushing swing from the behemoth. "Roger that. Let's finish this."

With the battle lines drawn, each member of the Task Force squared off against their respective foes.

Alpha vs. Titanax

David, in his Alpha suit, faced off against Titanax, the elephant-gorilla hybrid. The massive creature towered over him, its muscles bulging as it let out another ear-splitting roar. Titanax charged forward, swinging its colossal arms like wrecking balls. But David was quick, dodging each blow with precision. He countered with energy blasts from his suit's arm cannons, aiming for Titanax's legs to slow it down.

"Come on, big guy," David muttered, dodging another punch. "You're gonna have to do better than that."

Titanax roared in frustration, swinging down with a massive fist that David barely avoided. Using the opening, David ignited the thrusters in his boots and launched into the air, firing a volley of missiles that exploded across Titanax's broad chest. The Kaiju stumbled back, bellowing in rage as it tried to swat David out of the air.

But Alpha wasn't done. With a burst of speed, David flew in close and unleashed a powerful punch to Titanax's jaw, causing the beast to stagger. Titanax shook it off, but David wasn't giving it a chance to recover. He flew in low, circling around to the back of the Kaiju, and unleashed a barrage of energy blasts into Titanax's spine. The Kaiju howled in pain, clearly beginning to tire from the relentless assault.

Reese vs. Felonix

Meanwhile, Reese squared off against Felonix. The Kaiju cheetah was fast—blindingly fast. Every time Reese tried to get a lock on it, Felonix was already gone, zipping across the battlefield in a blur of motion. The Valkyrie's sensors struggled to keep up, and Reese had to rely on instinct as much as tech to anticipate the creature's movements.

Felonix darted in, claws outstretched, aiming for a devastating swipe at Reese. He managed to parry it with a quick energy shield, but the force of the impact still rattled his suit. "This thing's faster than I thought," Reese muttered, trying to keep his focus.

Felonix circled him again, a blur of yellow and black, and Reese decided he needed to even the playing field. He activated his Valkyrie's speed boosters, pushing the suit to its limits. The thrusters roared to life, and Reese took off, matching Felonix's speed as they zipped around the city in a high-speed chase.

Reese could feel the adrenaline surging as he weaved between buildings, dodging debris and staying one step ahead of Felonix's claws. "You're not the only one with speed, buddy," he said through gritted teeth.

Timing his move perfectly, Reese spun mid-air and unleashed a flurry of energy blasts, catching Felonix off guard. The Kaiju snarled as the blasts hit its side, but it wasn't down yet. Felonix lunged, claws out, and Reese met it head-on, slamming into the Kaiju with the full force of his suit's momentum. The impact sent both of them crashing into the side of a skyscraper, shattering windows and leaving a massive dent in the building.

Norah vs. Lynxara

Norah took on Lynxara, the sleek and deadly lion-like Kaiju. Lynxara's glowing blue eyes locked onto her, and the Kaiju let out a low, menacing growl. The Valkyrie's sensors picked up on the energy radiating from Lynxara—some kind of electric charge that coursed through its body.

"Great," Norah muttered. "Electric powers. Because this wasn't hard enough already."

Lynxara lunged, its body crackling with electricity, and Norah barely managed to dodge the attack. The air around them sizzled with energy as Lynxara's claws sparked against the ground. Norah countered with a series of quick plasma shots, aiming to keep the Kaiju at a distance, but Lynxara was fast. It zigzagged toward her, dodging most of the blasts and leaping into the air with a powerful swipe.

Norah raised her energy shield just in time, the force of the attack sending sparks flying. Lynxara growled, electricity surging through its body as it prepared to strike again. But Norah was ready. She charged up her suit's power core and unleashed a concentrated energy beam straight at the Kaiju's chest.

The beam hit Lynxara dead-on, sending it skidding back across the street. The Kaiju roared in pain, its fur smoking from the attack, but it wasn't down yet. Lynxara's eyes glowed brighter, and the creature snarled as it prepared for another charge.

"Come on," Norah said, gripping the controls. "Let's see what you've got."

Blake vs. Aquila

Blake, of course, was having the time of his life facing off against Aquila, the shark-eagle hybrid Kaiju. Aquila swooped down from the sky, its massive wings casting a shadow over the city as it let out a piercing screech. Blake, unfazed by the terrifying creature, grinned inside his suit.

"Oh, man, this is like the best day ever," he said, aiming his arm cannon at Aquila. "I'm fighting a flying shark-bird! How cool is that?"

Aquila dived toward him, its beak glowing with energy as it prepared to fire another blast. Blake activated his thrusters, dodging to the side just as the energy beam scorched the ground where he'd been standing.

"Nice try, bird-brain!" Blake taunted, circling around for a counterattack. He fired a volley of missiles at Aquila, the explosions lighting up the sky as they connected with the Kaiju's side.

Aquila screeched in anger, flapping its wings to create a powerful gust of wind that nearly knocked Blake off balance. But Blake wasn't done yet. He activated his suit's flight mode and took to the air, chasing after Aquila as they soared over the ruined city.

"Come on, let's see if you can keep up!" Blake shouted, pulling off a series of aerial flips and rolls. Aquila roared in frustration, but Blake was too fast, zipping around the Kaiju with all the agility of a seasoned pilot.

With a grin, Blake lined up his shot. "You're going down, birdy!"

He fired off a charged energy blast, hitting Aquila right in the chest. The Kaiju screeched in pain, its flight faltering as it spiraled toward the ground. Blake followed it down, ready for the finishing blow.

As the four Valkyrie suits battled against the Kaiju hybrids, the city of Miami trembled from the sheer force of the fight. Alpha, Riese, Norah, and Blake were holding their own, but the hybrids were relentless, each one a monstrous threat in its own right.

"Let's finish this," David growled over the comms, his eyes locked on Titanax. "We take them down, here and now."

Blake, still buzzing with excitement, couldn't resist one last quip. "And after that—pizza, right? I'm starving."

The battle between the Task Force and the Kaiju hybrids escalated into a chaotic dance of power, destruction, and tactical brilliance. Blake, Norah, Riese, and David found themselves facing not just monsters but cunning adversaries who were adapting to their every move.

Blake, in his green-and-silver Valkyrie suit, squared off against Aquila once more, charging in with a barrage of energy blasts. But this time, Aquila didn't just fly into the attacks blindly—she banked hard to the left, using her massive wings to create a wall of sand, temporarily blinding Blake. "Wait, what? Sand attack? This isn't a Pokémon battle!" Blake groaned as he struggled to regain his bearings. Aquila had clearly learned from their previous encounters, moving faster and with more precision. She circled Blake like a predator stalking its prey, looking for an opening.

Meanwhile, Norah faced off against Lynxara, the lion-hyena hybrid. Lynxara had started using hit-and-run tactics, striking from the shadows, darting away, then attacking from a different angle. Norah tried to anticipate the creature's movements, but Lynxara was learning, adapting to Norah's defensive maneuvers. As Norah raised her energy shield to block a lunge, Lynxara feinted, suddenly switching directions mid-leap and slashing at Norah's suit from behind, tearing a chunk out of her armor. "Okay, that was sneaky," Norah muttered, her hands flying across her controls to stabilize her suit.

Riese was locked in a battle with Felonix, the cheetah hybrid. At first, he thought he could outsmart the Kaiju by using his suit's superior agility, but Felonix was no fool. It had started to mirror Riese's movements, darting in with precision strikes, matching the Valkyrie suit's speed. Riese fired a volley of missiles, expecting Felonix to dodge like before, but this time the Kaiju didn't evade. Instead, it sprinted directly toward Riese, weaving between the explosions and closing the distance. Riese barely had time to react before Felonix was on him, slamming into his suit with a speed that rattled his cockpit. "Whoa! It's learning to take risks!" Riese shouted, quickly boosting himself backward to gain distance.

Alpha, meanwhile, faced the colossal Titanax. The elephant-gorilla hybrid had grown bolder, using its massive bulk and strength to its advantage. It swung its powerful fists with terrifying precision, each hit shaking the ground beneath them. Alpha had landed several solid blows, but now Titanax wasn't just relying on brute strength. The Kaiju was beginning to anticipate Alpha's strikes, parrying them with his thick arms and countering with devastating force. As Alpha went in for another punch, Titanax ducked low, grabbing Alpha's arm and using its own momentum against him, slamming Alpha into the ground. "These things aren't just strong—they're learning how to fight!" Alpha's pilot, David Bennet, growled over the comms, clearly frustrated but impressed.

The realization hit the entire Task Force at once: these Kaiju were not mindless monsters—they were fighting as a team, learning their enemies' weaknesses and adjusting their tactics on the fly. Blake, still dealing with Aquila, saw the Kaiju coordinating with subtle movements, shifting their positions to cover each other's vulnerabilities.

"They're not just fighting us, they're studying us," Blake said, his voice serious for once. "These hybrids are getting smarter every second."

"Yeah, I noticed that too," Norah replied, dodging another slash from Lynxara. "It's like they're figuring out our patterns and countering everything we throw at them!"

"We have to switch it up. No more predictability," Riese added. "If we fight like we always do, they're going to outsmart us."

The Task Force regrouped, their minds racing to come up with new strategies. They couldn't just rely on brute force anymore—they had to outthink the Kaiju hybrids, who were proving to be more intelligent and coordinated with each passing second. As the four of them faced off against their respective opponents, they knew they were in for the fight of their lives.

Blake grinned as he swerved away from Aquila's talon strike. "C'mon, bird-brain! I've seen toddlers throw tantrums with more coordination!" He circled back, noticing how Aquila favored her left wing more and more, slowing her down.

"Norah, she's getting predictable!" Blake called through the comms, his voice full of energy.

"You're one to talk about predictability, Blake," Norah shot back, smirking. "You've used that insult like five times now."

"I'm consistent, thank you very much," Blake retorted, locking onto Aquila's next move. "Let's see how well you fly with your wings clipped!" He sent a volley of missiles straight at her left side, where her wing flapped sluggishly. The explosions ripped through her feathers and scales, sending Aquila spiraling toward the ground.

Aquila screeched in frustration, slamming into the beach with a resounding crash. Blake swooped down, landing in front of the downed Kaiju, posing dramatically. "And that's how you clip a Kaiju's wings!" he shouted, puffing out his chest.

Alpha's voice came in over the comms, low and gravelly. "Blake. Don't get cocky."

Blake blinked, looking around. "Me? Cocky? Never!"

Meanwhile, Reese was engaged in a high-speed duel with Felonix, the cheetah hybrid. The Kaiju's speed had surprised Reese at first, but he quickly realized that Felonix had a pattern—every time it bolted forward, it gave a slight twitch in its back legs. Reese smirked inside his suit. "You're fast, but I bet you can't keep that up forever."

Felonix blurred into motion, lunging at Reese with terrifying speed. But Reese was ready. He waited for the exact moment when Felonix twitched, then fired a grappling hook from his suit. It latched onto a nearby building, yanking him out of Felonix's path just in time. The Kaiju skidded to a halt, confused.

Reese swung back around and planted a solid kick right in Felonix's side, knocking him off his feet and sending him tumbling through the sand. "Oh, look who's on the ground now!" Reese taunted. "Maybe you should try walking more—you know, enjoy the slower things in life?"

Alpha's voice chimed in again. "Reese. Don't."

Reese rolled his eyes. "Yeah, yeah. Not cocky, just confident."

Norah, meanwhile, was facing Lynxara, the lion-hyena hybrid. Lynxara was clever, using her agility and strength to stay close to Norah, preventing her from using her suit's long-range attacks. But Norah had noticed something. Every time Lynxara lunged, she hesitated for a split second, as if expecting a trap.

"Well, if she's expecting one, let's give her what she wants," Norah muttered. She activated a decoy hologram, making it look like she was preparing for a frontal assault. Sure enough, Lynxara pounced, aiming straight for the fake Norah.

In the same instant, the real Norah leaped over the Kaiju, landing behind her. With one swift strike from her energy blade, she knocked Lynxara off her feet. "Boom! Outplayed," Norah said, grinning.

"Nice move, Norah!" Blake cheered.

"Thanks," Norah replied, a smile in her voice. "Told you I'd handle it."

Alpha's voice came through the comms again, stern as ever. "Norah."

Norah sighed. "Is that going to be your new catchphrase, Alpha?"

While the others were handling their battles, Alpha had been taking on the behemoth, Titanax. The elephant-gorilla hybrid was the strongest of the Kaiju, and even Alpha was starting to feel the strain of the fight. Titanax had landed several brutal hits, but Alpha wasn't going to let him win. He studied Titanax's movements, noting how the creature always shifted its weight before swinging its massive trunk.

David, inside the Alpha suit, gritted his teeth. "You're big, but you're not smart enough for this."

Titanax roared and charged forward, his tusks gleaming. But Alpha was ready. He dodged to the side at the last second, then slammed both fists into Titanax's back, sending the massive Kaiju crashing into the ground. Titanax let out a pained bellow, struggling to get up.

Alpha stood over him, raising his arm for the final blow. "It's over, Titanax," David said, his Batman-like voice echoing through the suit.

But just as he prepared to deliver the finishing strike, his HUD lit up with a massive energy reading. Something big was coming.

"Hold up," David muttered. "Something's incoming."

The rest of the team noticed it too, their scanners lighting up with the same readings.

"What the heck is that?" Reese asked, his tone wary.

Norah's eyes widened as she glanced at her screen. "It's huge... whatever it is."

Blake, still rubbing the spot where Aquila had blasted him earlier, squinted at his monitor. "Well, I guess this beach party just got a new guest. And here I thought we were the main event."

Alpha's voice came through the comms, more serious than ever. "Get ready, team. This is far from over."

Chapter 22: The Black Valkyrie

A deafening boom echoed through the skies above Miami, so loud it momentarily drowned out the distant roar of the defeated Kaiju. The Task Force froze, their eyes snapping toward the source of the sound. Above them, a sleek black-and-gold Valkyrie suit streaked through the air like a hunting bird of prey, casting a dark shadow over the ruins of the city. It flew with a precision and speed that left even the most advanced Task Force suits in awe.

"Uh, guys?" Blake said, pointing upward. "Is it just me, or does that thing look... expensive?"

As the new suit landed in the middle of the city with a force that cracked the ground beneath it, dust and debris exploded outward in a cloud. The suit was sleek, angular, and somehow more predatory than Alpha's. Its armor gleamed under the Miami sun, shimmering with an almost unnatural golden glow, and its movements were fluid, like a panther stalking its prey.

"Who is that?" Norah muttered, backing up a step, her sensors going haywire. "There's no way that's one of ours."

Alpha's eyes narrowed behind his visor. "Everyone, stay sharp. This could be—"

Before he could finish, the black-and-gold suit moved, fast. It lunged at Alpha with shocking speed, swinging a bladed arm toward his head. Alpha barely managed to block the strike, his arm vibrating from the force of the impact. The two suits clashed, sending sparks flying as their metal limbs collided.

"Reese, with me!" Alpha ordered, his voice a growl as he parried another strike. The mysterious Valkyrie was relentless, its movements calculated and aggressive, each blow delivered with ruthless efficiency.

Reese, already revved up from his fight with Felonix, didn't need to be told twice. "Finally, a real fight!" he yelled, launching himself into the air and coming down hard on the black suit's left side. His impact sent the enemy suit staggering, but only for a moment.

The black Valkyrie spun with inhuman speed, catching Reese off-guard with a counter-punch that sent him flying backward into a nearby building. Reese crashed through a wall, groaning but still conscious. "Alright... that's gonna bruise," he muttered, climbing to his feet.

Blake, watching from a distance, was practically vibrating with excitement. "This is insane! It's like watching a Batman versus Iron Man crossover! Alpha! Please tell me we're gonna find out who's under that suit because I'm calling it now—it's gotta be someone evil, right?!"

Alpha grunted, ducking under another wild strike. "Focus, Blake!"

Reese recovered quickly, his suit's systems recalibrating from the hit. "Alright, I've had enough of this guy," he muttered, charging back into the fight. This time, he was ready. As the black suit lunged again, Reese dodged at the last second, using his grappling hook to snag one of its legs. With a powerful tug, he yanked the enemy off balance, giving Alpha an opening.

Alpha moved in, landing a heavy blow to the black suit's chestplate, sending it skidding backward across the cracked pavement. But the pilot inside was skilled—too skilled. The black Valkyrie recovered almost instantly, its visor glowing with a menacing red light as it re-engaged.

The fight became a blur of movement. The black Valkyrie was impossibly fast, its strikes brutal and precise, but Alpha and Reese fought with the synchronicity of a team who had faced impossible odds before. Alpha blocked and parried, his powerful strikes meeting the enemy's blows head-on, while Reese darted in and out, using his agility and speed to harry the black suit from the sides.

"Who is this guy?" Reese grunted, managing to land a punch that sent the black Valkyrie stumbling.

"No idea," Alpha replied, his voice as cold and calculating as ever. "But they're using tactics I've never seen before. This isn't just a random mercenary."

The black suit spun, locking onto Reese once again. It raised its arm, and for the first time, a weapon emerged—a glowing, crackling blade of energy that hummed ominously as it powered up.

"Uh, Alpha?" Reese said, backing up. "I don't like the look of that."

"Neither do I," Alpha muttered, his sensors flaring with danger warnings.

The black Valkyrie struck, slashing its energy blade at Reese. He barely dodged in time, the blade leaving a molten scar across the ground where he'd been standing moments before.

Blake watched from a safe distance, still geeking out. "Oh man! This is like a boss fight in a video game! Do you think he has a second phase where he sprouts wings or—"

"Blake, shut it!" Norah snapped, her fingers flying over her controls as she tried to get a lock on the black suit. "We need to help them!"

Alpha and Reese worked in tandem now, attacking from different angles, forcing the black Valkyrie to split its attention. But whoever was piloting it was just as smart, just as tactical. It blocked their strikes with a fluidity that suggested a deep familiarity with combat.

"I've got an idea," Reese said, breathing heavily as he barely dodged another energy blade swing. "But you're not gonna like it."

Alpha's eyes narrowed. "Do it."

Reese grinned, charging straight at the black suit. "Here goes nothing!" Just before the enemy could strike him again, Reese activated a high-powered shockwave from his suit, releasing a burst of energy that disrupted the black Valkyrie's systems for a split second.

It was all the opening Alpha needed. He closed the distance in an instant, landing a heavy punch straight into the black suit's visor. The force of the blow sent it crashing to the ground, sparks flying from the impact.

The black and gold Valkyrie suit, despite being knocked down, was far from finished. Its systems flickered back to life, and with a sudden burst of energy, it propelled itself off the ground, re-engaging Alpha and Reese in an all-out assault. The fight became a blur of motion as the enemy pilot fought with a tenacity that even Alpha hadn't anticipated.

David, aka Alpha, blocked a vicious punch aimed at his head, his arm vibrating from the impact. "Blake, Norah!" he growled through the comms, ducking under a follow-up strike. "Feel free to join in anytime now!"

Blake's voice crackled through the comms. "Well, you know, I figured you had it covered, big guy!"

Norah rolled her eyes, her hands flying across the controls. "He means we're coming in now, Blake. Less talk, more action."

Blake rocketed forward, followed by Norah, their jets leaving trails in the air as they joined the fray. The four Valkyrie suits now surrounded the black and gold intruder, each one working in tandem to land a strike. The battle intensified, the clash of metal on metal sending shockwaves through the crumbling city.

Reese darted in first, aiming for a high-speed punch to the intruder's side, but the black suit twisted out of the way with lightning reflexes, delivering a sharp counter that sent Reese stumbling back. "Okay," Reese muttered, shaking off the hit. "This guy's not playing around."

"Neither are we," Norah said, her eyes narrowing as she locked onto the enemy's weak points. "I think it's time to test out the Omega Killer shot."

David's voice came over the comms. "Do it. We need to end this now."

Norah didn't hesitate. With a quick flick of her wrist, her suit's most powerful weapon, the Omega Killer, powered up. A blinding light began to gather at the barrel of her arm cannon, crackling with raw energy. "Alright, buddy, time to see what you're really made of."

She fired.

The blast shot across the battlefield like a beam of pure destruction, slamming into the black and gold suit with a force that shattered the nearby pavement. The enemy suit staggered, sparks flying as its systems took a massive hit. The impact sent it crashing to one knee, the once-imposing predator now visibly damaged.

"I got him!" Norah shouted triumphantly.

But even as smoke billowed from the intruder's armor, he wasn't done. With a defiant roar, the black Valkyrie surged forward again, its movements more sluggish but still dangerously fast. Blake, ever the opportunist, zoomed in next, charging up his plasma cannons. "It's my turn!" he yelled, firing off two bright blue blasts of energy.

The plasma shots hit the enemy dead-on, sending it sprawling back. Reese followed up, landing a solid punch to the black suit's torso, denting the armor further. "Not so tough now, are you?" he quipped, smirking beneath his helmet.

David finished the assault with a devastating punch, hitting the black Valkyrie so hard it crumpled to the ground. The enemy suit seemed to power down, its lights flickering out, the once-formidable foe now lying motionless in the rubble.

Alpha stepped forward, his chest rising and falling with heavy breaths. "Good work," he muttered, glancing at the others. "But we're not done yet. We need to find out who's in that suit."

Blake tilted his head, looking down at the black Valkyrie with a curious expression. "Please let it be someone cool and mysterious, like a ninja or an ex-secret agent."

Norah rolled her eyes. "Focus, Blake."

David's visor flickered as he scanned the area. His attention snapped to the ground, where the four hybrids—Titanax, Aquila, Felonix, and the fourth—had been. But the area was empty.

"They're gone," Alpha said, his voice grim. "The hybrids slipped away while we were fighting."

Reese cursed under his breath. "Those things were smarter than we thought. They used the fight as a distraction."

David nodded. "They'll be back. But for now, let's focus on figuring out who our new friend is." He motioned toward the crumpled black and gold suit.

Chapter 23: "The Ultimate Valkyrie"

A low, menacing laugh echoed across the team's comms, sending a chill through the Valkyrie suits.

"Did... did anyone else hear that?" Blake asked, his tone half-joking but tinged with genuine concern.

Suddenly, the crumpled black-and-gold Valkyrie suit on the ground began to twitch. Dark liquid started oozing out from its cracks, pouring over the suit's surface like molten metal. The fluid shimmered and glowed, rapidly mending the suit's damaged parts. Within moments, the once-battered armor was whole again, and the suit's lights flickered back to life.

Norah's eyes widened. "No way. That thing's... regenerating?"

Blake stared in disbelief. "Oh, that's just great. Why can't we ever fight normal evil robots? They always gotta have some creepy, sci-fi superpower!"

The laughter returned, louder this time, dripping with arrogance. "Did you really think it would be that easy?" a voice sneered. "You're dealing with something far beyond your comprehension."

Reese's eyes narrowed. "Vance," he growled.

"Ahh, the smart one speaks!" Vance's voice was practically singing. "Yes, it's me. Doctor Vance, if you please. But let's be real here—titles don't matter when you've reached the pinnacle of power."

David, in the Alpha suit, took a step forward, his tone cold and commanding. "Vance, what the hell have you done?"

The black-and-gold suit stood tall, glowing menacingly as Vance continued to taunt them. "Oh, you mean this?" he said, as though he were discussing a casual hobby. "Just a little something I cooked up, using the data I gathered from Omega's biology. You see, Omega's blood had... remarkable properties. It helped me create the ultimate Valkyrie suit. Self-healing, adaptive combat capabilities—everything your pathetic suits could never dream of being."

Blake chimed in, trying to lighten the situation, "Okay, first off, rude. Second, if you think that suit is cooler than ours, you clearly haven't seen me in slow-mo, buddy."

Vance ignored him, his voice taking on a dangerous edge. "You're nothing compared to me. Nothing! Do you know why? Because you're weak. You always were. Strayer made sure of that, didn't she? Shut down my project, humiliated me, called me a failure!"

David clenched his fists, his voice low and threatening. "You're not a victim, Vance. You're a monster."

"A monster? Oh no," Vance replied with a sickening chuckle. "I'm a visionary. Strayer couldn't see what I was capable of, but I'll show her. With this suit, and my hybrids, I'll prove her wrong. The world will bow to me. I'll have the power to reshape everything. Strayer won't be able to stop me. None of you will."

Reese's voice cut in, calm but biting. "You sound insane, Vance."

"Oh, I've heard that before," Vance said, his tone mocking. "They always say that, right before they realize just how wrong they were. I'm not insane, I'm enlightened. Power... true power... is all that matters. The rest of you are just ants. General Strayer? She'll regret ever crossing me. You'll all regret it."

Blake let out a mock gasp. "Oh no! Not a power-hungry villain with a grudge! Gee, haven't heard that one before. Is this the part where you start monologuing about how much better you are than us?"

Vance's voice grew colder, more unhinged. "Laugh all you want, boy. But I've outgrown your jokes. I've outgrown all of you. With this suit, I'm invincible. You can't beat me. This is the future of warfare—of domination—and I hold the key."

Norah's fingers twitched over her controls, her eyes narrowing as she tried to find an opening. "He's too far gone," she muttered. "He's not going to stop."

"Let's make sure he does," David said, his voice steady. "We take him down, here and now."

Blake, still trying to keep things light, added, "You know, for a guy who's all about power, Vance, your suit's got a lot of talking and not a lot of actual fighting. Just saying."

Vance sneered. "You want a fight? Then I'll give you one. But don't say I didn't warn you…"

The black-and-gold suit flared to life, jets igniting as it launched itself at Alpha and Reese with a ferocity they hadn't seen before. The battlefield exploded into chaos once again, but this time, Vance fought with a brutal precision, as if the suit had somehow learned their weaknesses from the previous encounter.

Reese blocked a vicious strike aimed at his midsection, grunting as the impact nearly sent him flying. "This thing's faster!"

David ducked under a series of rapid punches, trying to find an opening. "Stay sharp, Reese! This isn't just about speed—it's learning as it fights!"

Blake and Norah moved in from opposite sides, firing their plasma cannons to flank Vance. The blasts hit him squarely, but the black suit absorbed the energy, glowing even brighter. "Is that all you've got?" Vance taunted, throwing his head back with a deranged laugh.

Blake narrowed his eyes, a determined grin spreading across his face. "I've got something special for you, Vance!" he shouted, reaching for the controls of his suit. The air crackled with energy as he attempted to charge his Omega Killer shot, the weapon's core glowing brighter and brighter.

David glanced at him, a mix of concern and encouragement. "Just be careful! We don't know what that suit can do now."

"Trust me! This'll teach him not to mess with us!" Blake shot back, feeling a rush of adrenaline. He could almost picture Vance's shocked expression as the massive blast erupted from his suit. "Omega Killer, charging…"

With a booming sound, Blake unleashed the shot, a beam of pure energy aimed directly at Vance. But just as the blast flew toward him, the black-and-gold suit raised a shimmering force field that absorbed the shot entirely. The energy shimmered and twisted, then exploded outward, sending shockwaves rippling through the air.

"Is that the best you've got?" Vance called, a sneer twisting his face behind the visor. "You're going to have to do better than that, Blake! It's so cute how you think you're a threat." He lunged forward, and the battle began anew.

The four Kaiju Task Force members squared up against Vance, but he was a whirlwind of speed and strength, taking them on one by one with mocking ease. He danced around Blake, striking with precision before spinning to catch David off guard, his fist colliding with the side of Alpha's suit with a thundering crunch. David staggered, trying to regain his footing as Vance turned his attention to Norah.

"Oh, what's this? The girl wants to play?" he taunted, eyes glinting with malice. "How adorable! What's next? A tea party?"

Norah glared at him, anger fueling her determination. "I'd rather have a battle, thank you!" She charged forward, her mech's fists raised, but Vance sidestepped her with ease, moving with an agility that seemed to defy the weight of the suit he wore.

"Look out!" David shouted, but it was too late. Vance summoned an energy sword, a blade of crackling light that extended from the gauntlet of his suit. With a swift motion, he slashed at Norah, cutting through her mech's left arm like butter.

"Oops! Did I do that?" Vance laughed mockingly as the severed arm fell to the ground, sparks flying from the exposed wiring.

"You jerk!" Norah seethed, her remaining arm instinctively raising to fire. In a flash, she unleashed a full-force blast from her right hand. The energy shot hit Vance squarely in the chest, sending him reeling back, but not without a wild grin plastered across his face.

"Ah, that's more like it!" Vance laughed, staggering but recovering quickly. "But you'll have to do better than that! You think your little toys can beat me?"

Blake clenched his fists, watching the fight unfold with a mixture of horror and determination. "We can't let him keep the upper hand!" he shouted, trying to rally the team. "We need to combine our strengths!"

"You mean like a super awesome team-up?" Norah quipped, reestablishing her footing and trying to bring her systems back online. "I'm in! But someone's got to take that sword away from him before he does any more damage!"

With that, they formed a quick plan, coordinating their attacks while Vance continued to taunt and insult them.

"Oh, look! The 'Kaiju Task Force'—so adorable! You think you can work together against me? It's like watching a group of toddlers trying to build a Lego tower! How precious!" He spun on his heel, taking aim at Blake next.

Blake dodged and rolled, barely avoiding a heavy punch from the suit. "Not today, Vance! I'm not a toddler; I'm a powerhouse!"

"Ha! Keep dreaming!" Vance shouted, slashing with his energy sword again. The blade whirled through the air, narrowly missing Blake as he sidestepped. The energy crackled ominously, and Vance laughed maniacally, clearly enjoying himself.

The chaos of battle swirled around them, but Vance remained a whirlwind of energy and taunts, dodging their combined assaults with uncanny agility. Each time they thought they had him cornered, he'd slip away, launching a counterattack that sent sparks flying. He ducked under Blake's punch, spun around Norah's plasma blast, and retaliated with a swift jab that nearly knocked Reese off his feet.

"Is this really the best you can do?" Vance mocked, his voice dripping with derision. "A team of wannabe heroes! Pathetic! I've seen training wheels do better!"

"Shut it, Vance!" Blake yelled, his fists clenched in frustration. "You're not as invincible as you think!"

"Aw, but it's cute how you believe that," Vance sneered, a wicked glint in his eye. "Maybe I should save you all the trouble and just send you back to the nursery!"

David, watching the brutal back-and-forth, could feel the anger bubbling within him. This wasn't just a fight anymore; it was personal. He couldn't let his team continue to take the brunt of Vance's psychotic insults and relentless attacks. He raised a hand, signaling for them to hang back.

"Everyone, fall back! I'll take him on one-on-one!" David shouted, his voice steady despite the adrenaline coursing through him.

"Are you sure?" Norah asked, concern etched on her face.

"I can handle him," David assured them, determination blazing in his eyes. "Trust me."

As his team stepped back, David stepped forward, confronting Vance with newfound resolve. The two faced off, sizing each other up. The tension in the air was palpable as they circled one another, the sounds of battle fading into the background.

"Ready for a real fight, Alpha?" Vance taunted, his energy sword crackling ominously. "I've been waiting for this moment. I'll enjoy watching you fall!"

David took a deep breath, the weight of the battle hanging heavy on his shoulders. He charged, and the clash was immediate, the sound of metal on metal ringing out through the city. Vance met him blow for blow, the two exchanging powerful strikes and deft dodges. Each swing of Vance's sword was met with a punch from David's Alpha suit, the two locked in a fierce battle that showcased their skills and determination.

Vance ducked low and lashed out, his sword slicing the air as David barely sidestepped the attack. "You think you can take me on in my own game? You're slower than a three-legged tortoise!"

David responded with a powerful uppercut, which connected squarely with Vance's jaw. Vance staggered back, momentarily stunned. David pressed the advantage, following up with a series of punches, each one landing harder than the last.

"Is that all you've got?" Vance spat, wiping blood from his lip. "I expected more from the so-called 'Alpha.'"

David gritted his teeth, channeling all his strength into one final blow. "I won't let you hurt my family!"

With a roar, he lunged forward, but just as he did, Vance sidestepped with a speed that took David by surprise. The energy sword arced through the air, slicing through the Alpha suit's armor as if it were paper.

David's eyes widened in shock. "No!" he shouted as Vance's blade ran his suit through, piercing the suit's core.

The Alpha suit began to disintegrate, particles scattering like dust in the wind. David felt the world around him fade as his suit fell to the ground, his consciousness dimming as horror struck his team.

"ALPHA!" Blake screamed, the sound echoing through the chaos. Norah and Reese echoed his cries, their voices a mixture of despair and disbelief as they watched their team leader fall.

"Ha! How's that for a power move?" Vance laughed, his voice booming with sadistic glee. "You thought you could take me on, but look where that got you! You're nothing without your precious suit!"

As David's form vanished, the siblings felt a surge of rage wash over them. Their grief transformed into determination as they rallied together, eyes blazing with fury. They surged forward, united in their resolve to avenge Alpha's defeat.

"You think you can win against us?!" Blake shouted, channeling his frustration into his movements. "We're not done yet!"

With renewed fury, the three of them attacked Vance in unison, striking with a combination of plasma blasts and physical punches. Vance's smirk faltered for just a moment, surprise flickering across his face.

"Wait, what?" he stammered before blocking a punch from Norah. The team pressed on, their attacks unrelenting.

"I hope you're ready for a real fight, Vance!" Reese yelled, joining in as they worked together to outmaneuver him.

Vance retaliated with a sweep of his sword, but the siblings dodged in perfect sync, their teamwork showcasing their resilience. They refused to let Alpha's sacrifice be in vain, driving Vance back with every strike.

As they continued their assault, Vance's taunts began to fade, replaced with grunts of exertion and frustration. "You're just delaying the inevitable! I'll crush you all!"

The fight raged on, each member of the Kaiju Task Force giving it their all against Vance, but he was a whirlwind of chaos, effortlessly dispatching them one by one.

Reese was the first to fall. He charged in, fists swinging, but Vance sidestepped him with a wicked grin. In one swift motion, he unleashed a power blast that sent Reese flying through the air, a streak of light against the night sky.

"REESE!" Blake yelled, watching helplessly as his brother sailed away, crashing into the ground miles from the battle. The sound of his suit's systems failing echoed faintly in their comms as the dust settled, leaving a chilling silence.

Next up was Norah. Determined not to let Vance gain the upper hand, she launched a barrage of plasma blasts. But Vance anticipated her moves, easily dodging and then sweeping in to strike. With a flick of his energy sword, he sliced through the knees of her Valkyrie suit, leaving her to tumble to the ground with a crash.

"Norah!" Blake cried, but his focus was soon diverted back to Vance, who now turned his full attention to him.

"Looks like it's just you and me, kid," Vance taunted, cracking his knuckles. "Time to show you how a real fighter does it!"

Blake straightened, a grin breaking across his face despite the dire situation. "Oh, please! I've fought my share of freaks! You're just a second-rate villain in a wannabe superhero costume!"

"Oh, I'm the villain now? How original! What's next, are you going to tell me I have a 'big bad' lair somewhere?" Vance scoffed, lunging forward.

"You might want to check your ego at the door, buddy," Blake retorted, dodging to the side just in time to avoid a slash from Vance's energy sword. "You're about as intimidating as a cat in a pillow fight!"

As they exchanged blows, Blake kept up the banter. "Seriously, is this suit made of paper? Because I feel like I'm just scratching the surface here!" He threw a punch, which Vance blocked with ease, countering with a kick that nearly sent Blake flying.

"Funny, I thought you'd be tougher! Where's the little brother who took down Kaiju?" Vance sneered, launching a flurry of attacks.

Blake ducked and dodged, his heart racing. "Oh, you know, probably somewhere regretting his life choices—like fighting you!"

With every quip, Blake fueled his own courage, determined to protect his family. But Vance was relentless, a storm of energy and malice, and the gap in their strength quickly became evident.

"Prepare to disappear, joke!" Vance shouted, gathering a swirling ball of energy in his hands. Blake's eyes widened as he realized what was coming.

"Oh no, not the vaporize! Anything but that!" Blake cried out, throwing his arms up defensively.

But it was too late. Vance unleashed the energy blast, and it hit Blake squarely in the chest.

A blinding light enveloped him, and for a moment, the world seemed to pause. Blake felt himself disintegrating, the sensation of being torn apart coursing through his suit as it vaporized around him. He gasped, the pain overwhelming, as he was swallowed by the light.

"NO! BLAKE!" Norah screamed, her voice filled with horror.

But just like that, Blake was gone, leaving only an empty space where he once stood.

Vance let out a triumphant laugh, the sound echoing through the devastation of the city. "This is what happens when you play with fire, kids! You get burned!"

Standing among the ruins of their fallen comrades, Norah's heart sank. The fight wasn't over, but the loss of Blake hung heavily in the air, a chilling reminder of how high the stakes truly were.

As Vance stood among the wreckage, a maniacal grin spread across his face, basking in the glow of his supposed victory. "You see, children?" he shouted, his voice echoing through the devastation. "This is what happens when you dare to challenge me! I've transcended mere biology! With the power of Omega running through my veins, I've become unstoppable! The General should have known better than to mess with a genius like me! I'll show her! I'll show the world!"

But as Vance continued his self-indulgent monologue, he failed to notice the subtle glow emanating from Norah's right arm. With her left knee and other systems incapacitated, she focused all her energy into the only functional part of her Valkyrie suit. Gritting her teeth, she powered up the cannon, adjusting the shot settings with determination.

"Vance!" she shouted, her voice breaking through his villainous tirade. "You might want to wrap it up! I've got a little surprise for you!"

"Surprise? I don't think so!" Vance scoffed, waving her off. "You're too late to—"

BOOM!

A blinding flash erupted from Norah's arm as she fired a devastating shot straight into Vance. The impact was immediate and violent, sending him hurtling backward, his wicked laugh cut short as he soared into the air. He tumbled, arms flailing, before crashing into the ocean with a tremendous splash.

The city fell silent, the echoes of battle fading as Vance vanished beneath the waves. Norah, panting and exhausted, watched as the ripples spread across the water's surface. "Not defeated... but gone for now," she muttered, shaking her head in disbelief.

Just then, the sound of helicopters roared overhead, and military aircraft filled the skies, their presence breaking the tension in the air. The familiar sight of armored vehicles and soldiers streaming into the area provided a wave of relief. Ground troops rushed toward them, led by General Strayer herself, her expression a mixture of concern and determination.

"Norah! Reese!" she called, rushing to their side. "We need to get you out of here. Are you both okay?"

Reese, still dazed from his earlier flight and the loss of his suit, nodded weakly as he clutched his side. "I think so... just a little bruised."

Norah, still processing everything that had happened, added, "We... we fought Vance. We were winning until... until Blake..." Her voice trailed off, emotions swirling as she struggled to accept their loss.

General Strayer's eyes softened as she placed a hand on Norah's shoulder. "I know it hurts right now, but we'll get through this together. We need to regroup, assess the situation, and find a way to deal with Vance once and for all."

With that, the military personnel assisted the siblings, helping them to their feet. As they were ushered toward safety, Norah cast one last glance at the ocean, where Vance had disappeared. The battle may have been won, but the war was far from over. They had a madman to track down and a world to protect.

Chapter 24: Whispers of the Past

The rhythmic sound of waves crashing against the shore echoed in Blake's ears as he slowly drifted back to consciousness. The salty breeze whipped against his battered face, and every part of his body screamed in protest. Pain shot through him like electric jolts, making it hard to focus on anything but the ache that pulsed within him.

"Where am I?" he thought, struggling to open his eyes. As his vision swam into focus, he realized he was lying on the sand, the cool grains sticking to his skin. "I survived," he mused, a flicker of hope breaking through the fog of agony. "I wasn't vaporized..."

Just then, the sound of footsteps approached, heavy and deliberate. Blake's head lolled to the side, and through blurry vision, he caught a glimpse of boots, sturdy and familiar. His heart raced. "No way..."

As if summoned by his thoughts, the figure leaned closer. Blake squinted, and to his shock, he thought he saw his father, David Bennett, standing above him. The rugged features he had longed to see, the reassuring presence he had thought he would never feel again—his father was here. "Blake," David's voice rang out, deep and filled with warmth, "I've got you."

With surprising strength, David lifted Blake into his arms, cradling him against his chest. As they moved, Blake's mind raced with questions. "How... how is Dad here? We're miles from home... from Rockland County..."

"Don't worry about that right now," David said, his tone calm yet urgent. "We need to get you inside. It's not safe out here."

Blake struggled to make sense of it all as David carried him toward the mouth of a cave that loomed in the distance. He felt the warmth of his father's body against him, the familiar scent reminding him of better days. It was a stark contrast to the chaos that had just unfolded—the battles, the loss, and the madness of Vance.

As they entered the cave, the coolness enveloped Blake like a gentle embrace, and he caught a glimpse of flickering light from a small fire crackling at the back. David set him down on a pile of soft moss and blankets. "Stay here," he said, firmly but gently. "I'll find some water and supplies. You need to rest."

Blake tried to speak, to ask questions, but the words caught in his throat. The pain and exhaustion pulled him under again, and he felt himself drifting, the cave's darkness swirling around him. In the background, he could hear his father moving, rummaging through supplies, a soft murmur of reassurance punctuating the air.

As he faded in and out of consciousness, fragments of memories washed over him—laughter at family dinners, long hikes in the woods, late-night talks filled with dreams and aspirations. Each memory was like a wave, crashing over him, pulling him deeper into the safety of his father's presence.

But just as quickly as the warmth enveloped him, doubt crept in. Was this real? Was he dreaming? The chaotic memories of the battle with Vance, the pain of loss, and the echo of his father's absence loomed large in his mind. "I can't let this be a dream," he whispered to himself, determination mingling with desperation. "I need to wake up... I need to help my siblings."

As if sensing his inner turmoil, David returned, kneeling beside Blake with a small bowl of water. "Drink," he urged softly, cupping Blake's chin to lift his head gently. "You need your strength. There's more we need to talk about."

Blake took a sip, the cool liquid soothing his dry throat. "Dad," he croaked, his voice barely a whisper. "How are you here? What's going on?"

David sighed, a look of understanding crossing his features. "It's a long story, Blake. But for now, just know that I'm here for you. We're going to figure this out together."

With those words, Blake finally let himself relax, allowing the weight of everything to settle on his weary bones. The comfort of having his father by his side, even in this surreal moment, ignited a flicker of hope within him. Together, they would face whatever awaited them in the aftermath of the chaos.

Back at the Task Force Building

General Sarah Strayer stood in the dimly lit briefing room, her eyes sharp and steely, but something deeper simmered underneath—grief. Reese and Norah sat across from her, their expressions tense, shoulders heavy with the weight of their losses. Sarah took a deep breath, her voice low but stern.

"You disobeyed direct orders," she began, her eyes boring into them. "I told you to wait. To stay put until we had a plan in place. But you went after Vance and the hybrids anyway."

Reese, still reeling from the battle, clenched his fists. "We couldn't just sit there and do nothing while people were dying. We—"

Sarah slammed her hand on the table, silencing him. "You cost us more than you realize! Blake... Alpha... They're gone because you couldn't wait! Do you even grasp what that means?"

The room went silent, the weight of her words hanging like a storm cloud. Norah's voice trembled as she spoke, barely a whisper. "We saved lives. Hundreds of people, maybe thousands. Wasn't that worth it?"

Sarah's eyes softened, but her lips remained tight. "Yes," she admitted, her voice barely more than a whisper. "Yes, you saved lives. And for that, I'm grateful. But we lost family today. And I don't know if I'll ever be able to forgive myself for that."

Reese blinked, confused. "Family?"

Sarah inhaled sharply, fighting to keep her composure. "There's something you both need to know. You deserve the truth after everything that's happened." She paused, her eyes glistening with the emotion she usually kept buried under layers of military precision. "Alpha... was your father... He wasn't just some soldier chosen at random to lead the Task Force. He was... a friend."

The words struck them like a blow. Reese and Norah sat frozen, their minds scrambling to piece together the fragments of what she had just said. Their father? Reese's mouth opened, but no words came out.

Sarah's voice cracked as she continued. "I've known David since Desert Storm. He saved my life. He was a man who would give everything—everything—for the people he cared about. That's why he was chosen to be Alpha. His willingness to sacrifice, to step into the fire no matter the cost... that's why he was the perfect candidate."

Norah blinked, her vision blurring. "Why didn't you tell us before?"

Sarah shook her head, her hand brushing away the tears she refused to let fall. "It wasn't my place. David didn't want you to be burdened by his role. He wanted to protect you, even from the truth."

Reese slammed his hand on the table. "You knew this whole time? You let us fight alongside him without telling us who he was?"

Sarah winced at his anger but held her ground. "It was his choice, Reese. He wanted to protect you in more ways than one."

Norah's voice cracked. "He died for us... didn't he?"

Sarah nodded slowly, tears threatening to spill. "Yes. He died a hero, like he always was. But don't let his sacrifice be in vain. You two—you are his legacy. You carry that with you."

There was a long, heavy silence. The weight of everything—Blake's loss, David's sacrifice, the truth—hung between them, raw and unspoken.

Sarah straightened, her voice resolute but filled with deep, personal sorrow. "We have a lot to answer for. But right now, we honor their memory by finishing what they started. This fight isn't over. Not by a long shot."

Reese and Norah exchanged a glance, both reeling, but with newfound resolve hardening in their eyes.

For their father and brother. For everything they had lost. They would fight.

Milton Keynes UK
Ingram Content Group UK Ltd.
UKHW021908231124
451423UK00006B/616